EPILOGUE OF MUNDANITY

THE COPPER CHASER

Vincent Rollo

I would like to thank my mother for always encouraging my creative spirit and for all the long hours she spent editing this book.

I would like to thank Ziyu Dong, a friend from high school, who drew the beautiful cover art.

And finally, I would like to thank you. Thank you for taking the time to read this book.

I hope you enjoy reading *Epilogue of Mundanity: The Copper Chaser* as much as I did writing it.

1

2045

A haze of ichor splattered across Prost's face. The final insult delivered to him before his enemy toppled over, never to rise again. He could taste it, even through the mesh of a mask that protected his mouth. It tasted like copper. Reflexively wiping the blood away, Prost looked down at his enemy. The creature lay sprawled on its back, twitching like a beetle.

Hardened copper covered most of its skin, and a liquid of similar color oozed from a deep gash on the back of its neck. A *Mechatolly*, as the government first started calling them fifteen years ago. That name just stuck. People had no idea what these creatures were back then. No idea how far the parasites would spread.

Prost spat the foul metallic taste from his mouth before wiping the blade of his knife on his pant leg. Mechatollies were predictable: with enough experience, as Prost so happened to have, dealing with them wasn't much trouble at all. But life had a funny way of making things hard on humanity. The Mechatollies weren't the only abomination that roamed the planet.

His eyes drifted to where his primary weapon, an axe, had gotten stuck. The metal had wrapped around the vines of a *Florid*. They were a more intelligent type of beast but sought to kill humans all the same.

Flowering vines ripped from the creature's skin, creating something of a barrier between any attempt to harm the creature and its *human* host. Of course, each variant had their own weaknesses, and when all else failed, all one had to do was destroy the parasite controlling the body; a Metalide and Antherus.

With a few good tugs, Prost freed the axe from the Florid. Its corpse slumped to the ground with an unsatisfying squish as sap oozed from the vines. He glanced back at the warehouse behind him, littered with bodies, Florids and Mechatollies alike. There were a few minutes before the parasites would begin to hatch. Fending them off was a feat best avoided. He looked up: a few platforms hung from the ceiling. Overlooking the warehouse was his companion, Neil.

Neil was the cautious type and preferred to avoid dirtying his hands, both in fights and in business. Despite that, he still joined this pathetic attempt at a search and rescue for Prost's wife, who had been missing for more than a year by now. He was slender and had short hair that was always brushed back away from his eyes.

It was unusual to see Neil without some sort of formal wear, even when he ventured into the alloy zones– hotspots overflowing with the abominations– where they found themselves presently. At least he was a good shot and kept the lurkers away.

"Neil," Prost called out to his companion on the rafters, but silenced himself as the sound of frantic footsteps rushed towards the building. He prepared himself for another fight with the infected, and Neil raised his rifle. The screams of a man surprised them.

"Don't shoot! Don't shoot!" A stranger screeched, darting into the warehouse through an unlocked door. He was clearly shorter than Prost and could maybe reach five and a half feet tall if standing upright. His dirty clothes hid his thin frame and had long, unkempt hair that almost made Prost mistake him for a girl. Not that Prost could judge, as his hair was longer than the strangers, only, his had been braided and pinned into place. The stranger's fingernails were long and cracked; his lips were dry– it was clear that wherever he came from was inhospitable to him.

The young stranger was running towards the Prost– or rather, was running away from someone else. Though he couldn't see Neil's face, Prost could feel Neil's eyes burning holes into the back of his neck, scolding Prost for something he had yet to do.

"Don't do it, Prost," he imagined Neil was muttering. Neil trailed the stranger with his rifle, though was yet to fire in fear of hitting Prost.

"Please– man– you gotta help me," the young stranger was out of breath but attempted to tell Prost of the situation as quickly as he could. "I thought I could trust them– but they turned around and robbed me! They're gonna kill me– *please–* please help me. I'll do anything."

Before Prost could tell the man to leave him out of it, the door once again burst open. Three strong men rushed through, armed with a homemade knife, a spear, and the leader of the three had a gun. Prost acted before he could think about the consequences of his actions, pulling the young stranger behind him and raising an axe against the three aggressors.

"Leave it. There's nothing more you can take from him," Prost spoke with brazen confidence, rolling back his shoulders as he prepared for an inevitable fight. Neil remained hidden and ready to help, though nevertheless was internally screaming at Prost for this act of heroism. Neil never would have risked his life for some random man, not because he was the leader of a city that needed him, but because it didn't make any sense to do so. The risk wasn't worth the cost.

But that's not how Prost saw things. He was desperate– desperate to save someone– *anyone.* If he couldn't save the love of his life, then at least he could save the life of a stranger.

"You clearly ain't seen much of anything if you think gear is the only thing you can steal from someone," the man in the front said. He was just as confident, not showing a hint of fear as he examined the battle-worn Prost.

"I told you to leave it," Prost hissed, raising his axe as the three slowly began to approach him.

"Alright, sure. We'll do that. But you just gotta do one thing for us. Just leave those pretty weapons of yours and walk away, hm? And you can keep the boy."

"Keep dreaming." Prost snarled, tightening his grip on the handle of his axe.

The first man sighed, clicking his tongue as he shook his head. "Why are they always like this? *Boy.*" The first man snapped, looking over Prost's shoulder to the stranger he was protecting. There was the sound of a click. Prost knew instantly what it was: the hammer of a gun being drawn back. The end of the barrel was pointed at the back of Prost's head now.

"I'm really sorry, mister," the young stranger murmured, "but you should really just do as they say. Please."

Knowing that he had no choice but to comply, Prost slowly began to lower his axe and looked between the four aggressors, figuring out who was closest. He glanced up at the rafters, crouching slowly as he waited for the explosion of a gunshot. Neil relaxed his hands and steadily exhaled, slowly squeezing the trigger as more of the young stranger's body became exposed while Prost crouched down.

The pop of the gun shattered the tense silence of the warehouse, marking the start of their fight. A scream ripped from the young stranger's throat as he crumpled to the ground behind Prost. He dropped the gun in his hand and clutched his right shoulder as blood seeped between his fingers.

The three aggressors instinctively looked back towards the origin of the bang. The first man fired a shot at Neil and managed to clip the barrel of the rifle with frightening accuracy.

Prost lunged towards the man with the gun first, thrusting the axe down upon his center mass. The first was quick to fall, and Prost was quick to shove his fist into the face of the next closest bandit, clipping his chin. The third extended a knife-wielding hand towards Prost, which he was quick to catch. Sliding his foot in front of the bandit, Prost used the momentum from the stab and slung the bandit over his shoulder, slamming him into the ground.

"Prost!" Neil yelled, "behind you!" Neil floundered for another weapon as Prost turned around. He was too late. The young stranger already had his gun raised and was pointing it at Prost. No doubt, to take revenge for his fallen comrades.

Prost looked down at the gun pointed at him; a shiver danced down his spine. *"Is this it?"* Prost wondered silently, his tired expression twitching into a frown. *"I'll never see Silvia again?"*

A second pop of a gunshot rang through the warehouse, and a body hit the floor.

2

The world seemed to stand still, as if nothing else existed beyond the warehouse. Prost's breath hitched and his heart seemed to stop. But time waits for no man. Prost heard one bandit fall behind him, one who would have taken his life if the young stranger had not intervened. The young stranger lowered his hand and cast the gun to the side. It slid a few feet before stopping. The only noise left was Neil as he climbed down and the stranger's pained breathing.

"Why?" Prost huffed. His gaze returned to the boy on the floor. He propped himself up but stayed seated, pressing his hand back onto the wound.

"He was going to kill you."

"They were your comrades. You could have killed me instead, but you didn't. *Why*?"

The young stranger shook his head. "They were the farthest thing from *comrades*."

They were quiet for a moment, and Prost could piece together the relationship between the young stranger and the aggressors. He could hazard a guess that the young stranger was less of an equal and more of a captive. Neil ran up behind Prost, keeping himself behind him and placing a hand on Prost's shoulder to get his attention. "There'll be more. We need to leave. *Now*."

Prost ignored Neil's comment, continuing to focus on the young stranger. "What's your name?"

"*Prost*," Neil hissed in protest.

"You owe me this." Prost glanced back at Neil, which temporarily silenced him. "Name." Prost turned back to the young stranger.

"Jamie. Jamie Ptak."

"You'll die out here. Come with us." Prost held a hand out to Jamie, though Neil was quick to hold Prost's arm back.

"Enough of this. We can't accept him– I won't allow it. He's a danger to Crawford and there's nothing stopping him from killing us when we become inconvenient like those people did." Neil knew exactly what Jamie was thinking because Neil would have done the exact same thing.

That's what terrified Neil. It was obvious who was going to win the fight, even if the aggressor had managed to ambush Prost while his back was turned. If Jamie wanted to live, his best choice was to appeal to Prost's protective nature, which he had flaunted earlier.

"You *owe* me this, Neil. If he gets out of control, I'll handle it. Besides, look at him. He's weak and wounded– and he saved my life. We can't leave him to die. I know you'll be able to figure out a way he can help out."

Neil glanced down at Jamie, huffing in annoyance but not saying anything further to dispute Prost's will. It was clear on Neil's face that the gears in his head were beginning to turn and he was quickly hatching a plan on what to do with their newest resident. Prost turned back to Jamie, once again extending his hand for Jamie to take. Jamie glanced between the hand and Prost but quickly took it, fearing that the offer would be rescinded as soon as it was extended.

The three left the warehouse, leaving the bodies of the aggressors and all the marred behind them. Yet Jamie couldn't seem to peel his eyes away from the dead marred, despite also wanting nothing more than to leave this place.

3

2042, four years earlier

For five years, picking locks and squeezing through impossibly tight places was all that Jamie did, only having stopped once Neil and Prost found him and took him away from his captors. He rarely spoke. Anything he did say fell on deaf ears, anyway. Against Jamie's wishes and innate drive to survive, he was often sent into danger, claustrophobic, and dark places– alone.

Sometimes they would send him out to survivor camps as a lamb in need of rescue. A small boy, weak and frail. Once the survivors dropped their guard to help him, the cultists would swoop in before the survivors realized that they had been duped. It was the same scam they were trying to pull with Prost and Neil.

In the beginning, Jamie tried to run or hide, though he would be put into isolation after every failed attempt. There soon came a point when he had stopped trying to flee all together. His spirit had been crushed; there was no hope of escape. The only path to survival was adaptation.

Jamie often looked back on one job in particular with great fondness. By this time he had stopped resisting his captor's orders. A wound he sustained during his capture, while they targeted his own hometown, had mostly healed.

On this day, the cultists traveled deep into the alloy zones, searching for the marred. While the parts themselves would fetch a pretty penny, like the copper, seeds, petals and sap, there was high demand for the marred themselves– dead or "alive". A successful hunt would feed the group for a month.

But as with anything, reward wouldn't come without risks. After all, managing to capture the marred was only one battle in a long war. The matter of transport and whether they could actually be sold would decide if the endeavor was worth their time. The cultist's saving grace was Tampica, the third kingdom, whose hunger for more Florids could never be satiated.

A cultist by the name of John sat next to Jamie on the ride to this particular mission. He was the only one of the cultists who spoke to Jamie like he were a real person, not an object to be used. Sometimes it even felt like John enjoyed Jamie's presence, despite Jamie's lack of charisma. A fault they both shared. The man himself was built similarly to Jamie, but stood a bit taller and walked with a heavy limp.

Typically, John was the infiltrator, not Jamie, though John had lost most of his abilities after being shot during the assault on Silverton. For now, Jamie was his replacement, but it wouldn't stay this way. If John recovered the cultists would have rid themselves of Jamie. It never came to that; Jamie had made sure of it.

Despite both of them being hyper-aware of this predicament, they were still with each other. "Did you sleep well?" John asked with a damaged voice as he looked at Jamie with genuine interest. For reasons beyond Jamie, John was still brought along on missions despite his injuries.

Jamie nodded in answer to John's questions. He spoke little words.

"Are you feeling ready for today?" John asked in an attempt to coax something out of Jamie.

Jamie shrugged his shoulders with little movement. Everything he did was minimal; how he moved, how he talked.

John chuckled, something he did often to break the silence, though was thrown into a coughing fit. After being shot during the raid on Jamie's town, he had to drag himself out of the burning mine and, as a result, inhaled excessive smoke.

The cultists had no way to treat him; Jamie wondered if it was better to put John out of his misery, but this most likely came from a place of self-preservation and less of a genuine want to relieve John's suffering. It wasn't that Jamie cared for revenge, either. He wasn't so angry that he became violent: he couldn't even begin to scratch at the walls in the pit of despair he was buried in.

Once John's breathing had returned to normal, he continued to speak. "Don't worry about it. If we fail, those metal bastards will crystalize again in three days, anyway. And the Florids… eh… they'll relax soon enough. We can come back," John paused, trying to think of something nice to say. "Tampica will feed us well if we find Florids. The Mechatollies are just a bonus. Either Crawford or Minerva will buy them, but they don't pay as much. They're stingy bastards. Maybe the others will let you watch the bidding."

Jamie shrugged. He never spoke to John, but John would talk anyway.

"Just get in through the vent and open the door for us– them. You ever been to school? That's where we're going."

Jamie shook his head.

"You're lucky, boy. The few times I went was hell," John laughed and would cough again. This time a spot of blood landed on the back of his hand, which he wiped onto his pants with little regard.

With the slow turn of his head away from the window, Jamie would stare at John with an expressionless face. Despite his uninterested look, Jamie's gaze was as sharp as ever. He wondered if John ever thought that death would be a welcome release? Recovery was impossible; John could hardly move. He was as much a prisoner as Jamie.

Before such thoughts could simmer for much longer, Jamie was caught off guard by the halting of the vehicle. They were here. Jamie uncurled his arms from under his knees, jumping out of the wagon without a word of consideration for John. At the helm sat a begrudged driver.

She said nothing to Jamie aside from a grunt and a nod of her head to get going. At least the horses, which brought them there, glanced in Jamie's direction without an angry scowl. They seemed disinterested more than peeved. There was no need to pay much mind to a replaceable prisoner, after all. Even the horses knew that.

Three cultists were already walking inside the premises of the school. They passed several buildings before stopping in front of the gym. Two stood in front of the door while the other made their way to a vent. The one beneath the vent beckoned Jamie to stand next to him.

"Open this," the cultist told him, handing Jamie a knife. Jamie would take it and hold the blade between his teeth before climbing onto the shoulders of the bandit. Once he had found his balance, Jamie grabbed the knife from his mouth and jammed it into the rusted screws.

The blade flexed with the pressure, but the screw would give before the knife could be damaged. The process repeated itself six more times: once per screw. Jamie would pocket the rusty screws before placing the blade back in his mouth. It was the dull side, of course, but Jamie still attempted to avoid placing his tongue against it regardless, as the thing was probably never cleaned. His fingers wriggled through the gaps in the vent as metallic dust powered his hands.

With a few forceful tugs, Jamie managed to pry the vent cover off the wall, carefully passing it down to the cultist beneath him. Even the cultists, who often threw caution to the wind and asked questions with the business end of a gun, understood the importance of being quiet in moments like this.

Alerting the Mechatollies too early would surely end with the capture of none. Florids, meanwhile, were much easier to alert accidentally but didn't often coexist with cocooned Mechatollies. The marred, by default, would fight members of the other side the second they spotted each other.

Even if the Mechatollies were already cocooned, any Florids that had wandered inside would surely have woken them. This wasn't to say co-habitation was impossible– just exceedingly rare.

Jamie's eyes narrowed as he poked his head into the gym, adjusting to the lack of light. As it got easier to see, he noticed a few brighter splotches of color amongst the abyss. Then he heard shuffling of feet. Had the cultists come during the day, the Florids within would have surely flocked towards the vent; attracted to the light like moths. For now, they remained docile– completely unaware of the looming danger.

"Mechatollies," the cultist asked in a hushed whisper. Jamie remained silent, waiting for the cultist to ask again. "Florids?" Was their second guess. Tapping his finger gently against the top of the cultist's head signified a correct answer, as Jamie grabbed hold of the wall. He flung himself inside, slowly lowering his body down using mostly upper body strength.

Once his feet were securely on the ground, Jamie took the knife out from between his teeth. The door was only twenty feet away, though in the darkness the distance could have easily been two-hundred. He crouched, dropping low to the ground. Better to take it slow– remain small and unnoticed.

His right hand traced the wall a few inches in front of him so that he couldn't veer too far off track. Half a foot was about as far as Jame could see. His left hand, meanwhile, clutched the knife with a white-knuckled grip. Falling into a rhythmic pace, Jamie slowly began making his way towards the exit where the cultists were waiting outside.

This dance had been going well for Jamie until he picked up on a Florid, somewhere between five and ten feet in front of him, that was breathing with great difficulty. The Florid's haggard gasps were strained, like a hole had been torn through its neck. Jamie would take a few steps forward, then the Florid would gasp and he would freeze. Shuffle shuffle. *Gasp*. Shuffle… *gasp*.

This pattern repeated itself without much variation, though with each step the gasping grew louder. The Florid never moved, only able to wait for Jamie's approach. Then he saw it. Clearly it was a child, likely his age. Though the Florid itself was certainly much older than that. The Marred aged differently from humans. Mechatollies practically didn't, seeing as the hosts were dead anyway. Florids did age, just very slow.

Jamie looked into the creature's eyes. It could voice no words– not even a peep came from the usually talkative parasite, though the Florid said all that it had to. This was a horrible life. Not even a Florid deserved to be pinned down like this, bound to the floor with broken bones and smashed beneath rubble. Jamie could not imagine being locked behind those eyes. Out of control, and worse yet, unable to go anywhere. In a way, it reminded him of John.

Vines wriggled out from between the squishy eye and the socket holding it in place, absently searching the air in front of the Florid's face.

The process looked painful.

A small flower, one that had been there before Jamie's approach, dripped from the Florid's eye like a teardrop. Never before had he been close enough to appreciate the strange, almost mystical beauty of these creatures. Monsters from which he had hid his whole life from but now seemed docile; at peace.

Most of the flowers on the boy's body were wilting, though a few remained in their prime. Even in this decaying state, the flowers seemed to spin like a dancer's flowing dress. The edges of the petals looked sharp, though they were anything but. The home of what should have been an Antherus only revealed a gaping hole, much like the mouth of a starving baby bird. The parasite couldn't infect Jamie, even if it wanted to.

The pair stayed petrified in the dying silence, silently gazing into each other's eyes. The Florid with some form of terror, while Jamie a childish fascination. It was dying. Yet Jamie didn't seem to care about the creature's suffering. He dragged a hand along the vines, plucking a flower from their flesh.

The surface of the petal was smooth and had an almost velvety finish. Jamie wasn't sure if this had hurt the creature, but it gave no indication of being in pain. Only an instant had passed, though an infatuation which would span a lifetime had been born.

4

2046, present day

It had been a few months since those peculiar men rescued Jamie. Prost visited him the most, though he had grown closer to Neil while he was recovering. The most progress in his relationship with Neil came after he had figured out what to do with Jamie.

When Jamie had arrived, they shaved his head, which was for the best, as the long hair that fell almost to his waist was beyond unsafe.

In this time he had also come to learn that Neil was the leader of Crawford, an affluent city which he recognized, as his former captors had done business with them in the past. Prost was supposedly Neil's bodyguard, though Neil was the one accompanying Prost into the alloy zones. Although it was obvious, even to Jamie, that the two were at odds– how good of a bodyguard could Prost really be?

To be truthful, Crawford was terribly boring. Nothing like the group that had control over Jamie before he came here. Most people would reason that not being forced to worm your way around infested buildings in search of scrap, all while being held hostage, would be a good thing. Really, he had just gone from a dingy prison to a lavish one.

One thing Jamie noticed about Crawford was their very sturdy walls. They dwarfed the encompassing houses and were far too tall and dangerous for Jamie to consider climbing. Jamie had no idea how they built the thing, but he could occasionally see the remnants of construction when he climbed the right buildings. The mundane-era walls, which once blocked the highway traffic from the town beside it, were used as a base. From there, Crawford used anything sharp and heavy they could find to fill the holes.

It was during this time– when he could finally see the horizon– that Jamie felt his mind return to a familiar question: was the world being kept out, or was he being locked in?

At least in the old group he was periodically allowed to roam freely– like a dog on a short leash. In Crawford, Jamie was but a house pet that nobody wanted. He usually walked around the city to clear his mind: the closest thing he could get to exploration within the walls.

Today he decided to explore the west end of the city. There were less highrises there, mostly stalky buildings. First, he came across a small two story mall; mostly empty. Stores from the mundane days had never been fully removed, and signs were left up.

Quick n Speedy Mart, *Atom Radio*, a martial arts studio, and a phone place. He was literate thanks to the books in his hometown. There wasn't much to do for a young child in an isolated and well protected town, such as his own. The same could not be said for his handwriting, which was nothing short of atrocious.

Jamie was naturally curious. Being sheltered all his life made him want to see all he could before his death, despite the danger. For the past few years, Jamie never went where he wasn't prompted to go. Obeying the beck and call of the cultists was his one and only duty, after all. Being able to walk as a free man was a surreal but pleasant experience.

Despite risking tetanus and exposure to all sorts of chemicals from the decaying mall, Jamie decided to go inside. Three of the stores were empty, but *Atom Radio* seemed to still be functional. Clearly somebody maintained it. The door was locked, but a key was hidden underneath a welcome mat, which Jamie found after a minute. The security was surprisingly lax, considering the care put into the station.

If it weren't for the dirty and boarded up windows, he could have mistaken the studio for being in the center of the city. Jamie stepped into the reception, looking at the front desk and a few chairs placed against the walls. There was a door with a red label. It read: *Recording Room*.

Now that seemed interesting. With a small push the door gladly opened, revealing a room overflowing with cables and sensitive equipment. Jamie's eyes lit up, quickly taking in the unfamiliar sights. Half of the electronics were things he had never seen before, only hearing about them through stories adults told him of the mundane days.

He could only imagine how expensive all this working equipment was. All of that copper currency spent, and for what purpose? Communicating with other settlements would be an obvious answer and was the first thing that came to mind. Though clearly there were other uses for these machines. A label made of tape entitled *city wide announcement* pulled his attention.

It certainly wasn't something he wanted to press. Jamie could only imagine how much trouble he would get into for breaking into the studio. The last thing he needed was to draw attention to himself. The thought of how many hours he would need to work at his mediocre job to pay for just one of the tech pieces inside was deterrent enough.

Before curiosity could get the better of him, Jamie decided to flee *Atom Radio.* Nothing good would come of staying somewhere he wasn't allowed. Jamie glanced around to make sure nobody had seen him leave, then continued on his journey. Next on his list was inspecting the wall.

It was a marvel of human might– a mix of mundane era engineering and Crawford's ingenuity. Piles of junk cars, fridges, anything. They plugged the holes in the pre-existing wall, which was built before the marred crippled society. The wall was something Jamie desperately wanted to get on top of.

He scaled the mall, the one housing *Atom Radio*, by way of a rusted ladder on the side of the building. With a running start, he'd be able to make it to the ledge of the concrete wall and throw himself over it.

If there was one thing he learned from his captors, it was how to be agile. Agile and quiet. Jamie jumped on his toes a few times, glancing between the edge of the building and wall as he gauged the effort needed to make the leap. He jumped a few more times, readying himself to run. He had achieved harder acrobatic feats in the past.

"Hey!" Jamie heard a voice call from beneath him. Jamie spun around, straightening himself in an awkward manner. His eyes darted frantically, searching the streets below for who had caught him. It was Neil. "What are you doing?" Neil asked in a bewildered tone.

Jamie croaked, having to figure out what to say to explain himself. "Just… running. On a roof. I like running on roofs."

Neil eyed Jamie with suspicion, seeing through the lie. "You should come down. It's not safe up there."

With a quick nod, Jamie turned to descend the building. Then he joined Neil on the street below. "Sorry for… going up."

"It's fine." Neil waved a hand dismissively. "Were you going to sprint off the edge or something?"

Jamie nodded. "I wanted to sit atop it. To see the outside."

"No! It's too dangerous out there. There are marred of all sorts roaming outside of the walls," he stated firmly. Neil seemed upset at first but had calmed after a look of revelation dawned on his features, though what he was about to say wasn't a spur-of-the-moment idea. "Leaving could be on the table for you." It was hard to tell what Neil was thinking; his body never betrayed his mind. The few expressions he did make seemed deliberate, as if they were planned before he had even started speaking.

Unlike Neil, Jamie was not so subtle. He practically jumped into the sky, his face flushed with surprise before it settled to a wide-eyed stare. "Really?" He exclaimed.

"I'll tell you what. I send you to Ivette. She keeps an eye on you, teaches you how we do things here. If you still want to go out, I'll send you. What do you say?" Neil extended his hand to shake on the deal.

Jamie nodded with excitement, quickly grabbing hold of Neil's hand and shaking it with unexpected fervor for a man of his size. "Yes– yes I–" Jamie stumbled over his words, having difficulty speaking over his excitement. "I'd like that."

5

2040, six years earlier

The massacre of Silverton was sudden and shocking. It was over before it had even begun. As the winter storms grew fiercer, so did the remaining survivors. On a particularly cold day, a group of three strangers had found the gate and were allowed refuge in Silverton's stronghold.

Unbeknownst to the villagers of Silverton, these three were no unlucky stragglers. They were escapees from a sect of notorious cultists. One that Silverton, in its island of isolation, knew nothing of. While the cultists presented themselves as raiders in need of food, what they really wanted were bodies: ones that they could transform into the horrible creatures they called pets. *Florids.*

Upon the first sign of a threat, the council of Silverton ordered everyone to stay within the confines of the nearby mines, from which the town got its name. The mines were a mile away from the snowed-in village, and the council had hoped that the homes would be enough of a distraction for the alleged bandits. It was not.

Jamie and his best friend, Amanda, were never content with waiting for things to happen. The pair had snuck away from the main group, intent on discovering what it was that had been plaguing their parent's minds.

They had made a hideout during their years spent inside, utilizing one of the pre-existing air ducts and expanding it. A rustic, mud-covered board concealed the entrance, invisible to the untrained eye.

"What's going on up there, Amanda?" Jamie whispered into the crawlspace, glancing around the tunnel. The pair was alone for now. "Can you see anything?"

"There's too much snow. Get in here– help me push the hatch open." Amanda was inside the crawlspace, trying to force her bodyweight against the outer vent to open it. The small burrow served as a much needed break from the bleak mines and their moist walls; sometimes their only view for months on end. The air duct opened up to the surface but had been snowed-in. It was useless in its current state.

Jamie sighed softly, laying down on the floor and wriggling his way through the opening of the crawlspace. The entrance was small; just barely enough so that they could fit inside. However, after the entrance laid a room the size of a large closet. There was enough room to sit upright. Countless years of shoveling had more than paid off in this moment.

Amanda and Jamie both leaned their arms against the hatch, fighting against the bulky snow. In rhythmic unity, they heaved their shoulders against it. Shove after shove would open the hatch by a half inch until they could fit their hands through the gap.

Their fingers clawed at the snow, acting as tiny shovels as they carved away. The final result produced a small peephole that faced the town. The snow reddened the tips of their fingers, though they disregarded the pain in their excitement. Amanda looked intently through the hole as Jamie waited, but she was silent for much too long.

"Well– can you see anything?" Jamie whispered impatiently, watching her stern face as she continued to closely study the town.

"It's dark. Give me a second," Amanda was silent for a moment longer. "I see some lights down there. Could just be the sheriff and his people." She conceded after a pause, glancing down at Jamie. "Let's close this up. It's freezing." She grabbed a rope attached to a knob on the hatch, pulling it shut. "I bet they found an… animal or something. They always try to get into town during the winter. Wonder whose house was broken into," Amanda questioned.

"You don't think it has anything to do with the stalkers, do you? Those– those *bandits*. I heard their leader scream something to the sheriff. They're supposed to return soon. A week, he said." Jamie crawled over to the exit, glanced over the still empty tunnel, then wriggled out. Once Amanda had joined him in the tunnel Jamie would conceal the entrance. A gentle smear of mud would cover the seal almost completely.

Amanda patted herself off, making sure there was no dirt stuck onto the snow that melted on her shirt. "That would explain why so many of the wall guards aren't inside."

"What if they find us here?" Jamie whispered, a shudder running down his spine at the idea of being attacked. Seeing his fear, Amanda attempted to cheer Jamie up by making light of the situation.

"You seriously didn't hear him say anything other than one week? What, like, *I'll be back! Fear my wrath*!" Amanda mocked the stranger, laughing softly.

Jamie shook his head, crossing his arms at the teasing. "I went back inside before more guards could get there. The last thing we need is for Sheriff Tam to get us on his radar *again*."

"*Ugh*... always so scared of punishment! That's why you need someone like me around. A smooth talker that ain't afraid of a little scolding." Amanda draped her arm over Jamie's shoulders, guiding him back to the main area of the mines. It was a few meters in and large enough for all the villagers. Not that there were many remaining.

Many of the villagers stayed within the main area. It provided great warmth and a place for idle chatter. Most chalked up their retreat to the mines as another failure in the power grid. Some shared the same sentiment as Amanda and Jamie. A rabid animal, which would soon be dealt with. Then they could return home. No one worried about the *bandits*. They hadn't seen how desperate the people of this world had become.

The cultists stayed just out of the town's walls until well after sunset. For a few hours, everything was fine. The group seemed to have left, and the patrollers found themselves at ease in their safety. Though that was wishful thinking. Within thirty minutes of midnight, the cultists had returned. An erratic man approached the wall.

He walked without a worry of being shot as he approached the gates of Silverton, just as he had before. This was the same cultist who had made demands one week earlier: the same one Jamie had told Amanda about. A smug look was plastered on his face as he sauntered towards the guards. The weight of his threats did not seem to weigh on his conscience in the slightest. Even a massacre did not faze him. "That town of yours is looking real empty!" The leader yelled up to the sheriff, who had refused to leave the gate since first contact.

"Our town is fine. It will be better once you leave!" Tam, the sheriff, retorted. The wall guards' bows were not yet drawn, though they were trained on the leader, nevertheless.

The leader simply cackled. A sick, twisted trill of a laugh. It did not sound human. "It is nearly midnight. I hope you have made the right choice! At least for… the sake of the people you've tucked away in those mines."

"You bastard!" One of the guards hissed, nearly firing an arrow at the leader. The guard next to him forcibly yanked the bow away with some effort. That guard was only the most confident of the bunch. It was clear the others were anxious to draw their bows and attempt their shot at the leader. Despite their hostility, the leader continued to wear a vile smile at them. These people did not worry him. He had seen much loftier attempts on his life.

"*All of you*! Steel yourselves. The council members will be here soon. Then this incident will be behind us," the sheriff commanded, looking over at the other guards. It seemed to calm them, albeit only slightly.

The guards would no longer shoot the leader at the sight of a stray cough, but they were still on high alert. Sheriff Tam turned away from the cultist leader, going to collect the demanded crates of food. It was Silverton's peace offering.

A single cultist slinked out from the tree line, approaching the leader. He seemed to chuckle at whatever it was she had said. The pair then watched as the gates opened, revealing the crates of food and the village behind them. All Silverton could spare was ten crates of food.

The leader was silent for a while. Each passing second rattled the guards. They gripped their bows, adjusting the position of their fingers every few seconds. The leader seemed surprised. Though it didn't last long. "Is this your offering?" He asked, "Is this *all* your lives mean to you? Ten… *measly* crates?" The leader huffed in frustration. It was almost childish.

The sheriff looked at him, his heart sinking into his stomach. This would not do. He would have to persuade the leader to be content with what they had given. "We cannot give anymore! Else we will starve–"

"Then starve!" The leader roared. His face pinched together in a terribly unnatural way.

The guards looked at him in stunned silence. The man who once seemed reasonable, albeit with a few loose screws, became senseless at seemingly the push of a button. He breathed heavily, looking at the sheriff as he attempted to compose himself.

With a wave of his hand, the cultists hidden in the trees started to collect the crates. Nearly twenty-five people emerged from the woods. Far more than what would be needed to grab the crates. A show of power. The leader turned and left with the same calm demeanor he approached them with.

6

2046, present day

The day was a momentous one. Crawford held its head up high, proudly standing among the few communes that had succeeded in this vast wasteland. Neil was in the middle of a speech, preaching about pride, wealth, and community. "These have been the ten best years of my life!" Starting to finish his speech, Neil raised a glass above his head, addressing the crowd a final time. "As long as we remain with one another, I know the future will hold true. To another bountiful year!"

Though only a year had passed, Jamie had already changed a considerable amount. He was slightly stronger and a much better traceur than before he arrived at Crawford, which pleased his trainer and Neil. But much to Ivette's dismay, his hair had regrown to a slightly offensive length, which he normally tied back instead of cutting.

Jamie sat off to the side, watching as people cheered and toasts were made. He felt happy for all of them, but mostly he felt relieved for managing to contain his urges to leave for nearly a year.

This was a time of celebration, but despite how he felt, Jamie couldn't bring himself to rejoice alongside the others. Much had changed in the past year since his arrival in Crawford. Even though these were all small issues, adjusting was a long and difficult process. Trivial matters, like making friends and learning to talk with people, which would come easily for most– not Jamie. It was an unusual feeling, and Jamie struggled to describe it at first: contentment.

But none of those things were what was troubling him at this moment. Such a cheerful celebration was surreal for him; he had never seen something like this before. Not even in Silverton.

Looking upon his dominion with a subtle smirk, Neil had been carefully surveying each section of the party to ensure that everything was as it should. And he was undoubtedly satisfied with what he saw. That was until his gaze fell on Jamie. He left his pedestal once everyone's attention had shifted onto each other, walking off the stage and towards Jamie. He placed a hand carefully on Jamie's shoulder, jolting him from a hypnotizing thought. "Are you alright? You look a bit pale."

Jamie shook his head slightly, glancing at Neil. "It's freezing." Jamie rubbed his hands against his face, getting a laugh out of Neil.

"That's why you've got to join the party with the rest of us."

"It must have taken a while to find all this stuff. I can't even remember the last time I was at a party like this. Probably not since the mundane days… back when there were actually people around to celebrate with."

Neil knew what Jamie was thinking. Even though Jamie had developed a good wall to hide behind, he always seemed to be completely exposed around Neil. "It is better here, you're right. But it's not better for you, is it?"

This seemed to hit the nail on the head, as Jamie's grip on his cup tightened just slightly. It hadn't gone unnoticed by Neil, who looked at Jamie with a subtle nod to tell him what was going on. "I'm tired of being trapped behind walls, Neil. I appreciate all you've done for me. I really do. But I don't want to wait for death to find me sitting here." Jamie fell silent, looking at the cup in his hand. Every few seconds the trembling of his fingers, a product of the cold, sent the contents of the cup sloshing about– though never spilling over.

Even if for only half a second, Neil's demeanor shifted. A smile, barely noticeable, slipped onto his face. Then it was killed by an expression of concern. Neil leaned over Jamie's shoulder, whispering into his ear.

"You know, Jamie… you don't *have* to sit behind these walls. You could be an agent for *me.* A thorn which protects the blossoming flower of Crawford. Become one with the *Pale Roses*." Neil placed a hand on Jamie's, trying to calm his iron grip on the cup.

Jamie turned his head towards Neil. A shiver ran down his spine, as if he had heard something he shouldn't have. Despite that, Neil's words were comforting. The conversation that the two of them shared a year ago resurfaced in Jamie's mind. Neil watched quietly as

Jamie sorted through his thoughts, understanding that he was close to accepting the proposal. "I– I could?" Jamie tried to remain hesitant.

Neil watched for a moment as a pleasant smile crept onto his face. "Of course, Jamie. I knew since the day I saw you, you could– *would* be perfect for this task. Now I am certain I was right." Jamie nodded, feeling his heart begin to crawl up his throat like a spider. "As much as I would love to pour over the details now, this is a time of celebration. Business has no place here. Come tomorrow morning, I want you to meet Prost in the library. Do *not* tell anyone, say you'll be joining the expeditions outside of the wall if you must, but don't mention the copper. This is *highly* classified business."

"I understand." Jamie nodded, glancing away for a moment before returning his gaze to Neil. By now Neil had leaned back in his seat. "My lips are sealed. Locked up tight– key thrown away," Jamie spoke with fervor. That got an amused chuckle out of Neil.

"Free yourself of worry, Jamie. This night is to be *filled* with enjoyment and laughter. Then, come morning, we'll gain another pillar to hold up our wonderful lives. *You.*" Neil squeezed Jamie's hands softly, an attempt at comforting him one last time. "I should be speaking with others now, can't keep the people waiting, after all. See you tomorrow." Neil patted Jamie's shoulder, getting up from the chair and walking over to other groups of minglers. He seamlessly integrated himself with other people, talking the night away.

Jamie, meanwhile, would end the night where he started it: watching others dance, sing, and laugh. Nothing more than a spectator. It was as if he were the sole viewer of a mediocre movie in a lonely theater. A feeling that he had not felt in a very, very long time. Yet the sensation was not at all unpleasant– it could almost be described as peaceful. Because this was who Jamie was: a spectator.

The night was beginning to drag on, and Jamie decided to leave before he ended up staying until dawn. He finished the drink before sliding his coat on, slipping outside. It was dark; the air was crisp and burned his nostrils like peppermint. The streets were dark, illuminated only by the stars and the semi-present moon. Save for one person, it was empty. If not for the rumble of the party and the well-maintained surroundings, Crawford could have seemed abandoned.

Snow crunched beneath Jamie's feet as he approached the person outside: Prost. He wasn't smoking at the moment, but Jamie could still smell the floral scent of the petala he was always huffing. It was a type of depressant crafted from a by-product of Florids: the seeds within the flowers. There were flakes of burnt paper in front of Prost.

"I thought you'd be home by now," Jamie said as he approached, standing by Prost's side and observing the desolate city in front of them.

"Guess I decided to hang around a bit longer."

"Did you see the others off? Sicaren and Natty just left, didn't they?"

Another roll of petala was pulled from Prost's coat as he nodded at Jamie's question. The petala was quick to find a home between Prost's lips. He held a match's flame between a cupped hand and the end of the blunt, letting the fire warm his fingers. Prost took a long drag of the petala before pulling the blunt away from his mouth, letting the smoldering ash die in the snow in front of them before taking another huff and continuing the cycle.

"I… still feel like I haven't really thanked you. For… bringing me to Crawford, and everything. What if I got you some of those things you like smoking? I bet I could get my hands on some." Jamie's spirits were buoyed after hearing he would soon be going on expeditions. Otherwise, he wasn't the type to gush over others.

Prost shook his head, speaking in a tone more humored than usual. "That's above your paygrade."

"Come on, Prost! Seems fair, on account of you saving my life and all."

"What I mean is…" Prost removed the blunt from his mouth to make his voice clearer. "The only place that you can reliably get your hands on these is Tampica. They're not kind to strangers."

"Well how do you get them?"

"I don't. Neil gets them for me. They're my sop." Prost took another huff. He was nearly a quarter through. Jamie opened his mouth to ask for an explanation, though Prost was quick to continue. "Not that it matters."

"Why? I mean… why does he give it to you?"

Prost shrugged, lifting the blunt in front of his face and rolling it between his fingers. The burning end seemed to be alive, dancing in the cool winter night and leaving streaks of indulgence in the air.

"They're too good to quit. Just like I can't quit him," was what Prost ended up saying.

"I don't think he's half bad. I mean, he's rough around the edges. But so am I. And so are you. It's what draws us to each other."

Prost glanced over at Jamie for the first time tonight. He chuckled at the statement, taking another drag of petala before acknowledging with a "maybe."

"How did you two meet, anyway?"

"We've all done things just to stand here tonight. I don't believe in fate. I think everything that brought us here was of our own actions, and for that we're responsible. You shouldn't let what those people did to you then affect what you do now."

"I don't." Jamie fought, defensive at the accusation but knowing it was true. He wasn't sure where this was coming from.

"And you shouldn't let Neil's choices lead to what you're about to do."

"Being a copper chaser?"

Prost froze at the mention of the copper chaser. He was quick to hide his expression beneath his hand as he continued to smoke. "I'm just saying that things aren't what you think. You should be wary of him. Weary of me."

"I know *why* he's sending me out. I'm fine with that. If it's benefiting the city that gave me shelter, then I'm fine with that. We all have to pitch in somehow, don't we? I can hold my own out there."

"He's doing this to get back at me," Prost thought, though knew how insane that sounded. So he didn't say it aloud. He bent down, extinguishing the rest of the blunt in the snow. Prost knew that those

things made him anxious. *Paranoid.* Yet he would always find a way to smoke more.

"You're right," Prost relinquished. "This is the price we pay."

"We were placed on this path, Prost. That path is what led to our encounter on that day. But you were still the one that saved me." Jamie grinned. Prost recognized the look: Jamie was up to something.

"Just don't get caught up in Neil's path thinking it's your own. It'll bring you nothing but trouble."

"Maybe his path will reveal a perfect payment for my savior," Jamie teased with a wide grin.

"Goodnight, Jamie." Prost rolled his eyes, and Jamie scoffed in disbelief.

"Seriously! Just tell me what you want and I'll get it. Anything, anything at all. My offer expires never. Think it over tonight and tell me tomorrow. I'll start looking for it the second my first expedition starts." Jamie patted Prost's shoulder, taking a few steps down the road before Prost's voice called to him.

"Wait!" Jamie turned around to look at a stationary Prost. "A favor. That's what I want. I'll tell you what it is when I need it."

Jamie smiled, lifting a thumbs up before waving goodbye. Then he continued down the road, disappearing into the night.

7

Once the morning sun rose, Jamie burst out of his apartment like an escaping prisoner. He bolted down the stairs; the stale wind in the stairwell whipped past him, as if he were cutting through the air itself. Nothing else in his life had ever moved him to leave his bed– at this hour no less– as fast as he did now. Jamie looked upon the empty street as he collected his thoughts. No one was up early in the morning, especially not after a night like yesterday.

He started walking towards the library, glancing up at the sky; a twinge of orange sunlight peeked through the tops of buildings– none taller than four stories. The air was crisp, but not cold. Spring would soon be upon them.

Never before had he been able to feel the morning breeze in solitude, though Jamie suspected that would change once he started working for Neil. His gaze fell from the sky, returning to the streets in front of him– laser focused on the ever closer library, as if worried that it may run off at any moment.

In a quick, single motion, Jamie reached for the doors and looked inside, though didn't wait long before entering. The library was quiet, lacking the usually busy and frantic librarian. Neil always valued knowledge and proper records keeping, which is why Crawford had a library at all.

He closed the door behind him; it creaked softly as he did so. Then Jamie stepped forward, opening his mouth to call for Prost. But before he could do anything, a hand clamped over his mouth– grabbing him tightly while an arm wrapped around him; he was trapped. Whoever it was had been hiding behind the door as Jamie entered. He flailed his arms around in an attempt to wriggle free, throwing his head back before biting down on the stranger's hand.

"Ah– *shit*! Calm down," Prost hissed as he released Jamie, shaking the bitten hand; the skin of which thankfully remained intact. A mark of Jamie's teeth, however, was left on Prost's hand. "I was going to reprimand you for not paying attention. Though I suppose you did well enough," he sighed, crossing his arms.

"I'm... sorry?" Jamie apologized, but he wasn't sure if he really should have, considering how Prost grappled him.

"Don't apologize to your attackers. Come along." Prost brushed past Jamie, walking off to a side room. Jamie was always left absolutely bewildered whenever he talked with Prost. It felt like Prost was always doing one thing but saying the other. There was probably wisdom in what Prost said and did. Jamie followed suit not long after.

Prost was unmoving for a while after Jamie entered the side room, looking out at the library. Like he was looking for something– or someone– but not being able to find whatever it was he was searching for.

He resigned his efforts by closing the door. With a sharp turn on his heel, Prost faced Jamie and took a deep breath, as if preparing for a grand speech.

"I'm not entirely sure why, but Neil's decided you'd fit in well with us. And for some reason, you agreed to it." Jamie could tell Prost was disappointed but nonetheless wanted to support Jamie's endeavor. "And in order for you to stay, well... *alive,* you need to get caught up on how the world works. Doubt those cultists knew the same things we do." Prost tossed Jamie a book that looked like it was originally intended for children. Then he carelessly gestured to a small table with two chairs on either side of it. "Read this. It's basic, but it'll get you up to speed. There's some other journals and whatnot that go more in depth if you need... they're all in the library."

Jamie looked at the magazine cover for a few seconds, then flipped through a few pages. "This is very... uhm." The book looked like a child's arts and crafts project. He was looking for words to complement it, of which there were very few possible options.

"I'll have you know I made that myself." Prost crossed his arms, his gaze narrowing on Jamie.

"You?" Jamie closed the book quickly, looking up at Prost with a look of disbelief and amusement. "Such a liar. You would have used

the paper for rolling petala," he said in a joking tone reserved for friends.

Prost rolled his eyes half-heartedly, laughing at the statement: he had smoked just before meeting Jamie. "Neil put it together. Now, I'll be back in a half hour, so sit tight until then." Prost closed the door silently behind him as Jamie sat down, starting to flip through the magazine.

He couldn't tell what the magazine used to be about, as the old text was completely covered with new information and infographics. Even the occasional, very detailed drawing graced the page. They looked out of place compared to the rest of the artwork. Fittingly, the book was entitled *Marred Survival Guide.* It detailed general concepts about Florids and Mechatollies. There were a lot of *fun facts* which were usually more gruesome than fun.

Most of the words were illegible, having been worn with time. Despite that, Jamie was able to get a lot from the booklet, though most of the information he already knew. Whoever wrote this knew that Mechatollies would recrystallize after three days of inactivity. Neil certainly wasn't the type to stay out long enough to notice such a detail in the Mechatollies' behavior, but Jamie wasn't sure why Prost would lie about Neil being the author of the booklet.

A small card fell out from between the pages about halfway through. The note contained a handwritten message. The writing was delicate and well preserved, which was similar to the text inside, but was clearly written well after the booklet had been made.

Nothing to fear, new recruit! Everything will be just fine– trust me. I was once in your shoes, too. Luckily, this magazine will cover everything you need to get you started.

Please stay safe, and I wish you the best of luck on your journey. And soon enough, we'll get to meet face to face! Much love and happy harvesting.

– *S*

8

Jamie read the note carefully, rubbing the paper between his fingers. The writing seemed odd at first, though he dismissed it. Adults from the mundane days had an odd way of doing things. They had nice handwriting and frilly language. Nothing like people his age.

With a thump, Jamie closed the magazine. He had read all that he had to. Without anything to do, Jamie got a proper look at the surrounding room. It was dark, only illuminated by a small window which sat just below the ceiling. He idled patiently though didn't have to wait much longer.

As Prost swung the door open, brutish as always, his eyes darted towards the notecard on the desk. At first he was unable to see what it said, so interrogated Jamie with his usual spunk during his approach. "Are you writing love letters now? Who taught you to write, huh?"

With a scoff, Jamie held the card out to Prost. Jamie's handwriting was nowhere near as nice as the one on the notecard. Prost examined the card. A strange look smeared on his face. Something of surprise. Maybe shock. He would shove the card away into his pocket, as if trying to distance himself from it. Then he slammed a bag onto the desk in front of Jamie, speaking before Jamie could ask any questions.

"It should all be there… Neil had this bag set aside for a while now and had to dig through storage to find it. I think he fell asleep while he was looking. Didn't answer my knocking earlier," he prattled on, gesturing for Jamie to look through the bag as he took out a small list of the items inside.

Jamie unzipped the bag, laying out the items on the table. A uniform, a couple knives, a lock picking set, a journal, a strange device, and a flask. "What's all this for?" He asked, looking up from the table as he did.

"Basic necessities. The uniform is the same one I'm wearing now… and… all the time, really. Yours isn't as cool though." He wedged his thumb beneath a small, stitched on heart that covered a bullet hole. Prost had never seemed so prideful of anything else. As for the uniform itself, well, there was nothing much to be said about it. It was a black, long-sleeved turtleneck, a durable pair of dark blue jeans, and a pair of boots that would last a lifetime.

"You know how to sew?" Jamie questioned in disbelief, quirking a brow at the almost unrecognizable heart. The lines were so uneven and poorly planned that it made the pattern look incredibly lopsided.

Prost shook his head as a subtle frown appeared on his lips. "Most of the Roses wear this. It's the costume Neil dresses us all up in. Anyway, you'll see the other three more now. Natty and Sicaren are anxious for a new friend, I'm sure Ivette would be happy to see you again. Most of the copper goes to either Natty or Sic. They're good people. You'll like them," Prost cleared his throat, putting the paper away. "I'm getting sidetracked… the knives are good for harvesting and combat, you should take them to Natty whenever you come back. She'll show you how to care for them. Lock pick is obvious, Ivette should have taught you how to use that," he fell silent for a moment, watching Jamie fiddle with the butterfly knives before glancing at the strange device.

Pointing at the contraption, Jamie looked up at Prost for guidance. "What's this for?"

Shrugging, Prost inspected it closer before concluding that he did, indeed, not know what it was. "I dunno. Something about reading copper in the air. You'll figure it out."

Prost took the knife Jamie was playing with, quickly flicking it open and then closing it again in a fluid flick of his wrist. "Spring loaded knives are better, but harder to maintain. Just practice when you have nothing else to do. You'll get the hang of it." Prost handed the knife back to Jamie, who was trying to replicate what he just did. Prost grinned at the sight: Jamie looked like an elephant trying to carry an egg on its tusk. Before long, he continued on with the remaining two items. "The journal's for recording your expeditions. Neil will tell you more before he sends you out."

"Why do you know so much about this? Were you a copper chaser back in the day?" Jamie didn't look at Prost, continuing to focus on the butterfly knife. He picked up the name copper chaser from the book– supposedly being the title of the job he was about to begin.

Prost shook his head, sitting on the chair opposite the one Jamie was sitting on. "I've worked as Neil's bodyguard for eight years now, but I'm more like hired company for conversation… that way we can *watch out for each other.* I picked up most of it from him. He likes to talk to me about these kinds of things. Everything he's not sure about. Plus the…" Prost fell silent. His face said that he just spoke of something he wasn't supposed to.

"Hm." Jamie didn't seem to have paid attention to what Prost said, too absorbed in trying to properly fold and open the knife. Prost watched Jamie for a moment longer, sighing softly as he looked up at the lone window.

"Neil's going to be planning your route today. Just– enjoy the rest of the day. Get into your uniform tomorrow morning and go to his office. You probably won't leave then, but he'll need to get you ready. Mentally, that is." Prost stood, finally snapping Jamie out of his trance. "Tomorrow morning. Uniform. Neil's office." Jamie nodded as Prost left the room, quietly packing everything back into the bag.

9

When the following morning rolled around, Jamie got dressed in the uniform he had been provided. He looked at himself in the slightly damaged mirror, putting on his usual jacket before finally looking away from the reflection and leaving the unit.

Jamie walked down the street again, searching for Neil's office. In truth, he hadn't been there often, except for when he first arrived in the city. Despite this, he remembered clearly where the building was. It was hard to miss and instantly recognizable, much like Neil.

Traversing the vaguely familiar halls, Jamie looked for items that had remained in his memory to guide him. He found Neil's office on the second and final floor of an older building, close to the heart of the city. It offered a good vantage point, which oversaw most of Crawford and all the major buildings.

When he stood before the office door, Jamie pressed his ear against the wood and would listen for any noise inside. Once he confirmed that no one was speaking, Jamie knocked on the door to announce his presence. Hopefully, Neil wasn't in a meeting. Jamie wasn't good at introductions.

Neil called to him from behind the door.

"Come in!" Jamie cracked the door open, looking at a still busy Neil. He glanced up at Jamie to acknowledge his entrance, though looked back down at his papers to finish up. Prost was leaning on the wall behind Neil, his arms crossed as they normally were. Watching Jamie intensely, as Prost did with everyone else. "Just– close the door after yourself. I'll be just a minute."

Jamie closed the door quietly, sitting on the chair opposite the side of the desk that Neil was working on. The chair was large, almost engulfing him completely. It was also very loud; crumpling as Jamie sat down and groaning as he fit into place. The noise was unpleasant– especially to Jamie, who valued silence.

Everything in Neil's office was very well kept: not a single trace of defilement to be found, even with the most keen of eyes. Some of the windows were likely once broken, though they were replaced in such a way that would make it difficult to tell if there was ever any damage.

It almost seemed normal– something that the elders would describe from the mundane days. By the time Jamie was done looking around the room, so too was Neil with his work.

Neil placed the papers in one of the desk drawers, smiling warmly at Jamie. Then he looked back at Prost, speaking to him. "Why don't you take a walk, Prost?" Jamie glanced at Prost, who hadn't moved an inch since he first entered the office.

Prost's gaze hadn't lifted from Jamie, either. But the focused look in his eyes had softened and melted away completely. Jamie couldn't put a name to the look, yet Prost seemed almost sad. As if there were something he wanted to say to Jamie, but was unable.

But his mind was quick to move elsewhere. There was nowhere that could really be considered *safe*, not even Crawford– but this seemed a little excessive to Jamie. Wouldn't Prost's skills be better used outside of the walls, or to defend it?

It was obvious that Neil was a smart guy, so why would he waste manpower to have a bodyguard in the heart of one of the sturdiest cities; one that hadn't ever been breached? *Why not let Prost leave the walls?*

Jamie forgot the thought when Prost interrupted it by speaking. "I'll be outside." Prost was defiant in an inconsequential way, as always. He pushed away from the wall, walked out of the door, and closed it behind him as he left.

His footsteps trailed off after a few seconds, staying just outside the room. Close enough so Prost could run inside if needed, but far enough away so as not to encroach on their conversation.

Neil watched Prost as he left, then returned his focus to Jamie. He interlaced his fingers before he spoke. "Have you ever killed someone, Jamie?" He became quite serious as he asked, carefully watching Jamie as he answered.

"Not… directly. I mean– I suppose I did. But I didn't… shoot them, or anything." Jamie thought back to the bandits– *the cultists.* He trapped their leader in a burning mine.

Of course, that was a life or death moment, but either way, he wasn't the one doing the killing; the fire was to blame. There was also a sickly man whose life he *had* stolen– robbed with his own two hands. But for that Jamie felt no grief: there was mercy in the man's death. So Jamie felt no need to spare Neil any details.

"But you know that by leaving these walls, someday you'll be forced between keeping your life or taking another's, don't you?" Jamie nodded, and Neil continued after a pause. "My main… goal is to keep you safe and healthy. When you get back and have any regrets, my shoulder is yours to lean on. Regardless, whenever you return, swing by my office. I'll be in charge of distributing the copper and I would like a debrief of what happened outside. Information is vital, you know."

Neil leaned over to one of the drawers, taking out a map of the area surrounding the city. "How far will I be traveling?" Jamie's eyes scanned the map, recognizing a few familiar roads.

"A decent way away. Some of our cars will be driving to one of our allies a few cities over in a couple days. They'll take you most of the way there, but the rest will be up to you. They'll drive out to the west." Neil pointed at the main road which left through the west side of the city. "They'll be halfway to the city of Minerva before you jump off. One of our people heard that there may be a group of Mechatollies hidden in the buildings of an overgrown town. They'll be back to pick you up in three days, so you have a bit of time to find them and harvest the copper, if they're really there."

This type of trip wasn't so uncommon for the drivers of Crawford. Minerva and Crawford had been long-time partners; even before both of their rise to riches.

Crawford had much to thank Minerva for, after all. Without them, Crawford would have remained a poor city, floundering about with the rest of the world. What use are cars when there is no fuel with which to power them? Not that Crawford relied on Minerva as they once did.

"How will I know where it is? I mean, if it was just off the road, someone would have found it already, right?"

"The road that leads to the town has been mostly destroyed and is overgrown, like most others. But there's a few markers to help pinpoint it. Ah– I have a map to give you, so once you're there you'll be able to find it. Hopefully," Neil said as he rummaged around in his drawers again, pulling out a map and a small compass. "Oh, that reminds me. I have something else for you." He turned around, going through some cabinets behind the desk.

"You really have a lot prepared," Jamie muttered, picking up and inspecting the compass.

"What would I be if not prepared? It's not like I can send you out with someone. Nobody is trained and honestly… I think they'd just get in your way. I'm sure you've learned on the job before." While Jamie had never told Neil exactly what happened during his time with the cultists, Neil was able to figure a lot out on his own, with the small bits here and there that Jamie told him.

He knew the cultists traded in Florids and sometimes copper. Neil also knew that Jamie would be the best suited to get inside places quietly when conventional methods wouldn't suffice. Subtly was key in alloy zones: this fact was ingrained in anyone who had ventured there, Neil included.

Neil presented a mask to Jamie, one that would cover his entire face. "This is my old mask. I haven't used it in a while, and I doubt I ever will again. It's kept me alive all these years, so I'm sure it'll do you good, too."

Jamie held the metallic mask, which was sturdy but light. The mask would secure to the face, which would do a good job staving away the Antheri– a parasite resembling an isopod. They couldn't infect someone without latching onto their tongue. Fabric could easily be chewed through, but this would certainly do the trick.

It looked a bit boring, though, which was probably for the best. No paint graced the slightly reflective surface of the mask, but that would soon change. Jamie's creative flair, which he had inherited from his mother, would not let a canvas go unpainted.

The mask felt like it was made of aluminum. There were adjustable leather straps with metal buckles to keep them in place. A secondary piece was dangling from the mask: another aluminum plate, which looked like it was meant to cover the back of the neck.

Unless the metal plate became loose or fell out of place, it also made the armor resistant to the Metalides; they resembled dragonflies made of copper in place of organic matter.

The parasites burned into the skin at the back of a victim's neck and fused to their spine. Infection was painful: once a host was infected, they lost control of themselves and the copper in their blood rose to lethal levels.

If not for how difficult something like this was to manufacture, let alone how it practically had to be tailor made to the user, Jamie was sure that the human population wouldn't have decayed to the point it had. It would take the parasites infinitely longer to infect the wearer.

"How'd you make this?"

"Natty made it for me, I think she used some scraps from the old junkers and the leather from old belts, or maybe someone who used to be a leatherworker. It was a while ago. Can't remember exactly. Why don't you try it on?" Neil tapped the arm of the chair as he spoke, diving deep into his memory in an attempt to recall the information.

Jamie flipped the mask around, looking at the inside before he put it on. There were a few thin, black felt pads to help cushion parts of the face. Mainly the nose, forehead, and under the eyes. It fit him well, which made sense, since Neil and himself seemed to have similarly sized faces.

The pads helped make it comfortable– as comfortable as a metal mask could be, anyway. He didn't tighten the straps, however, as he suspected that the mask would likely limit his ability to talk.

"I've taken a few good hits in that thing, too. And! I've *yet* to receive a broken nose."

"Natty really thought of everything when she made it, then." Jamie took the mask off before speaking and placed it down onto the table, looking back up at Neil.

"That she did." Neil nodded passively, leaning back in the chair.

"Where's your current mask?"

Neil sighed, shrugging. "On a mantle in my home. If you ever swing by, I'll show it to you."

Jamie thought for a moment, smiling softly before sharing his thoughts. "It's probably a mask more fitting for a noble than a copper chaser."

10

Jamie approached the line of cars. It was much too early for him. He had never particularly been a morning person, but he appreciated the tranquility of the early hours– this was anything but. With a flick of his wrist, Jamie would zip his jacket completely shut, and would then use that free hand to flag down one of the drivers. "Got any extra space?"

The driver looked at Jamie, glancing him over, as if trying to figure out who he was. "You must be that kid Neil said would join us. Sure, I got room. Sit up here with me." Jamie walked to the other side of the car, getting into the passenger's seat next to the driver.

He put his backpack on his lap, which, other than the items he was originally provided, now had four days' worth of food and enough water to get him by. The mask Neil gave him was clipped to the top of the backpack.

"This is your first time traveling out of the walls, isn't it? Never seen you leave with us before. Name's Patrick, by the way. But just Pat will do." Pat had one hand on the wheel; the other arm rested against the window.

He took his hand off the wheel to offer a handshake to Jamie and placed it back once Jamie shook his hand. He dressed as one would expect a member of a biker gang would, and had long, straight brown hair and a pale face that would go red whenever he was excited, which was practically all the time.

"Basically, yes. I'm Jamie."

"That's a pretty mask you got there, Jamie." Pat spotted the mask that Neil had given Jamie the day prior, though with a few alterations. The drivers had something similar to Jamie, though their masks only covered half of their faces.

The people inside the walls had even less protection, receiving only a simple cloth covering. However, this was better than most other cities, even affluent places like Minerva didn't issue any form of protection to their citizens inside the walls.

"I painted it last night." Jamie unclipped the mask from the bag, giving it to Pat so he could get a better look. The colors were dulled and seemed to all have a hue of brown to them, on account of their age and the filler used to prolong the lifespan of the paint. Other than the base, which had been painted black, a small bluejay with its wings spread was painted from the right temple to just above the eye-socket.

"That's nice," Pat affirmed. "What the hell are you doing with us? Surely there's some rich asshole who'd like a few paintings."

That got a genuine, albeit slightly awkward, laugh from Jamie. The two fell silent for a moment; the silent hum of the engine occupied the empty space. "These are quite a few cars. How do you have the fuel for them?"

"You been living under a rock or something?" Pat scoffed with subtle amusement at the notion, but it was more true than he thought. Jamie's blank expression explained that plenty. Pat begrudgingly explained, though not without a playful eyeroll. "Some... *geniuses* figured out how to get fuel from the Florids– or, not Florids, no. Something close to it though. Anyway, they pretty much launched everyone out of the dark ages. I think it is a special engine, too. No gasoline. I heard one of our own helped work on it, can't remember her name though. Super clean, super efficient. Even better than the cars before this all started, and those were pretty nice."

Patrick got excited by the prospect of cars. He must have been obsessed with them back in the day. "If you ever go where I'm headed, you could look at the farms– they're the heart that keeps Minerva's blood pumping. I guess that would make us the valves– we ain't nothing without each other. Anyway– in the farms they tie tassels around the plants' dangerous bits so you can see where they are. Apparently if you touch them you get paralyzed! Like a minnow caught in a jellyfish."

This all seemed a bit far fetched for Jamie, so he made a mental note to ask Neil about it later. "Why would a Florid produce fuel?" He looked at Pat with a questioning look though tried to be respectful.

"You ever brought a flame to a Florid? They burst up like a swab of paper doused in oil. You know, if you talk with that lady…" Pat paused, searching his mind for the name. "Oh yes– Natasha, that was her name. She was there, designing the engines and those types of parts, so she probably knows all about the biofuel that runs them."

Jamie thought for a moment if he recognized the name. He came to the conclusion that it was Natty; the name was similar enough and she was an expert in mechanics. "I'll talk with her when I return, then."

The driver yawned, nodding slightly. The large metal gate finally swung open and the line of five cars rolled out of the city. Jamie looked back at the wall as they left, it being the first time he could really appreciate it.

The wall was made of concrete but more importantly was tall and sturdy: a remnant from the mundane days. Any gaps were plugged with metal sheets, which were then reinforced with beams and cars. They wouldn't be knocked down anytime soon: the only way through would be to climb.

It was a feat of survival: an impenetrable barrier which kept the barbaric chaos from a peaceful civilization. It was nothing like the flimsy barricade which protected his hometown. Now Silverton's protection seemed more like a fence in comparison to the grand walls of Crawford.

"Neil makes us drive out to different cities frequently. Usually for trading, but today is more like gift giving. Minerva and Crawford are intertwined, even a fool could see that much. We have the cars and they have the fuel. But what do I know? I just drive the stuff to them, and sometimes I take a look at what's inside, you know?" Pat talked idly as the convoy pushed forward. The roads were certainly better maintained than others Jamie had been on.

"Have they been allies for a while?" At first, Jamie wasn't paying great attention to what roads they were taking out of the suburbs. It caught his eye when the convoy didn't drive straight out of the city. Instead, the snake of cars would deviate from the expected path at intersections, seemingly at random. It looked like there was some debris left on the roads not traveled, but it was too far away for Jamie to be sure.

"*A while* is an understatement. They're practically bound at the hip, like three peas in a pod."

"Three?"

The cut off from the suburbs to the forest was extreme. This was the first time Jamie was able to get a good look at the peculiar perimeter. Clearly the area had been well maintained, enough to keep even the vines from creeping too close to the houses in the abandoned suburbs. There was no obvious reason for this: no guards could see this far from the wall and nobody ventured here to appreciate landscaping. But Neil had plenty of strange habits and Jamie assumed this to be one of them.

Pat wasn't bothered by such things, unlike Jamie, who found the shift disturbing. It had become routine to Pat by this point. "Yeah, three cities. Oh– don't even get me started on Tampica. It's to die for. If I could, I'd go there every month. But they're pretty strict on who gets in or out of their city. Works great for me though, since I get to drive often enough, and there's hardly any travelers. Don't tell Neil I said this, but I think Tampica might be prettier than Crawford. Its walls aren't as brutalizing, so you get to see a lot of the surrounding scenery. Not like that's a problem here, if you live on an upper floor."

"Maybe I'll get to see if Neil lets me tag along until the end of the road."

"I'd take you either way." Pat wasn't so different from Jamie, and he extended his hand to Jamie to offer a pact. "What do you say? Let's visit Minerva and Tampica some time." Jamie glanced down at Pat's hand and smiled, taking him up on the offer and shaking his hand to seal the agreement.

The two continued to talk about their adventures for the rest of the drive. The places they had seen and the oddities that had been seared into their memories. Pat spoke the most, as Jamie had lost any form of charisma many years ago and wasn't very good in conversation. Lunch and a few other times when the cars stopped to refuel along the way was the only time their conversation was interrupted.

Throughout this time, Jamie had been keeping track of the road signs as they drove, looking out for the road signs he was told about before he left. It was a few hours after their departure until he finally spotted one that he could recognize. "Hey– pull off here, would you? This is it." He grabbed his bag, pointing towards the sign as they approached. Pat moved the car over to the side of the road and a few other cars rolled past.

"I'll be seeing you then, kid." Pat watched Jamie as he opened the door and left the car.

"I'll try to stay in this area on your way back. Look out for me. Please?" Pat nodded. "Thank you." Jamie closed the door, waving goodbye to Pat as the car sped off and quickly rejoined the rest of the convoy. Jamie enjoyed the silence for a few seconds before reaching for his mask, unclipping it from the bag, and securing it to his face.

Then he took a folded map out of his pocket, looking at the directions that Neil scrawled onto a small piece of paper. His handwriting was dry and concrete: as if a robot had written the instructions instead of a human. Once Jamie was certain of how to find the town, he placed the map away and pulled the bag back over his shoulders.

The mask didn't obscure his vision much, though the slight mesh which covered the eyes did make everything a bit darker. The change was nothing extreme; something his eyes could adjust to with ease.

As Jamie began walking, he rested his hand on a knife which hung on his belt– a normal knife, not one of those fancy butterfly knives he was given. He breathed in deeply, starting his trek into the woods and his search for the abandoned town.

There were two tools at Jamie's disposal that helped him with navigating the unfamiliar terrain. The first was a compass, which helped keep him from veering too far off course. It was small but reliable. The second was the copper tracer, which measured the copper level in the air. The number displayed usually stayed around .016 micrograms. As he continued to walk towards the town, the number gradually started to drop, until it sat at just .01 micrograms by day's end.

Throwing his things up in a tree, Jamie slept the night away wedged between a few branches. It was dreary and wildly uncomfortable, but safer than sleeping on the ground.

Each time he took off his mask to drink water, he looked around with paranoia; fearful that an Antherus was lurking behind every shadow. Thankfully, that night would spare him from any parasite encounters.

The following day started similarly, without any appearances of the parasites or their hosts, allowing Jamie to continue a safe voyage through the forest.

By this time, he had taken out the copper reader from his bag, carefully watching the numbers as they appeared on the heavily damaged screen. If the magazine he was given was right, the copper in the air should take a nose dive before jumping to unusual levels.

For now, the tracer seemed to be following a steady downward trend. The number on the copper tracer continued to drop before finally reaching its lowest at .005 micrograms. The number would hover at that level for a few meters before skyrocketing, peaking at .15 micrograms. He was close.

Looking up from the display, Jamie noticed that the trees were starting to thin out and were replaced with brush and other foliage. He crouched down, approaching the end of the treeline with heightened caution.

After a day of wandering, he finally saw something other than the seemingly endless trees: an abandoned town– his pot of gold at the end of the rainbow. While Jamie should have been overjoyed, he couldn't help thinking about Silverton. How easily they could have perished, just as this town had. Still, this couldn't weigh his mood down for long, and he continued pushing forward.

Jamie refocused his attention on the town, scanning for any wandering Mechatollies, though they were absent. No signs of Florid growth, either. They had unique, unmistakable flowers; Jamie remembered that. Not to mention, the flowers were absolutely stunning. So, in a way, Jamie was also disappointed not to see any.

Once Jamie was just a foot from the clearing, he drew his knife from its sheath, eyes keener than ever. It wasn't another moment before Jamie stepped out from behind the treeline, marking his first step as an official copper chaser.

11

The streets were empty. So were the alleys. On the one hand, the silence was relieving: he wasn't immediately attacked, and that worked well, considering his inexperience working alone. On the other hand, this meant that the Mechatollies were either not in the town or they gathered in the houses and were currently hibernating, which wasn't bad, since Jamie would be able to start his work on his own terms.

Once Jamie felt as safe as he possibly could, he dropped his defensive position and straightened his posture. The knife remained securely in his left hand. One could never be too careful; a lone Florid would wait until he dropped his guard to strike, as they had some limited degree of patience.

He approached the first house, closest to the way he had come. The windows were dirty and nearly impossible to see through, but intact. Circling the single-story house, Jamie surveyed its potential as a home base and tested each window to see if any had been left unlocked. Sneaking in was, unfortunately, not this easy: all the windows were either jammed or locked from the inside.

So Jamie returned to the front door and began to pick the lock with the tools he had been provided. With a steady hand, he carefully set each pin, working slowly but effectively. Eventually, he got to the last pin and heard a click as the door unlocked. Jamie smiled, breathing a sigh of relief as he conquered the first hurdle in what was undoubtedly going to be a long first mission. But he wouldn't delay for long, placing his tools back neatly into the box and stuffing it back into his bag.

Jamie's right hand wrapped around the cool, rusted metal of the doorknob as he drew closer to the door; pressing his body against it before slowly beginning to push it open. Jamie was ready to slam the door shut or defend himself with the knife in his left hand, but thankfully it didn't come to either of those options.

A subtle, anxious smile crept onto Jamie's face, though it was obscured by the mask. Step after step he took, slowly shifting weight onto his front foot and shifting it whenever the floorboards creaked–which was often. He played this game of Minesweeper as he ventured deeper into the house, checking room after room.

The house was heavily damaged. There was a leak in the roof, seeing as the ceiling had caved in over the dining room table. What was left of the dining room, anyway. Something– or someone– had come in and destroyed most of the wooden furniture, maybe for kindling.

The silver lining was that there was one room that could be considered secure. It was still in good shape– so long as one ignored a few dandelions that were growing through the floorboards. But this trumped sleeping in the wilderness, and Jamie would take anything he could get.

With a home base established, Jamie worked on making sure the house was secure before nightfall. It had already started to get dark– his navigation in the forest was incredibly time-consuming. Although tempted to sleep on a bed, Jamie slept on the floor, using his bag as a pillow. He couldn't get over the moss that had taken root in the damp mattress.

After breakfast the following morning, which consisted of a few sticks of jerky and a handful of nuts, Jamie left to begin scouting. He counted ten houses in total. All the other buildings had been destroyed or ransacked to the point that only the walls were left. Not that there was much in the remaining houses either. He had gotten through five houses without catching a single glimpse of copper.

The sixth house was a different story. Starting his usual routine, Jamie froze when he caught a flash of something shiny through the window. Something was inside; maybe what he was searching for. While a part of him wanted to rush in and check, his better judgement told him to finish surveying the houses, which he did. Thankfully, he wouldn't have to wait long, as he had sped through the rest of the houses and returned to the sixth house after just half an hour.

This began the slow process of picking the lock on the front door. Pressing his ear against the lock, Jamie could almost feel each pin as it dropped into place. They rocked around in his skull and the anticipation was surely going to kill him. He was so excited that he could barely keep his hands steady enough to finish the job.

When the final pin clicked into place, Jamie finally was able to relinquish his hands from the tools, letting himself relax– if only for a moment. With a gentle push of the door, Jamie's eyes started to dart around the room. Light flooded into the house like a flock of doves.

Then he saw it.

Copper plating branched out from the center of the room, creeping up the walls and stretching over the floor. Large stalagmites– made completely from copper– protruded from the ceiling and encroached upon the hallways below; copper needles stuck out from every wall and seeped into every crack in the floorboards.

Jamie struggled to contain his awe as his gaze slowly passed by each nook and cranny in the copper cavern. Eventually his eyes fell upon the source of all this metal: a Mechatolly cocooned in copper. It stood seven feet from the door, partially obscuring the other three which stood behind it. Their brilliance had not faded, despite the undoubtedly long years they had stayed in hibernation for.

The Mechatolly had tightly embraced itself before it was enveloped in copper, and its eyes, despite being protected by copper, held great satisfaction. The creature even seemed at peace, looking down at its crossed arms with a calm reprieve. Though the Mechatolly held itself in such a way that something felt lacking, like it was supposed to be holding something in its arms and not just itself. As if to hold an invisible child.

Jamie's grip on the door loosened as he fell into a familiar trance– captivated by the cocoon's haunting brilliance. He took the time to carefully study it, appreciating its features: it had been years since he was last free to see a copper cocoon, and he would be damned if he didn't savor this moment. That terrifying stillness after a dormant volcano releases a quake across the land– the statue that imprisoned a killer, one which would not hesitate to strike once it was freed. But one could not neglect the motherly love that dashed across the creature's features, which seemed to make the danger melt away, much as one's own mother would.

Still standing at the doorway, Jamie knew he couldn't wake them without a plan. Slowly he closed the door– making sure he was quiet; he didn't want to make any sound and disturb the Mechatollies inside. Glancing behind him at a house across the street, Jamie left his bag by the door, only keeping his knife on him as he walked over to the house. He opened the door, which he had left unlocked, as he thought of a plan while walking over to the kitchen. Jamie glanced at a window above the sink.

He pried it open with a bit of effort, sliding the window up and down a few times to make sure it wouldn't get stuck. The frame was made of wood and didn't screech while he tested it, though it certainly wasn't the easiest using the window. After a few more pulls and tugs, the window was able to be adjusted without a struggle.

Jamie cautiously got onto the counter, seeing if he could use the window as a quick escape. He jumped out of the house through the window a few times, then back inside. Once he felt confident that he'd be able to make it out of the window in a hurry, he returned to the front door.

The next part of this plan involved locking the door so that the next time it closed, it wouldn't reopen. For now, he kept the door open, placing a door stopper in until he actually returned to the Mechatolly-filled house. He surveyed the house for a little while longer before finally accepting it as an adequate jail for the Mechatollies.

Jamie returned to the house with the Mechatollies in it. He took a bell out of his bag and held it in a way so that it wouldn't accidentally sound before he was ready. With more caution than last time, he reopened the door, checking that the Mechatollies were as he had left them. Indeed, for in a tomb of copper they had remained. He bounced on his feet, looking back at the house he had prepared and recounting his steps.

Without making any sudden movements, Jamie would turn his head and return his gaze to the Mechatollies. He imagined the rush of the chase. The pounding of his heart as he scrambled away from the agitated Mechatollies, who had just been awakened from their slumber. In truth, he had never done this before– that is, intentionally waking the Mechatollies and, furthermore, using himself as bait. Which made the plan that much more thrilling; at the very least Jamie could say that he had done what no one else was bold (stupid) enough to try.

With a deep breath, he released the clapper in the bell, and with a sharp inhale to balance the act, Jamie committed himself to his plan– ringing the bell. Death's bell struck fear into his mortal heart. It was a decree that signed a warrant for his head; a dinner bell for a parasite ready to devour him. His hair stood on its ends, and his skin prickled in an attempt to flee from his foolish body.

Just a few chimes would suffice before the town returned to silence. Peace lasted only a few seconds. At first, it sounded like an egg cracking. Then the noise got louder; like the snapping of cold wax. The fingers of the copper cocoon started to wiggle, and glimpses of skin broke through the shell as metal leaves fluttered to the ground.

Then the Mechatolly's hand started to move, stretching and flexing and contracting to remove copper remnants as it continued to free itself. Copper fractured at the elbows, then the shoulders. It clawed at the copper on its body, peeling off loose flakes of metal. Its feet made the noise of an apple being torn in half as it first stepped out from the anchor which kept it glued to the ground.

As the Mechatolly freed its body, its attention then turned towards its head. The copper broke at the neck as it swung its head around like a hammer. Then it lifted its hands, pressing one row of fingers on its lower lip and the other row on the upper lip. Like a snake, it pried its jaw open to an unnatural degree, revealing rows of broken and copper-capped teeth. With a swipe of its arm, the Mechatolly scratched away the copper that covered its eyes and spotted Jamie as soon as it opened them.

The Mechatolly began to stumble towards Jamie, breaking up the copper at its joints as it moved. Escaping from the cocoon took no more than twenty seconds but was so haunting that Jamie wished it had taken longer. He tossed the bell onto his bag, which was still slumped against the wall next to the door. Before the Mechatolly and the rest of its companions could gain any more ground, Jamie spun on the ball of his foot and began to sprint towards the other house.

The Mechatollies gave chase, quickly regaining their usual speed and keeping in step with the copper chaser. Jamie heard the ever-approaching footsteps get louder and louder. Heard metal scrapped against metal. Like a swarm of angry bees, whose nest he had just stomped on and proceeded to set on fire for good measure.

Jamie dashed through the house, swinging into the kitchen and diving through the window. He rolled a few feet away from the window as he softened his fall to avoid injury. One of the Mechatollies, the one with the caring face who also led the pack, had attempted the same but lacked Jamie's agility.

Only one of its arms managed to breach the window, while the other shoulder bashed against the sides. Wood cracked as copper armor rammed against it. Each charge as the Mechatolly attempted to free itself sent scraps of paint and copper jumping towards its prey. Towards Jamie.

The plight of the creature momentarily petrified Jami, who continued to watch the struggle from his seat on the ground. The gnashing of its teeth, which had caused the Mechatolly to cut itself. Copper dripped from the wounds in its mouth, leaving a horrid stench in the air. A mix of metal and rot.

With a bit more force the Mechatolly finally pushed through; leaving a deep gash on the window where its arm escaped from as a wooden chunk fell to the ground beneath it. The creature would soon be free. It grasped at everything within reach, flailing its arms in a poor attempt to leverage itself out of the small escape hatch. Its companions, which once helped it, now trapped its legs inside the house. Even that would not last long.

Jamie threw himself upright, gaining an additional foot of distance until his back was pressed against the house next door. This bump snapped Jamie from his fearful trance and he took a better hold on his knife.

With his free hand, he grabbed the Mechatolly's hair and raised his knife in a threat to take the creature's life. The Mechatolly let go of the windowsill, grabbing Jamie's arms– trying to prevent him from getting the better of it. The two struggled for a few seconds, pulling and pushing against each other's grips. Its grip had slipped from Jamie's hand during the struggle. Not a moment after he had regained his freedom, Jamie plunged the blade into the nape of the Mechatolly's neck, slashing through a dragonfly-shaped marking and killing the Metalide attached to the host's spine.

With a harsh shove, he managed to force the body back through the window as the deceased Mechatolly's companions attempted to clamber over its corpse to reach him. Not wanting a repeat of what just happened and unwilling to kill another Mechatolly, he grasped the bottom of the window, slamming it shut before the rest of the pack could get any closer and stick their spindly fingers under it.

They scraped the window, and the copper made a horrible screech as the Mechatollies dragged their hands against the glass. While he would have liked to take a moment and enjoy the victory, there was still work to be done to ensure the trap was airtight. Jamie bolted away from the window, going back around to the entrance of the house and slamming the door shut.

12

Jamie was sure to close the front door quietly, and he could hear that the banging on the window had lessened dramatically. There must have been one that remained, while the other two followed Jamie back to the door. They clawed at the door, slamming their weight against it, but having lost the vigor they once had. Eventually, that quietened, too. Until there was nothing more than a whisper of the wind to liven the town.

They assumed Jamie to be out of reach, lost. No need to risk getting hurt by a door that didn't budge. Sometimes they would keep doing whatever it was that they had been doing, like mindless robots that needed to execute a task. And sometimes they just gave up and forgot what it was they were doing. Jamie thought they were more likely to keep doing something if others were, but he hadn't spent enough time watching their habits to be sure.

Jamie stepped a few feet away from the door as his labored breathing slowly began to calm. He adjusted the mask, ensuring that it hadn't loosened when he fell. Then he made his way back to the house which originally sheltered the Mechatollies.

For now, he didn't bother with the copper. He kept his knife unsheathed, carefully looking for any Mechatollies that may have been left behind. The house was left empty; no animal would linger in such a toxic place. The copper helped to preserve the old house, strengthening it and keeping it from the harm of mold and termites.

He walked inside, looking for a room. A bed, more specifically. It's not like he was tired, no. Rather, he needed the blankets and sheets laid on top of it. He had to shake off the metal dust, which rested delicately on the child-sized bed. There were copious quantities of copper: everywhere he looked there was more and more, building and growing off of previous layers. It was a painting with new details every time you looked at it. A sweet perfume that both enticed and confused you.

Once Jaime had gathered all the sheets he could, he rushed back over to the makeshift prison of a house. Jamie bent down in front of the door, squishing the bedding between the gap in the door and the floor. Before he lured the Mechatollies inside, he meticulously inspected the house for any holes which could allow the parasites to escape.

Thankfully, all he had to worry about were the gaps in the door and an old air conditioner, which the Metalides would surely find and use as an escape hatch if left uncovered. He had covered the vent with a few sheets and blankets, then weighed it down with garden pots. All the padding should be enough to keep the parasites inside the house, so long as he didn't provoke them. Regardless, he would stay as far away from the house as possible– enough for them to be ignorant of his presence.

Once he was content with the security measures, Jamie returned to the original house. He took his bag in with him and shut the door behind him as he entered. Jamie set the bag down next to the first cocoon, taking some thick gloves and a small handsaw out from a protective pouch. He took his other gloves off before wearing the ones from his pouch.

The first pair of gloves, which he always wore, was mainly to avoid small cuts and to freely grab Mechatollies without worry of being scratched. The leather pair from inside the bag was much sturdier. He wouldn't have to worry about slicing himself on the copper as he worked with those on. He would wear them more often if they weren't so restricting and bulky.

Once Jamie laid all of his tools out, he began cutting a circle around the base of the cocoon. Sometimes it would make a harsh grating sound, though this was never very loud. Not to him, anyway– sometimes the noise would rile up the Mechatollies. He would hear the chimes of a copper choir singing from the homely cage, though it was quick to fade once the noise quieted.

This sound resembled wind chimes, if instead of whimsical, a demented conductor played them. Jamie glanced in the direction of the other house– not as if he could see it, since the copper-covered door blocked his view. After a few seconds, the rattling stopped, and a few seconds after that, Jamie continued his work.

His hands were shaking softly as he worked, only making more noise as the saw tapped against the copper. Though his hands did not shake from fear, the additional noises did nothing to soothe his nerves. He yanked the saw out from under the cocoon, removing his mask for a moment as he wiped his face. His hands were numb; his knuckles were white.

He thought to himself while he rested, "*there must be an easier way to do this.*" Jamie lifted the mask, resting it atop his head as he inspected the saw. He glanced back at the butchered base, looking for the deepest cut. He loosely put his mask on before he continued working, jabbing the saw under the copper and leveraging it against the floor.

The cocoon started to crack along where the cuts were made, finally beginning to pull away from the floor. He would move along the base of the cocoon, jabbing and prying the copper every few inches until most of the base had been removed from the ground. When he got to the last sliver of copper, he stopped, not wanting the copper statue to fall and agitate the Mechatollies next door. He grabbed the shoulders of the statue, rocking it back and forth to weaken the last bit of copper attached to the ground.

After a few rocking motions, the copper had cracked enough to be lifted from the floor with relative ease. Jamie rested the base on the floor, gently leaning the cocoon flat on the ground.

Now he could finally get a closer look at the statue. Its body was nearly cracked in two; remnants of when the Mechatolly burst forth from the copper prison. The face, which was once pleasant and full of warmth, now seemed cold.

The copper was sturdier than it looked and unwilling to move even an inch with his strength alone. He returned to his bag, rummaging around in the pouch. He put his saw down next to the bag and after a moment pulled out a lopper. One of the handheld ones: small enough to carry around but enough for cutting the thin layers of copper cocoons.

Once he returned to the cocoon, he started to cut the copper into manageable sizes. Starting with the legs, Jamie moved onto the head, and finally finished with the torso and arms. He just needed to process the copper enough for him to be able to carry it around. The outside was spiked with copper thorns, but the inside was as smooth as marble.

He left the dismembered copper corpse in a pile in the corner, continuing with the other three cocoons. The sun was already starting to set once he finished processing the last cocoon. It felt like Jamie's arms were about to fall off, but he was just thankful to be done. And to top it off, he was left with more copper than he could have imagined. Jamie inspected the pile of copper as he thought about how to bring it all back.

An idea came to him quickly. Jamie turned into the bedroom, taking the remaining sheets off the bed. He laid the sheet flat on the ground, leaving the elastic side upright. Carefully, so as not to cause a ruckus, he collected the copper and put it into the sheet before tying the ends together once he was done.

Then he layered the sheet with two other sheets, hoping that it would be enough to keep the copper from slicing a hole at the bottom and spilling out. It looked a bit like a sack once all the sheets were nicely tied together. He was about to put his knife away when a small imperfection near its hilt caught his eye.

At first, Jamie had thought that his carelessness had caused the damage, though he soon realized that the imperfection was deliberate. It was not haphazard scratches but rather two letters carved into the blade with intention.

It made the initials *S.O.*

Jamie wasn't sure what it meant and chalked it up to being the initials of the previous owner, or perhaps the bladesmith that maintained it.

After this inspection, he finally put his tools away. First, he stowed the leather gloves and replaced them with his original pair. Then the saw, the lopper, and finally the knife. He put his bag back on, grabbing the copper-filled sack with both hands and was surprised by how light it ended up being. He wondered how much copper his efforts would amount to. By this time the sun had already set, and the moon was the only light source that illuminated the town.

He set up camp in the house he had inspected earlier. When morning came, he could just take his bags and leave. He wouldn't even have to think about the house with the Mechatollies in it. The house was nicer than Jamie remembered, but that was likely a product of his tiredness. An office was Jamie's choice of lodging within the house. It was far from the door and seemed the least affected by the passage of time.

As he checked the room, he came to a realization: this house, much like all the others, was rather run down. As was to be expected, of course. Termite damage, scratches, dust, and the like. The house in which the Mechatollies roamed, however, was in near-perfect condition. Granted, it was still sprinkled with dust, but it was as if no animal was courageous enough to get anywhere close to the house. Upon further consideration, even the paint on the outside of the house was less damaged than that of its neighbors.

At first, he considered that the constant movement spooked critters, but that wouldn't explain the lack of termites or the incredible preservation. Plus, the Mechatollies would have rotted long before he got there if they weren't cocooned. And the abundance of copper on the walls meant that they must have been hibernating for quite some time. There had to be another explanation.

He rested the copper-filled sheets next to him, using his bag as a pillow yet again as he continued this wordless debate. The copper must have killed the mold and the termites, re-enforcing the structure of the houses. Did the same thing happen within the body of a Mechatolly? Yes, Jamie thought that seemed logical.

Placing his thoughts to rest, Jamie tried to do the same and fall fast asleep. He laid out a few stolen sheets, stiffly resting on top of them. It was going to be a long night.

13

"So, tell me about it." Pat had been driving for a while now and was quite tired, but kept a friendly demeanor. Thankfully, he hadn't been waiting long before Jamie emerged from the treeline.

Jamie shrugged slightly, throwing his bag and the sack of copper into the backseats. He closed the door once he was sure that the cargo was properly secured, joining Pat in the front of the car. "I got lost, but it was fine. Had a few odd dreams. Nothing interesting." Pat had waited until Jamie fastened his seatbelt before he started driving. Neil was very strict about safety measures outside the walls. Unsafe behavior– especially if it ended in injury, was a quick route to termination.

A lot of other settlements would buy cars from Crawford, as they were among the best considering how safe, silent, and efficient they were. However, that was almost the only thing Crawford had going for it. It was a lucrative business, albeit a fragile one. At least they lacked competitors, and cars from the mundane days were easy to come by, even if they couldn't run without repairs. Jamie was now a vital part of these operations, making sure that there would be enough copper for necessary repairs.

"Those… sheets. What's in them? Sounded metallic." Pat sped up a bit, rejoining the convoy.

"Some copper. Nabbed it from the Mechatollies." Jamie shrugged it off, as if this was no big deal.

Pat was silent for a while, looking through his rearview mirror at the sheets. He broke the silence with a bit of laughter, patting Jamie's shoulder. "Wish I had that much courage at your age. Right, then. Give me a good story."

Jamie started to detail the events that led up to the gathering of the copper. He mostly talked about how he lured the Mechatollies away from the house. To him, that was really the only interesting part of his trip. As much as he would like to make the whole experience as grand and interesting as possible, Jamie was far from a storyteller.

"So, you killed one of the Mechatollies. How'd you deal with the parasites? Don't tell me you set the house on fire. *Did you?*" Pat asked with a mix of concern and excitement.

Jamie shook his head. "If I burned the house, any marred in the forest would come running. *And I… lack the skill to cut the parasites out*, even if I could have gotten to the corpse." Jamie paused, thinking back to the events that followed the killing of the Mechatolly. In a way, they're more dangerous dead than alive, as the parasites in the Mechatollies usually only emerge after killing the host. "I locked the body up in the house with the others. Seemed to work well enough, but I definitely didn't take my mask off after that."

"So the parasites are just… *hanging around?* That sounds dangerous. But you couldn't really kill them in that state, either."

"Yes… you're right." Jamie nodded, looking at the road ahead of them. He thought about what had happened in the hours leading up to his departure from the town.

Jamie wasn't just going to leave the Mechatollies in the house. At least not originally. That would be foolish and incredibly dangerous. He was planning to burn the house just before he left to find the road. That way, if anyone was nearby and went to investigate, Jamie would be long gone. Yet he never did.

Fear had gripped Jamie before he was able to commit the act. He had set the sack of copper down within arm's reach so he could depart as quickly as possible once the fire started. A can of particularly potent biofuel, one of Sicaren's own designs, was held with both of his hands.

It would have no trouble starting a bonfire with the house as its fuel. The parasites would simply burn up, and the Mechatollies would probably suffer the same fate. It would be easy. It was easy– of course. He just had to pour the fuel around the house and take a match to it. Easy. *Easy.*

Jamie couldn't do it. He could! No, he couldn't.

As Jamie clutched the can, his fingers quickly became numb from the constriction. If he had applied any more strength, he would have crushed it. Not out of anger or frustration. Out of fear. Terror gripped him, like vines wrapping around a Florid. It dragged him into the ground, pulling him from reality.

He felt unwell; his blood ran cold. It was spring, but he was freezing.

He felt as if he were fifteen again. He got horrible flashes of what happened on that freezing winter day. The sight of those Florids running rampant. Flames bursting from their skin– the pops, like firecrackers, caused from a flower combusting.

What would a Mechatolly sound like once it was set ablaze– running about as it writhed in agony? Jamie shuddered at the thought, putting the can of fuel away in his bag. He would not find out today. He could not destroy those creatures he was so fond of– he just couldn't let go.

Jamie was hardly left alone with his thoughts for long, and Pat woke him from his trance with a nudge of his shoulder. Back to the car his mind had returned, looking at Pat with question. "You okay there, Jamie? Got real quiet." Had Pat not been focused on driving, he would have looked at Jamie to check on him. For now, all Pat could offer were a few cursory glances.

"Yeah– yeah. I was just thinking, that's all. I have much to discuss with Neil." Jamie gripped his neck, forcibly silencing the anxiety which rose from his voice.

Other than the occasional bump in the road, the trip was running smoothly. It was a well established route for a reason. Pat and Jamie had been sitting silently until there was maybe just an hour left until they reached the city.

"I'm starving," Pat grumbled, leaning against the seat. "Me and the other guys are going to grab food once we get back. You should join us."

Jamie considered the offer for a moment before responding. "I think Neil wanted me to report back to him on my return. That's the first thing I should do, is what he made it sound like."

"Alright, but next time you better be there. Else I'm rolling up to Neil's office myself and demanding your immediate release!" Pat grinned. Jamie nodded, observing the enthusiasm for a moment. Pat was a jolly guy. Laughed and smiled at everything. It seemed genuine enough to Jamie. But that's what a lot of people were like. Guarded at first, but really happy people. No, not happy; mostly just lonely, so they overshared. That's why Pat was such a chatterbox, like everyone else. It's also why Jamie was so quiet; the world was his friend and he told it everything he couldn't tell other people.

"Of course. Wouldn't want that." Jamie noted, returning his focus to the road. He wasn't sure why this conversation was coming as such a struggle to him. Normally he could at least trick the other person into carrying the conversation for both of them. At first, he thought it was due to sleep deprivation, but Jamie was quick to think of a new reason: he was already ready to set forth on a new adventure.

Jamie leaned his head against the seat, watching the tops of the trees as the convoy continued to Crawford. His tourism would have to wait until his talk with Neil.

14

Jamie's body jolted awake as Pat nudged his shoulder. His gaze flicked to the right, where Pat, who was holding the passenger-side door open, was standing. Then he looked outside. They must have been driving for a long while, as the sun had already started to set. The convoy had made it back to Crawford, but for how long, Jamie wasn't sure. The keys were already out of the ignition, and the other cars in front of them were dark, though some of the drivers were nearby.

"How… what time is it?" Jamie sat upright, sluggishly grabbing his things.

"We got back not long ago. I tried to shake you awake for a bit, but you were in pretty deep. So I unloaded the car and just now was able to wake you up. Guess you needed every minute you could get." Pat smiled softly, going to the back seat and grabbing the copper-filled sack as Jamie hopped out of the car.

"Thanks, Pat… getting rest out there wasn't… *the easiest.*" Jamie took the sack from Pat, each closing their respective car doors.

"Oh, I quite remember. Now– I've got a dinner party to get to, and you've got important people plans. Hopefully, this won't be the last drive we have with each other." Pat extended his hand and, after a moment of adjusting his grip on the sack, Jamie returned the gesture. They shook on it before going their separate ways.

The walk to Neil's office was no easy task. Each step felt like an additional pound added to the sack. A part of him wanted to lie down on that very sidewalk and take another nap. It had been some time since Jamie had been to an alloy zone, and the comfortable life he enjoyed within Crawford had made him forget the perpetual fatigue the alloy zones tended to induce.

At least the walk didn't take much longer, and Jamie's internal complaining distracted him from his aching legs. After a quick but tedious flight of stairs, Jamie knocked on Neil's door and rested his head against the wooden wall next to it, waiting. This time, Neil himself had opened the door. He looked at the sack for a moment, smiling softly. "I take it your first escapade was a success? Ah– please sit." He extended his hand for the sack; Jamie was more than happy to relieve himself of that heavy burden.

Jamie walked over to Neil's desk, setting his bag down beside him. "Yeah. It was fine."

"You don't sound fine." Neil had put the sack in a side room, joining Jamie at his desk.

"I'm just tired."

"Jamie," Neil trailed off, looking at him for a moment. As if he were studying Jamie. "You're upset. You don't have to hide it... just tell me what's wrong."

"I," Jamie breathed deeply, straightening in his chair. "Can– can we talk about this tomorrow?"

"We should address this now. Else it may fester into a greater problem."

Jamie opened his mouth to rebuttal but was unable to come up with anything. He slumped deeper into the chair, looking over at the glass doors on the other side of the room. Neil took notice of this, looking over to where Jamie did.

"Have you seen the garden? Let me show you." Neil rose from the chair and walked away from the desk, opening the glass windows.

Jamie joined him shortly, looking at the rows of flowerbeds. Neil walked over to the edge of the balcony, resting his hands on the white fence. He caressed the petals of a nearby flower, smiling softly. Jamie was looking around at the flowers, focusing on the one that Neil was playing with.

"I should have destroyed that house. Set fire to it– at least the parasites would have been killed quickly. But I… I guess I've never liked breaking things. I dunno. I've just been thinking about it. If I should have… acted differently. Acted at all," Jamie lamented.

There were many types of flowers, some recognizable and others not. Jamie could recognize the flower that Neil was looking at, though couldn't place where he had seen them. Having gotten what he wanted from Jamie, Neil laid off and moved onto a different topic.

"Gardening is quite nice. It takes my mind off business. Flowers are… fragile, delicate little things. In need of special care; of my care. Then they can blossom into their full potential with my guidance. I suppose you have a lot in common."

Jamie was silent as he thought about what Neil had said. He wasn't sure if he should feel insulted or take it as a compliment. "Thanks…?"

Neil turned back to Jamie, taking slow and methodical steps towards him. "We should celebrate your first successful mission, wouldn't you agree?"

"I'm not one for parties." Jamie occupied himself with a small fern, which attempted to free itself from the rest of the garden patch. He played with the small green curl at the end of its arm, stretching it but careful not to damage it, despite being a weed.

"Few are. But that doesn't mean we can't do anything. Join me back inside when you're ready." Neil brushed past Jamie, sliding a gentle hand on his shoulder before leaving Jamie to solitude and returning to his office.

The fern would soon be exterminated. It wasn't pretty, like the flowers it ran from. Nor was it particularly obedient. Jamie released the curling section from between his fingers, watching as the plant bounced back into shape. Despite the force he placed on it, the plant showed no signs of damage.

With a quiet shutting of the doors, Jamie had rejoined Neil in his office. A bottle of wine and a single glass cup sat on his desk. On the other side sat a mundane-era juice box. It was starfruit. "Can't let you drink just yet. But a wandering trader brought this in and only asked for a room for the night, so I gave it to her." Neil nudged the juice box so it would be closer to Jamie.

"How'd you get wine?" Jamie asked, taking the juice box and sitting down. He observed it carefully before hesitantly poking the straw through the top. It must have been years since he last saw a juice box.

"This ah… associate of mine found it when they were setting up a community of their own. Gave it to me as a token of goodwill."

Neil placed the bottle away in the wall of trophies and took a sip from the glass. "Speaking of which, I have a gift for you."

"Another?" Jamie drank the juice box happily. It was sweeter than he expected, but left a horribly bitter aftertaste in his mouth.

"Mhm. A gun. I find them even harder to procure than a car." Neil again turned to the wall of trophies behind him, grabbing a revolver from one of the shelves. Then he placed it on the table, finishing his drink as he observed Jamie's reaction.

At first, Jamie seemed shocked. A working gun was rare, let alone getting the bullets needed for it. A gun was more of a last-ditch effort or for dealing with humans. Although Jamie quickly took note of the intricate patterns burned onto the wood and felt a deeper appreciation for it.

Flowers curled around the grip of the gun. They seemed almost alive, as if they could be swaying in the wind without a care, as flowers do.

"It's pretty," was all Jamie could muster before being pulled back to the design. He trailed his fingers along the wax-coated wood, feeling the well-preserved material.

Neil nodded, slowly tapping his fingers along the edge of the desk. "I want to introduce you to Sicaren and his lab after such a successful expedition."

This pulled Jamie's attention away from the gun, as his smile grew harder to contain. He had done well and his efforts had been rewarded.

15

"You've never met Sicaren, have you?" Neil walked alongside Jamie. They had started at his office and were making their way towards Sicaren's lab. It had been a week since their last meeting.

"I don't think so. You talk about him sometimes."

"He's certainly a man worthy of praise. Have you ever met a scientist before, Jamie?"

"Doubt it."

"Well, I'm sure you'll be amazed once you see him." Neil led Jamie into a smaller building, which was a ways away from any other frequently used buildings. It was also behind a chain-link fence, and Jamie couldn't recall ever going past it before. "He makes all of our fuel with the surplus from the auto shop. It isn't much compared to what we bring in from selling our cars, but it isn't nothing to sneeze at, either."

There wasn't much to look at once they went inside. It looked a bit like a waiting room with a few couches and a front desk, but lacked much else. There was a door just behind the front desk, which Neil led Jamie into. Inside there was a single desk and chair, with yet another door leading to a bigger room behind it. In front of the desk there was a big window, which let in most of the light and placed the larger room on full display.

Jamie looked through the window into the other room, staying by the desk while Neil opened the door. There was a man walking around in the other room. He held a bucket and would stop every few feet, taking out large metallic chunks of copper, which would slowly be pulled upward by an invisible force.

Although the man may have resembled a farmer feeding his chickens, these chunks did not serve as sustenance for whatever creature the man cared for. Sunlight took care of that for him. Instead, the metallic chunks seemed to fizz as they reached their highest point.

It reminded Jamie of soda, which he could only distantly recall from when he saw it on television as a child.

Some of the chunks looked very similar to the copper Jamie collected, except much more pristine. There was no grime or oxidation to speak of. Had the copper nugget been in the sun, it would have blinded those who passed by.

"Stay here." Neil walked up to the door, opening it while knocking on the tile wall to announce his presence. The noise got the attention of the man, who looked over to catch Neil waving hello. Closing the door behind him, Neil approached the man in the center of the room. They started talking, though Jamie wasn't sure exactly what about, since their voices were muffled through the walls. Neil laughed, playfully slapping the man's arm before turning back the way he came.

The man carefully shut the door behind himself and Neil, placing the bucket down next to one of the legs of the desk. He looked tired, as though he frequently worked through the night. Still, he had a friendly smile and seemed to take care of himself with what little time he had. "Hello, Jamie. You can call me Sicaren if you'd like. I've been looking forward to meeting you."

Sicaren had a couple of piercings on his ears and face, which were clearly done by different people of varying levels of experience. He had a subtle accent, too, but Jamie couldn't tell where it was from. Despite his intelligence and body jewelry, Sicaren couldn't have been that much older than Jamie, probably only ten or eleven when the marred appeared, making him in his late twenties. "Neil speaks of you often."

"I hope it's all good things," Jamie spoke in jest, offering a half-smile.

"Of course it's all good things!" Neil was quick to add. "You know, Jamie, when the marred started running around in his area, he was taking a tour of a lab. Like this one– but better. The scientists talked his head off so badly while they were hiding that he decided to become one!" Neil snickered.

Sicaren shook his head, smiling sheepishly. "It was a bit more complicated than that. And you didn't even tell the best part."

"Oh, yeah. This guy traveled almost an entire continent to get here. Anyone who thinks tourism is dead clearly hasn't met this guy."

"The scientists were American and attending a conference in Brazil. Since I had no family left, they took me with them to California. When fuel started to be developed, I tried to go to Minerva to help improve upon their inventions. Although I was… unfortunately rejected. I had nothing left to my name there, but Neil saved me. He needed to make fuel of his own, so he brought me back with him."

"Minerva really lost out when they rejected this guy. He's a one-man army, I tell you! The way he refines the sap is incredible. Thanks to him, we've got fuel for every situation. Even Minerva doesn't compare to us. Though I suppose specialization worked out for them." Jamie felt like he was intruding on a trip down memory lane, but did his best to follow along anyway, slowly nodding as Neil and Sicaren conversed so they knew he was listening. "But… I suppose I shouldn't bore you with the details. I'll be outside, join me once you two are done." Neil patted Sicaren on the back, quickly leaving before Jamie could ask anything about what was happening.

There was a brief pause after Neil's departure before Sicaren broke the ice. "Well… come along, then." Sicaren opened the door leading to the room he had been in prior to their arrival. "Have you ever seen a Medusa before, Jamie?"

"Medusa?" Jamie's eyes trailed over towards the jellyfish looking creatures. What was visible, anyway.

"Yes, thanks to them, the production of fuel became much more widespread. Oh– don't put your hands over the blue tarps and don't touch the blue tendrils. You'll be in for a rude awakening." Jamie looked at the blue tarps, which looked as if they were intended to collect rainwater. Above them was a strange, blue-tinted sack. It looked like a Man o' War jellyfish. "I heard you've got a lot of experience outside the walls, don't you?" Sicaren glanced back at Jamie before prattling on. "They're practically unheard of in the wild, outside of where they've been intentionally placed, anyway. I doubt you'll ever have to worry about a Medusa."

"Oh," Jamie stated plainly. Sicaren was starting to become unnerved by Jamie's short answers and copped by speaking faster– as if this would help hold Jamie's attention.

"Mhm. And– ah, they're good for fuel, too! Before, in order to get sap to turn into fuel, you'd have to extract it from the vines of a Florid. With a needle! It was horribly barbaric. Not to mention tedious, dangerous, and inefficient. The folks at Minerva discovered that they can get the same sap from the bell of the Medusa. People had already been refining the sap to make it less unstable, and some had the foresight to make it usable for cars. Minerva really took the north by storm in a matter of weeks. I don't know how they do it, but I know my method is more efficient than theirs." Sicaren stopped next to a Medusa, eyeing it with fierce intensity.

"I thought the tendrils were invisible."

"That's what Minerva thinks– apparently the first king owes our boss a few favors. Neil was able to get me some of their lab notes." Sicaren smirked, ready to impart knowledge and theories he had come up with onto Jamie, despite the fact that it would most definitely go over his head. It seemed like Sicaren was *really* desperate to have someone to talk to, even though a brick wall would have been more receptive than Jamie. "If you inject dye into an Antherus when they start developing in the flower of a Florid, they'll take on that color. But if you're too slow, it'll reject the dye and wilt. If you try to dye the tendrils after it's already become a Medusa, it'll be quickly washed away as the Medusa cleans itself. Then you just get nasty, unusable sap. I saw the farms once; they tie red ribbons along the ends of every tendril. Feel bad for whatever newbie they got to do that."

"You thought that was inefficient, too?" Jamie quirked a curious brow as Sicaren offered a giddy smile in turn. It seemed like Sicaren was captivated by his studies in the same way that Jamie was by his expeditions. Clearly Neil was either extremely lucky or very talented at finding the right people for his unusual jobs.

"Terribly so! The Medusa wastes extra energy because of the extra weight it has to carry for no reason. Since it spends more energy on lifting up its tendrils, it'll produce less sap, since it can't afford to spend the resources to work at full capacity. Else it'll starve. Also, I found that the type of debris that the Medusa is given will help determine the quality of the fuel and what type of fuel can be made." Sicaren continued to babble on about the relationship of copper and all the types of fuel that could be made from the sap.

Like a child forced to attend summer school by his parents, Jamie continued to follow Sicaren around; he was trying to stay focused on what Sicaren was saying, but more often than not became distracted by the unfamiliar objects scattered around the room. His focus circled back to Sicaren as he bent down and rummaged around a chest, grabbing a red can filled with bio-fuel from his farm.

Making sure that Jamie wouldn't drop his precious can of fuel, Sicaren carefully handed it over for Jamie to carry before grabbing another for himself. The can was heavy and nearly filled to the brim, but the weight wasn't something that Jamie was unused to. He could hear the contents within– it didn't slosh around like water but wasn't quite as thick as syrup. Before Jamie could open the lid to see inside, Sicaren began to lead him outside the farm.

Neil was waiting outside for them, idly taking notes on a tall pad of paper. Before the can of fuel would trade hands, Neil placed the pad away, hiding what he had written. "Thanks, Sic," Neil said; his presence was serene as always. Something Sicaren certainly needed after talking to someone who could almost be described as charismatic as a dead cockroach for the past few minutes.

"Of course. Good, that the kid knows what he's working for."

Neil nodded, watching as Jamie walked out of the fenced area. "He's a bit… shy around strangers. I think with some time, you two will become good friends."

"I hope he comes around quickly. That was exhausting." Sicaren shook his head. "I'll be back to my work, if that is all."

"Yes, it is. I'll be seeing you." Neil offered a faint smile in farewell, joining Jamie and helping him with the can of fuel.

16

The pair approached the line of cars, bringing the can to one of the drivers. The driver put it in their trunk, carefully closing the door and giving thanks to Neil. He waited for the driver to leave before speaking to Jamie.

"It is thanks to this convoy and yourself that our city prospers. You may not see it, but your job is the root of our success. Without copper, we could not build the cars that power the Northwest. No cars means no trade. No trade means no innovation." Neil turned to Jamie, placing a hand on his shoulder. Jamie was wondering why Neil was telling him this now and looked into his eyes with a familiarly skeptical glance.

"What I mean is, we need you to do well. And I say this with love. So just do as you've done, and we can make more cars. More cars mean more trade, which means more chances to go on expeditions. If you catch my drift."

Jamie nodded. "I'll keep up the good work, then."

"I knew I could count on you. Now, I'm sure you have preparations to make, so I'll see you when you return." Neil patted Jamie's back, walking away from him. Now that he was left to his own devices, Jamie walked around in search of Patrick. Thankfully, Pat wasn't too hard to find. He was tucked away in his car, fiddling with a rubix cube. Clearly, he was busy trying to avoid doing any extra work before the long drive out. Pat nearly jumped out of his seat when Jamie opened the passenger side door, throwing the cube out of his hands as if to dispose of the evidence.

"Hi– hey!" Pat stammered, speaking before he saw who it was. Pat sighed with relief as he watched Jamie get inside. Quietly thanking God that it wasn't his superior who came in. God forbid, that it was Neil.

"What's that thing?" Jamie asked, catching a glimpse of the cube which now sat between Pat's feet.

"A rubix cube." Pat bent down, presenting the scrambled toy of colors to Jamie. Jamie looked at it, almost reeling away from the foreign and strange object.

"What's it for? Why does it look like that?" Jamie frowned, looking at the current state the cube was in. The colors had faded, barely more pigmented than if the toy were pure white.

"That's because I haven't solved it yet. Look." Pat loosely held the cube with the tips of his fingers, taking a moment before unscrambling it with lightning-fast reflexes and astonishing precision. Despite this, the cube barely looked any different from when it was first presented to Jamie, but Pat seemed happy with the change.

"That's… cool," Jamie whispered, glancing at Pat's enthusiastic smile. Although Jamie was unable to notice the faint differences in the color, he could certainly admire how fast Pat was able to turn the faces of the cube without breaking it.

As the train of cars hummed to life and started its long journey, Jamie tested his wits on the cube. It was not his dexterity that was lacking, but rather his focus. His attention kept being pulled to a once-red tile, which had a few scratches on the paint. They resembled birds.

In fact, Jamie became so consumed by the rubix that he had nearly missed his stop, allowing Pat to drive right past it. A few hundred feet had passed before Jamie regained his senses. With a few frantic glances, Jamie attempted to place himself among the passing trees, requesting Pat to stop upon seeing a road sign he vaguely remembered Neil telling him about.

Jamie took a few moments to read the sign, recalling his instructions before getting out of the car. As usual, he waved goodbye to Patrick and waited on the side of the road until the car was long gone. Once he was alone, he turned towards the forest, pulling out a well-worn map and a compass. He started his journey towards his new hunting grounds.

The first thing Jamie did upon reaching the city was to find himself a nice ledge to perch atop. Nothing too nice. As many run-ins with the Mechatollies would show, any building which was too well maintained was likely infested with Mechatollies. Better held together buildings were always teeming with the marred.

Of course, the opposite extreme was buildings which were suspiciously degraded and overgrown with foliage. As the years dragged on, it was harder to find the dwellings of the Florids, as nature grew where it pleased. They were always much better than the Mechatollies at hiding, though the Florid's places of refuge had a large giveaway.

Those buildings would always be well forested– often completely obscuring the skeleton of the buildings they inhabited. But everything in the dense city was covered in weeds, along with the occasional tree. It took a keener eye than most to spot a building that wasn't infested.

Although this method certainly wasn't foolproof, Jamie was careful to avoid the heavily green-washed buildings. Most crucially, making sure that there were no flowers. When a Florid was left to rot, sometimes their bodies and the vines which grew from them would take root in the ground. A final effort to survive.

The vines flourished in the dirt– it's where they never should have left. The vines grew everywhere, given the time to spread, but they were betrayed by their signature flower. Though these flowers were harmless now, as they no longer harbored Antheri.

If those little parasites did manage to grow in the flowers of the unassuming vines, surely the copper trade would cease in its entirety. The cities would be too far gone to get even remotely close: they'd be swarming with the Florid's parasites. Jamie shuddered to imagine it. Parasites everywhere, blanketing the world in an eternal darkness. Eventually, they would make their way to human settlements. The consequences would be disastrous.

The city was very quiet. Nonetheless, it was welcoming, unlike the bustling chaos of Crawford. Despite Crawford's abundance of empty shelters, the number of residents was still jarring to Jamie. His skin crawled and his head spun whenever he got into a crowded room with all of them. Holiday gatherings were a nightmare.

But in the alloy zone, nobody was there to disturb him. It was just himself and the marred. Oddly, where he felt most at peace. At least the marred were easy to deal with and rather predictable. Not like the strange battle of wits that made up daily interactions or the intricate social webs people had. It was something Jamie had long since lost the ability to understand, let alone willingly participate in.

Jamie felt a lot like the building he had next decided to explore. It was considerably smaller than the highrises that towered next to it. In fact, the building almost seemed to sag in embarrassment as it shrunk away from the loftier structures beside it. Maybe this was Jamie's mind attempting to project his own feelings onto an inanimate object, but it almost felt as if it were looking down upon him and the surrounding scenery, lacking the confidence to stand tall with the others. There were several holes in the building, which likely deterred most of the marred from attempting to establish a shelter within.

As Jamie explored, he looked for any remnants of life. Both marred and not. Jamie had picked up a few notes on their behavior through the years. For one, both the Mechatollies and the Florids seemed to have an aversion to extended time outdoors. The exact reason why he was unsure, but he thought it had something to do with avoiding unnecessary risk to preserve the integrity of their hosts.

If the Mechatollies' hosts were truly dead, as Jamie suspected, they would naturally want to avoid the outdoors. Regardless of whether the mind of the host was dead or not, the parasite still remained the puppet master. Keeping out of nature's way and avoiding things like rain would stave off any erosion to the body it stole.

As he pushed through the building's entrance, he spotted a group of three cocooned Mechatollies. He removed his knife from his pocket, piercing the thin copper membrane and planting the blade into the nape of each and every statue. It was a shame to lose them, though to rouse the trio and draw the attention of others in hiding would be a fool's gambit.

Once the three Mechatollies had been taken care of, he made a second round and dragged his knife along their spines. Many expeditions ago, Jamie had observed another, much older hunter doing some copper hunting of her own. The hunter was much louder than Jamie would prefer, though clearly there was a method to her madness.

Upon killing the Mechatolly the hunter had been chasing after, she dragged a knife along the Mechatolly's spine, killing the parasites. Ever since, Jamie started doing the same. Because even though the Mechatolly was dead, the parasites within were still alive. Wriggling. Biting at flesh– tearing at their fleshy prisons.

Processing the corpses was the only way to ensure that the parasites wouldn't be back for revenge. Ensure that they would never rise again to infect another.

A mechatolly's ichor– it's copper blood, if it could even be called blood now– always ended up coating his hands whenever he processed the Mechatollies. The ichor oozed from the statues. But it was better than fire. At least Jamie could never lose control of his knife. There was no risk of losing control and destroying everything. Not like the usually destructive nature of an inferno that Jamie was so used to. The same destruction that he had unleashed before and swore to keep contained from then on.

Jamie walked in front of a statue, gliding a hand against its coarse copper face. It was so beautiful now– elegant: frozen in a single moment of bliss. But something sinister lay beneath the surface. Rot.

First the eyes and lips, then the nose and ears. Cheeks. But eventually the rot would slow down. The copper coursing through their veins seemed to be a ready deterrent for most of the decay, and what wasn't cured was quickly covered with copper and protected. That's why their mouths tended to be so mutilated: the cuts filled with copper, and the copper made more cuts. A sickening cycle.

Jamie shuddered as images of Mechatolly's teeth flashed in his mind. Jamie had seen Mechatollies eat a great many things during their active period. They usually ate the flowers and vines of dead Florids, though their stomachs made of molten copper could digest just about anything.

When they were *really* starving, a Mechatolly would eat copper. Sometimes the copper of other Mechatollies or copper which grew on the floor. On rare occasions, they would pluck the copper right from their skin, just so they would have something to eat. They always ate with mild satisfaction, despite the injuries they sustained while doing so. Sometimes they would attempt to chew the metal, which would leave their teeth cracked and broken. Though any injuries would always be refilled with more copper.

Their saving grace, at least when Jamie had to deal with them, was that they couldn't infect as efficiently as the Florids could. The parasites within a Mechatolly grew along their spine, after all. They only hatched when the Mechatolly was dead, or if the controlling parasite or host was too weak to continue on. Infection meant mutually assured destruction for a Mechatolly. The original host would die, but at least a new host would be attained by the parasites.

17

There was an entrance leading to the basement of the building, which Jamie checked next. At first, he had noticed nothing out of the ordinary. After a tug on a resistant door, Jamie noticed a small leaf peeking out from under the crack between the floor and the door. It could have belonged to anything, though Jamie suspected a Florid. Again he pried at the door, causing some rust along its hinges to fly off.

When the door finally gave way, it swung open as if it were trying to jump into his arms and crush him. He too was nearly sent flying back, though not by the fast-moving door. A wall of wilting vines, which clung to the meager light near the exit, confronted him. Just above his eyes was the face of a thin human.

Human was generous and calling them thin was for lack of a word to describe something smaller. There was more bone than meat, and it seemed that the Florid would soon perish from starvation. It didn't even have the energy to make Antheri, else Jamie would have already been swarmed.

The Florid stared at Jamie with big, bulging eyes. It was more bug-like than human. Yet it did not look upon Jamie with the usual aggression that he had come to expect. It seemed quite complacent, with a touch of sorrow. The spindly creature's jaw opened slightly, attempting to make a noise, but was unable.

Unlike their copper counterparts, the Florids seemed much more emotional and communicative. Some parts of their brains, it seemed, were left intact. They could be shocked and even perform something similar to a scream, unlike the usually idle expression on a Mechatolly.

In many regards, they seemed quite human. More so than the Mechatollies, at least. When a Florid was cold it would hug itself, shivering as it searched for shelter. It seemed to feel some degree of pain but was able to persevere whenever it was chasing a human. Much like the Florid in front of Jamie. It seemed hungry. Idly licking its lips as if there were food remaining between its teeth.

"*Poor bastard must have gotten stuck in here,*" Jamie thought, raising his knife to the top of the Florid's throat and piercing it where the Antheri lay. Blood poured from the wound as the marred's suffering ended.

It was unusual to see a Florid in such a state. A Mechatolly, sure. But a starving Florid was something Jamie had never seen. A Florid could use their leaves and the sunlight for sustenance in a pinch, so they only ever starved when they got trapped. Much like the one stuck in the basement door.

Despite his persistence, it seemed as though the only marred within the building were the four on the lower floors. There were occasional rodents, and one floor was even overflowing with beehives. It was the largest colony he had ever seen, but thankfully the buzzing wasn't loud enough to reach the ground level.

The noise from the hives was near deafening nonetheless; even with concrete and a thick metal door between it and himself. It seemed like an impossible feat for such a large hive to exist, but Jamie had yet to see the rest of the city. Actually, he didn't even bother searching that floor in its entirety. No Mechatolly would be able to relax enough to cocoon there, and a Florid would be quickly stung to death.

Quickly getting away from the large beehive, Jamie had found himself at the top of the building after a few more floors. At least, what remained of the building. It seemed like it should be taller, at least compared to the other buildings that were still standing. Still, the bigger the building meant the more Jamie would have to search.

While on occasion he would find an interesting trinket or knick-knack to bring home, sweeping a building was more often than not a monotonous task. Thankfully, this time he had only taken four hours to finish searching, securing the building, and setting up camp.

Once he was done, he returned downstairs and collected the copper from the three cocooned Mechatollies, which would take him just under two hours. Jamie had gotten very good at his job over the past year.

By the time he had finished his duties, the sun had started to set, and he found himself famished. His arms were limp from the exhaustion of the work, though he had gathered enough copper for this trip and pitched himself a rather nice tent.

Using what remained of the sunlight, he grabbed dinner from his pack and a pair of binoculars. This was a source of entertainment while he ate, though he would tell anyone who asked what he was doing that he was on the lookout for danger.

He held his dinner, a humble sandwich in one hand, and the binoculars in the other. Sitting down at the edge of the building, Jamie let his legs dangle off the side and swung them childishly. With a keen eye, he scanned the streets for anything interesting.

As he expected, there were no marred roaming the streets. It was starting to get cold as the sunset, so any marred wandering for food had likely gone inside by now. What intrigued him was a building deeper in the city center. It seemed to dawn a blanket.

Not a human-made one, but rather one made of vines. If he had thermal vision, the building would probably be glowing a sweltering white. He could only imagine how many Florids, dead and alive, resided within to make such a large mass of vines.

Despite the possible danger, Jamie considered going deeper into the center of the city to get a better look. This city was quite the oddity, and it was unlikely he would ever be able to return. He swore to himself that he would never let life slip through his fingers, which is what caused him to take such a job in the first place. It would be a shame to pass up such an opportunity.

But for now, Jamie would have to worry about getting a full night's rest before attempting the voyage. He got away from the ledge, moving the rest of his things into the tent with him before it got too dark to see properly. Placing his things away, he rummaged through his bag to find a glass bottle half-filled with dirt and a long string.

First, Jamie tied one end of the string to the door handle and placed the other end of the string, which was attached to the bottle, on top of the weather guard above the door. The dirt within the bottle was heavy enough to prevent a false alarm but light enough to be thrown to the ground if the door opened.

If anything tried to sneak up on Jamie as he slept, he would hear it. A lesson he learned the hard way after a Florid broke into his hideout half a year back. He was lucky enough to have still been awake at the time, but had started crafting these makeshift alarms ever since.

Returning to the tent, he lay on the ground. It was only mildly padded by using his bag as a pillow and his jacket as a bedroll. The only relief from the cold came in the form of placing whatever else he owned on top of his body. Next time he would have to bring a second, thicker jacket.

At the ceiling of the tent lay a small hole: an inch in diameter. Although it had been patched with some mesh and tape, he could see through it clearly. Jamie looked upon the encroaching stars with lazy awe. The small lights seemed to swirl in the abyssal night sky as Jamie fought to stay awake; his gaze danced from star to star until he fell asleep.

18

Jamie's face scrunched as a frigid breeze leapt through his tent, awaking from a mildly unpleasant dream. The face of a girl with a gap in her teeth. A sheriff. A doctor. The dreams. The memories. They faded from his mind as he sat upright, embracing consciousness.

The jacket, which hadn't been very useful at all, had at least not shifted from beneath him. This is what Jamie got for packing light. Though for longer expeditions such as this, which would last a week, it was better to have more food than comfort. Finding discarded cloth to use as bedding wasn't difficult, though food would be exceedingly difficult.

If he did run out of food, which often happened, it certainly wasn't the end of the world. The growths of the Florids were edible and surprisingly tasty to boot. The vines tasted a lot like asparagus, but the flowers were sweet and sat well in his mouth.

The seeds within the flower were the most interesting. They tasted like oranges, and Jamie would often use them to have something to chew on throughout the day.

The seeds also made good painkillers. They were a rather popular bartering item due to their versatility. Besides eating them, the seeds could also be smoked, as Prost so often did. People would grind down the seeds, then roll them up and take a flame to them. That's how Prost told Jamie it was done, anyway.

Zipping open the tent revealed that the rest of the roof was exactly as he had left it. Jamie crawled out, wrapping himself in his jacket and fully closing the zipper, as he had done to the entrance of the tent behind him. He paced around the rooftop to warm himself up, feeling the mask that sat on his face. He usually never took it off, and in thanks, the mask never slipped off his face during the night.

Jamie stretched himself out for another five minutes before feeling ready to head out into the unexplored alloy zone. He took a hatchet, a gun, a pair of binoculars and a copper tracer to know if any

Mechatollies were nearby. He was able to fit most of the things in his belt loops or his pockets, but had to hang the binoculars around his neck.

While he was leaving, Jamie was extra careful to tightly lock the escape hatch which led to the roof. The last thing he needed was all of his copper being stolen by bandits while he was out exploring. Worst yet, all of his gear. It would be terribly difficult and expensive to replace everything.

The first place on his list was the blanket of vines he had seen the night before. It was about five blocks down, but the roads were clear enough for him to walk through, so it wouldn't be long before he was there. As Jamie started his walk, he gravitated towards the center of the street. There was the occasional car blocking his path, which he would either vault over or go around.

It was better than the alternative of staying close to the buildings. Enigmas with malicious intent liked to lurk inside: humans and marred alike. It was better to stay near the cars, which had been stripped down to their skeletons and thus did a poor job of concealment. Jamie learned that lesson the hard way after watching who was likely a novice copper chaser be thrown into a panic during one of his expeditions.

First Jamie heard a yelp of shock, then a scream of terror. By the time Jamie had located the novice, the latter had pressed himself under a car. Perhaps if he had been chased by Mechatollies, whose eyesight was well known to be subpar, the novice would have survived. Unfortunately, it was the Florids who spotted him quickly once they approached his hiding spot. It was over before the novice could scream much at all.

Jamie shook away the thought as he got closer to the blanket of vines, reminding himself of the need to stay vigilant as he got deeper into the city. It would almost certainly be teeming with marred. He looked around carefully. At every car, every boarded window.

There weren't many marred hanging around the windows, much as he expected. No Florids seemed to be stalking him– at least not yet. So long as Jamie remained quiet, his chance of encountering a

Florid or a Mechatolly, for that matter, was relatively low. They usually didn't roam the city unless they were disturbed or awoken. Conserving energy and avoiding damage to the hosts was more important now that their human prey had begun to thin.

When he had finished surveilling, Jamie couldn't help but be pulled back to the blanket of vines. It seemed to stretch into space, appearing weightless as it swayed in the wind. A subtle aroma drifted from it. It smelled of roses and oranges. Jamie almost wanted to take his mask off to better understand the scent, though resisted the urge.

Getting closer would reveal the source of all the vines: corpses. A few hundred of them, maybe even triple that. Jamie suspected that this was the result of a culling, maybe from some unlucky scavengers or a foolhardy militia, instead of a grand battle between Florids and Mechatollies.

If it was a battle between marred, there would be more copper. Even right on the street, Jamie could see the skeletons of what were once Florids that were running away from the building. Their vines had ultimately found their way back to the building that they were so desperate to leave. Though the vines had rooted in the ground, they did not relinquish their former hosts and preserved the integrity of the bones. The vines from the countless bodies had entwined, creating the behemoth before him.

Next, he heard a low, constant humming from the vines. Bees. They happily sprang from flower to flower. There must have been thousands, as the sky above him seemed to tremble with great fervor. Both the beehive and the wall of vines must have been growing since the day the marred had emerged.

It was the only way to explain how large they had both become. The size of both masses was so large that it was almost nauseating to comprehend. Despite that, Jamie took pleasure in the poetic nature of this strange city. From death came life, and so nature reclaimed what it had lost, building on top of the ruins of the mundane days.

He could sit and look at it for hours, carefully observing every flower on the vine wall. Every flower was like a thumbprint; unique to each Florid. He had already noticed a few hundred which were noticeably different. Although all the flowers had the same basic shape, the colors and the spotting on the petals were all drastically different. With so many flowers, Jamie continued to imagine the graveyard which hid behind them.

Sometimes it felt like the sun itself was being swallowed up by the bees. They seemed to be squishing him downward and forced Jamie to look at the vines closer to the ground. It felt as though they were trying to reach for him– bring him into the fold. He resisted this temptation only because he valued his life and needed to see more of the world before he left it.

It was nearly a half hour before Jamie was forced to stop looking at the great wall of vines. A particularly meddlesome bee had started swarming around Jamie, and he didn't want to wait for more of its friends to show up. For a moment he debated returning to his home base, since there was still time left in the day before sundown.

The decision came easily. Jamie wasn't about to hide away in his tent if there was something new to experience. If something so peculiar existed closer to the border of the city, then he could only imagine the types of things deeper in. Prost sometimes told Jamie stories about marred mutants, though he doubted that Prost's stories were anything close to reality. Neil told Jamie it was likely more to scare him than to warn him. Prost was odd in that way.

Maybe he wouldn't find mutants, though Jamie would settle for natural wonders like the beehive and the wall of vines. Jamie walked through the main roads, weaving between the carcasses of cars. Usually he would have seen more marred by this point, though there were hardly any. The vines grew thicker the deeper he went and were so dense that he had to carefully navigate around them. Eventually he couldn't even see the pavement beneath his feet; it was all vines.

Every building showed some signs of marred inhabitancy. Vines and flowers; copper instead of concrete. Yet their makers were nowhere to be found. Jamie found this suspicious, and the lack of any activity had begun to unsettle him. He was quick to come up with a theory.

There was nothing left. No humans; even the animals were scarce. The largest non-marred creature he had seen was a rat, which fed itself on the vines. Most of the Florids had been killed, probably not long after the parasites emerged and the subsequent end of the mundane days.

Those that remained left in search of food or starved, much like the Florid in the basement. The Mechatollies, meanwhile, didn't need food in the same way that Florids did– they could eat pretty much anything because of the toxic copper in their stomachs which digested whatever was put in there. Jamie had, on occasion, seen them eating bark, metal, and other items that didn't seem to have nutritional value.

But most likely the Mechatollies had crystallized and hadn't awoken due to the lack of noise in their colonies. Partially why such large vine walls existed, as most animals wouldn't make enough of a dent to destroy the vines like the Mechatollies did.

Humans didn't bother to set up camp here yet. The city was too big and too far away from any existing settlements. There were many cities like this once– though none exactly the same as the last. Quiet. Peaceful. Though they were usually too far out of the way and didn't have much in the way of copper, which meant Jamie couldn't usually visit them.

The break was a welcome one, to be sure. Rarely did he have leisure time, let alone being able to actually relax during it. Not having to constantly look over his shoulder was a welcome change. As he got closer to the city center, the vine walls became more common. They were practically a dime a dozen. A stark contrast to most other cities, which had none. As the vines became more common, so did the bees, as he was able to see a few more hives.

They were pure, undisturbed. Nature was left to thrive without the brutality and desperation that humanity brought with it. It was as Jamie thought things should be. He never wanted violence, but it was the only language humans spoke. This he knew well.

Although the vines were a marvel, they were a reminder of how much death riddled the dense cities within the early days. People became infected and then were killed. Their fate was to be left to rot.

Jamie tended not to think of the great mortality from that time and tried to focus on the good that came from it. Even if others would think of him as mad for doing so.

He was much too young to remember the end of the mundane days and had never left his small village before the marred emerged. All that he could see now was the mosaic of flowers left behind. For the elders, such sights would only carry memories of tragedy. For Jamie, it was a symbol of prosperity and joy.

The largest wall of vines leeched onto the tallest building in the city. It wasn't exclusive to just one face of the building, but rather wrapped around it in its entirety. It was like a glove. A large, organic, pulsating glove.

Jamie took out his hatchet, cleaving at a few of the vines. They were hard to cut away, though they would eventually fall to the ground. Behind the wall, which was almost half a foot thick, lay the foundation for such a marvel.

Small roots penetrated the concrete. Even the greatest human structures could not withstand the unyielding vines. Jamie would pocket a few of the vines for himself to make food from, then keep the flowers as keepsakes. He plucked a few from the wall of vines before scurrying back to camp, placing most in his bag, though did start to eat a few petals.

Prost and Jamie were not so different in this regard. While Prost was a smoker and would be until the day he died, Jamie couldn't keep himself from gnawing on the Florid's petals whenever he found them. A habit Jamie undoubtedly picked up from Prost, though at least the petals weren't addictive like the petala Prost smoked.

By the time he returned to camp, it was already dark, and he had decided to skip dinner, embracing his comfortless bed. Jamie was quick to fall asleep.

19

2040, seven years earlier

It was always on quiet nights when Jamie had nightmares. As if his brain couldn't fathom a peaceful day and had to torture him in his sleep. The subject was always the same. It was a memory from many years ago, one which would loop endlessly until his pounding heart woke him up. The cold and unforgiving winter of 2040.

More accurately, the day he lost everything. The cultists who had been harassing Silverton had finally lost their patience and on this day they razed what remained of the villagers. The stronghold in the mine had been breached.

Amanda stood at the opening to the main space of the mine. Frozen in her tracks, she was unable to join the rest of the villagers in the main area. Jamie had run up behind her, looking at the scene for only a moment. It was a horrifying scene accompanied by a mystifying aroma, not too dissimilar to petala.

A barrage of burning Florids had infiltrated the mines, illuminating every crook with the inferno. They were spreading their fire with the villagers, latching onto them as if needing help but only worsening their plight. The only silver lining was that the Antheri had burned to a crisp: at least infestation was off the table, for now.

But this was no time to dwell on the sight, else they may also fall victim to it. Jamie grabbed Amanda's petrified hand, turning back and running deeper into the mines. He swerved masterfully through the web-like tunnels. Though all it would take is a single frantic Florid running in no particular direction to find them.

They ran for a long time. They ran until the light from the fire disappeared and the screams turned to whispers. They had been plunged into darkness, but for at least a moment, they were safe. Jamie pulled Amanda behind a support beam, pressing himself into the dirt walls. After their breathing had slowed, Amanda finally spoke. "We can't stay here. We have to get out. Back the way those things came from."

"But won't they spot us– can't we just escape through the hatch?" Jamie let go of Amanda's hand, peeking out from the support beam to look at the tunnels behind them. The Florids drew ever closer.

"Jamie. They're on *fire.* We can probably smell them before we even see the light. Let alone before they see us." Amanda looked up at Jamie, pleading with him. The ash on her face was cleaned by her tears. "We have to save my mom. Please– you would do the same for your family."

Jamie glanced away, guilt overtaking him. Jamie's family had gone south in search of supplies, along with many others. Would he be able to help them if it were his family instead of Amanda's? He was but a child. A scared, outnumbered, and cornered child.

Even through the darkness, they could find their way out. These caves were their second homes. But Jamie was nonetheless apprehensive. They could escape with relative ease now. In Jamie's mind, there was nothing they could do to help Amanda's mom. "What if we get lost?" An unpersuasive attempt to dissuade Amanda.

"What would you do without me?" Amanda shook her head, grabbing his hand now. "Just stay quiet. I'll lead us out of here." Jamie reluctantly followed Amanda, the two careful to deafen their steps as they walked.

If it were up to Jamie, he would wait there for as long as it took until those cultists and their captive Florids left. There was nothing either of them could do to save the others. But Amanda could take on the whole world if she wanted. That's why she turned back.

They walked without much incident for a couple of minutes. The Florids hadn't walked far into the caves yet; preoccupied with their neighbors at the front of the caves. But this didn't mean they were safe, and they would soon be reminded of this. Someone was sprinting towards them. Amanda quickly turned and dragged Jamie away from the noise, pressing against the walls of another tunnel.

The running got closer and closer until it passed. One of their neighbors, Miss Caddeswell, was running with a limp. Her leg had been severely burned, though she pressed on despite the pain. Amanda was about to reach out to pull her into the tunnel they had ducked into, though stopped herself just before she did anything drastic.

Miss Caddeswell's leg wasn't the only burning thing that was approaching. A light was running towards them: a Florid. It was much faster than Miss Caddeswell, but she had a head start on it. It dashed past Amanda and Jamie, not even noticing them as it chased her. Despite the fact that it was quite literally a ball of flames, the Florid gave chase without the slightest hint of pain or exhaustion. The pair didn't say anything, but secretly thanked their neighbor. One less Florid to worry about.

The pair looked down at the floor beneath where the Florid had been. A trail of ignited breadcrumbs led back to the entrance of the cave. It seemed to be a strange liquid, which was slimy in texture and slightly gelatinous. The substance resembled tree sap. It didn't smell like gas or oil, though it was burning with seemingly no end.

"You think that's what's keeping it from falling apart?" Jamie asked Amanda, speaking barely above a whisper.

"It looks more like the thing that's keeping it from extinguishing," Amanda answered. The two waited for a short minute before continuing their journey. They had a few more encounters with the Florids. Some were just wandering; others were chasing their neighbors around in the mines. Though the pair had yet to see Amanda's mother. This both relieved and frightened them.

In fact, they had traveled so far that they were nearly at the exit. It was completely unguarded, though they still could not leave. Amanda refused to until they found her mother, and Jamie would not leave without Amanda. The prospect of escape was tempting to both of them, nevertheless.

The pair could feel the cool air breathing down their necks. They peered out towards the entrance, looking at the small cut-out area of the boarded-up walls that the crate had used to cover. There was nobody guarding the entrance; they suspected that the group had gone further into the caves to hunt for people.

Click!

The pair glanced at the tunnel behind them. A cultist. Their eyes snapped forward, as if the cultist would cease to exist if they did not look at her. "Little rats trying to escape? Stay still. Or I'll kill you both." The woman's voice approached them, tying their hands together behind their backs with zip ties. "Turn around. *Now.*" The two turned around cautiously. Jamie couldn't look at the woman, but Amanda had no problem doing so.

"Where's–" Amanda started to speak, but the woman shushed her quickly.

"Don't speak unless I tell you to. Else I'll take your tongues." The woman re-aimed her gun at the two of them, her eyes narrowing. "Against the wall." She pointed her gun at the wall adjacent to the exit. Jamie moved quickly, but Amanda stayed where she was. Her outspoken nature would get her killed. "You deaf, girl?" The woman raised her gun at Amanda, who finally moved. She sat beside Jamie, looking up at the woman hatefully.

The woman looked at them for a moment longer before pulling out a walkie-talkie. Her gun was still in one hand, though no longer aimed at the two of them. "Where the hell are you guys?" She asked, though received no response.

Amanda leaned over to Jamie, whispering. "You think the bandits all died?" Jamie shrugged, watching the woman silently.

The woman clipped the walkie back onto her belt, looking at the two. "What the hell did I just say?" She grabbed her gun with two hands again. A deep frown creased her face like paper.

The three looked at each other for a while. It was mainly Amanda and the woman, as Jamie attempted to distract himself by counting the rocks on the floor. "You're a tenacious one. Bet you'd make a good pet. We haven't collected a child Florid yet." Her frown turned to a smile, watching a fuming Amanda.

She was about to provoke Amanda further but was interrupted by her walkie. A man's voice sounded. "Jess. Don wants us all to gather deeper in the cave. Bring any captured survivors." Amanda looked at the knife on Jess's hip, contemplating if she could grab it while she was distracted. The walkie clicked as the message fell silent: the opportunity slipped out of Amanda's hands before she could even finish the thought.

"Looks like your luck hasn't run out just yet. Come on. If you're slow, I'll feed you to our pets." Jess walked behind them, receiving instructions on where to go from her walkie. Jamie was looking for a way to escape as Amanda continued to walk forward without complaint. If Amanda's mother were alive, she would be here.

Most of their neighbors who had taken shelter here had been lost, either to the mines or the cultists and their so-called pets. There were twenty of them, including Amanda and Jamie. Among the other eighteen villagers, Amanda found who she was looking for: her mother. Eight of the cultists bunched together, and Jess joined them after setting Jamie and Amanda down. Much to Amanda's misfortune, her mother was on the other side of the tunnel, so their reunion would have to wait.

A few of their comrades had been lost to the tunnels; their walkies were unable to connect through the stone walls. The leader of the cultists, Don, was among the eight cultists but didn't lump in with the others.

He was walking in front of the line of villagers, listening to the walkie-talkie. Jamie could hear people talking and the sound of gunshots but couldn't make out what they were saying. "Good... good." He nodded, studying everyone's faces carefully. He bent down occasionally to get a better look at people, but never stayed at one person for too long. He started to pair people up with each other.

"Leave at sunrise. No matter what. We'll head south to catch the rest of them. They can't have gotten far on those bicycles." Everyone looked at each other nervously as tiny whispers started to spread among them.

Jamie and Amanda remained quiet as Don walked in front of them. "We can finally leave this shithole behind." Don grinned as he reached Jamie and Amanda. He grabbed Jamie's face, though didn't do anything further. His fingers were caked in ash, much like everything else in the mine.

Don looked at Jamie for a while longer, then at Amanda. He let go of Jamie's face, standing back up and continuing down the line. "What a creep," Amanda whispered. Don didn't seem to notice; the other voices overpowered Amanda's. Don kept walking until he reached the middle of the line.

He looked back at his subordinates, joining them for a moment to deliver instructions. Then each cultist stood in front of a pair. Don took two in the middle. The woman who had captured Amanda and Jamie earlier stood in front of them. She seemed unsure of herself. She seemed scared.

"In the great words of our prophet!" Don started. His words seemed well-rehearsed. "I release you from the suffering of our mortal tombs. Those who pass on should weep, for they are unable to embrace the Lord's gift to us! Those who remain should rejoice for what will come after," his voice bounced against the walls of the tunnels. Don's lackeys raised their guns at the pairs, not yet aiming for either one in particular.

Someone wailed; Jamie couldn't see who. They were shot the second noise escaped their mouths. Don flinched slightly, raising both hands to cover his mouth. The noise of the gunshot traveled throughout the mines. The remaining Florids would start to make their way towards the group. "I am a generous man. Half of you shall receive our blessings in this life, and the others must try again in the next," then Don fell silent, listening to the two pairs in front of him argue amongst themselves about who deserved to live.

The cultist who captured the pair still seemed unsure of herself, unwilling to take the life of a child with her own two hands. Amanda and Jamie looked at each other, unsure of what to do. Jess left the two as the occasional gunshot fired off. She approached Don, who had already made his decision.

Two crying people sat in front of him. Two dead people lay in front of him. She asked if he would do it. Then he killed her. Her body fell to the ground without the slightest hint of remorse. He didn't even flinch this time. The rest of Don's lackeys didn't seem to notice. Maybe they didn't care.

Don stepped over Jess's body and walked towards the pair, bending down in front of them. "The great prophet, have you ever heard his teachings? He told us that we must remember the words of every person: strangers, friends, and foes. To keep the remnants of them before their ascension. He also told us that those who speak without courage are destined to never accept the Lord's gift. So we should allow them to be braver in the next life as soon as possible."

"You people aren't normal," Amanda blurted. Although this was rash, it was certainly true, and for this she would not be punished. That is what the great prophet decreed, and Don seemed to be bound to his word. As she had said, these were no ordinary bandits.

Amanda's mother had at least survived the culling. Another was inbound. Florids had started to rush the refuge. For some reason, the cultists were doing their best to pacify the Florids instead of killing them.

"You two, you look young. Same age, right? Don't see that often. You must be friends. Is that true?" Jamie nodded quickly. Amanda nodded too, but never took her eyes off her mother. "Then what am I to do? I can't separate such close friends. Maybe I'll just kill both of you. You can't both have earned the gift of the Antherus in this life."

Amanda finally looked at Don. Her head snapped to look at him. "*What?*" She exclaimed.

"Then what'll it be?" Don asked, staring intently at Amanda. The last shot had been fired, and they were the final pair remaining. Three flaming Florids had been caught and put on a leash. Some new Florids, their neighbors, had started to arrive. Their vines weren't as thick or plentiful as normal Florids.

Jamie wasn't sure what to say and looked to Amanda for guidance. She seemed even more lost than Jamie. Her face tinted red, and Jamie could clearly see that she was biting down on her tongue to hold it back.

Then Amanda looked at Jamie. Her gaze was soft and full of uncertainty. Yet it did not fall on him long, as her eyes quickly jumped back to her mother. "Kill him," Amanda pleaded. "He'll never survive on his own! He's too soft– too timid. I'll be of use to you all! Spare me– please," Amanda's voice broke with her final word, but her expression was unwavering.

Don laughed, looking at a stunned Jamie. His mouth had fallen slightly agape as his best friend just tossed him to the gallows. The emotion was so overwhelming that he felt himself lose control over the muscles in his throat and was unable to speak a word in protest. Jamie knew Amanda was right. She had always been the braver of the two, and there was nothing for Jamie to say that could disprove that fact.

"If you're so confident, why don't you prove it? I'll give you this gun, and you kill your friend. Can you do it? Can you take a life?" Don studied Amanda, intently watching her as she spoke.

"I wouldn't hesitate for a moment." Jamie looked down, trying to hide the tears that welled in his eyes. How could Amanda be so cruel? She spoke as if their friendship had meant nothing.

Don fell silent, looking at Amanda for a while. At this moment, the world seemed to fall silent. The flames of the infernal Florids had extinguished; the sobbing replaced with a serene peace. Don heard the silence as well and understood that the time for games was over. He stood, ushering a final decree.

"Close your eyes, child." Amanda sighed with relief, looking at her mother. They would be together soon.

Jamie's eyes winced shut. A pop, which was shortly followed by a deafening bang, rang through his ears. Then the silence returned. Jamie thought of all the things he hadn't done. Of what he had yet to see. In his next life, he would be more of a free spirit, he swore it to himself.

Then he realized something. Death should feel much different from what he felt now. A tidal wave of noise hit him before he could open his eyes again. The fire that screamed louder than a barbarian stricken with mania. The sobbing which had turned to screeching wails.

For a moment, Jamie believed himself to be in hell, though he soon realized that he was still on Earth and that there was no difference. Opening his eyes, Jamie realized it was not his blood pooled on the floor; it was Amanda's. Her mother called for her, but Amanda could not answer.

"The prophet told us to be rid of snakes disloyal to the cause. She will have to learn in her next life." He looked at Amanda's corpse with little regard, as if he had killed a fly instead of a person.

Jamie watched Amanda with great horror. His muscles writhed with a desperate itch to escape, which he could not scratch. It was a scene he could neither tear his gaze from nor remember. Blood continued to flood the mines– not just Amanda's, but everyone who had been murdered on that day. It showed no signs of stopping– not until everyone in those mines drowned. Blood stained the pants on his knees. Jamie's mind raced, and he could feel himself beginning to sink into the red lagoon.

Though her lungs breathed no more, Jamie convinced himself that she was still alive. Like she was playing a game, not so dissimilar from the ones they always played. For a moment– a passing second that could be missed by the blink of an eye– Jamie could have sworn that he saw Amanda's fingers twitch. As if she were reaching toward him.

Jamie wanted to reach for her. To stop her death– to feel her warmth before it faded. Yet he couldn't. He was trapped: bound by those cultists, whose ropes around his wrists cut deeper than his skin and into his very soul. He was powerless.

20

2047, present day

"I had that dream again," Jamie confided in Prost after his return to Crawford. He had never been in need of counseling, but he found himself telling Prost, of all people, about his worries. While Prost was similar to Jamie in being somewhat uncharismatic and lacking in the skills needed to comfort someone, Jamie could under no circumstances tell Neil about what had been happening. Anything which could jeopardize Jamie's ability to leave the walls had to be eliminated or covered up, and this was one of them.

Regardless, it was still unusual for him to speak about his woes, as Jamie had been used to dealing with them by himself for several years now.

Prost also found this peculiar, but seeing the way that Jamie was carrying himself– full of doubt and shame– he knew he had to brooch the subject carefully. While he would never be able to soothe Jamie like Neil could, at least he could attempt to understand him.

With a quick glance around the street, Prost sighed softly and gestured for Jamie to enter his home. Jamie had just returned from an expedition and had yet to stow his gear in his apartment.

"Water?" Prost asked, pouring a cup despite Jamie's gentle refusal. He placed it next to the chair Jamie sat down on and proceeded to sit across from him. "Why didn't you meet with Sicaren? Aren't you friends with him?"

"I didn't want him telling Neil." Jamie picked up the cup but was yet to drink from it, tracing his finger around the edge. "I mean– I don't think he'd do it on purpose. But he's like me, you know? Would tell Neil if he asked."

Prost nodded, crossing his arms and leaning back in his chair. "Something's got you worried?"

"No," Jamie paused, feeling Prost's gaze on him, and sighed. "Yes."

"I'm not going to lure it out of you like Neil does, Jamie. You're gonna have to tell me."

"I was taken from my village around this time. I don't know. Brings back bad memories."

"And you think I can help?"

"Can I not just confide in a friend?" Jamie glanced up and was greeted by Prost's look of *don't bullshit me.* They both knew that Jamie wasn't the type of person to initiate conversation unless he needed something. "How do you deal with it? Your wife's passing, I mean."

"I try not to think about it. It put me in a dark place for a while. I guess I still am. But I know she wants me to be happier, so I do my best. For her." Prost's tone softened as he spoke, and Jamie saw a side of Prost that he hadn't seen before. And then Prost smiled, looking away as he recalled a fond memory.

While this wasn't advice and certainly nothing like what Neil would tell him, Jamie felt at ease. It was strange connecting with someone after such a long period of isolation. Relieving, nonetheless.

"I'll be leaving for another expedition in a few days. Won't you see me off?"

"I would like that."

21

A week later

It was close to the end of a rather uneventful year, making this the last expedition before the winter hiatus. Jamie was in the middle of processing Mechatolly cocoons and had nearly finished getting everything packed up into the bag, tying up the top so that nothing would spill out once he started walking.

It had been many months since his time in the city with the large beehives and vines that swallowed the concrete monoliths, but in slow trips like these, he found himself returning to those memories.

The thought of the trek back up the many flights of stairs to reach his hideout pulled Jamie back to the present moment with an annoyed groan. The bulky bag would certainly test his stamina, and that was all Jamie had to look forward to.

He went to stand, hearing a loud crack sound from behind him– it sounded like a gun. Something had wrapped around his arm, pulling him off his feet and causing him to be turned around before falling onto his face.

A pit of small copper needles greeted him, slashing his exposed neck as he fell. A stinging pain shot through his left arm, though dulled after only a few seconds.

Spinning onto his side, Jamie threw his working hand towards his gun, yet the swift movement of a boot pinned him back onto the floor. His arm had been trapped under him; he was stuck.

As Jamie tried to pull his face away from the copper needles, he felt a hard object dig into the back of his skull. A gun. "Don't think of moving," a woman's voice commanded with great authority. This wasn't her first time pointing a gun at someone. "Now let go of your gun." She released the pressure on his back, though only slightly.

It was just enough so Jamie could free his arm, but any sudden movements would mean a bullet in his brain. He didn't have any choice but to obey. So he slowly pulled his arm out from beneath himself and placed the firearm on the ground nearby.

Jamie reluctantly let go of the gun, looking up at his left arm that was still restrained. It looked like some sort of whip was coiled around it, an unusual weapon choice. He tried to look up further to get a look at her mask, but was unable to.

The lady grabbed his gun, and despite being unable to see her face, Jamie could feel her smug smile. She let the bullets from his revolver fall onto the back of his head before tossing it aside.

"You did a real great job for me, harvesting all that copper. For your reward… hm… I suppose I'll let you fight your way through the monsters outside instead of killing you. That is, if you can outrun them," she snickered, releasing the whip from around Jamie's arm.

He snapped his arm close to his chest, slowly flexing his hand as he checked to see if anything had been broken.

His arm felt uncomfortably tingly as blood rushed from his shoulder to the tips of his fingers. Feeling was starting to return to it. Jamie shuddered to imagine the pain once it did.

The lady walked over him, seemingly unbothered as Jamie picked himself up. He had to hold his knife in his non-dominant right hand, but he'd be damned if he just let her walk away with all of his copper without a proper fight.

He was about to lunge at her, but she was already aware of his attack– spinning around and whipping him with the butt of her gun.

"Next time I rob you, I might not be so nice. You better collect more next time, Bluejay." She watched as Jamie flew to the ground, naming him after the bird on his mask. The blow to his head had left him dazed.

Once she was satisfied with the damage she inflicted, she secured the bag and, with unusual confidence, threw herself out the window. No, she certainly didn't jump to her death. Upon closer inspection, there seemed to be a rope dangling alongside the open window.

It was occasionally visible depending on the way the wind blew. The rope was once attached to a carriage so that the windows could be cleaned. Now all that remained was a single line.

Jamie dragged himself over to a cubicle, hiding himself under a desk so he would be harder to spot when something inevitably came to investigate the noise.

He held his knife up to his chest, listening to the space surrounding him. The noise of the marred running up the stairs was already loud. Soon he would be swarmed.

The crack of the whip was loud– everything in the city must have heard it. By the time two minutes had rolled around, the marred had found the barricade Jamie had set up earlier. It wouldn't hold for long. The barricade grew weaker with each pound of weight thrown against it.

Florids which were on the lower floors had finally made their way up and started brawling with the Mechatollies. He could smell the blood and sap from the Florids and the ichor which poured from the Mechatollies.

The fights had bought him some time, but not much. He would be able to avoid them if he were fast enough, though the streets were the real problem.

Even as he sat hundreds of feet above the ground, Jamie could still hear the clamoring of the marred. The clattering of copper; the shrieks of the Florids.

He dragged himself out of the cubicle, carefully looking over at the barricade. The doors were yet to fall. Many injured lay on both sides, which worked well for Jamie. Had the Mechatollies been allowed to work uninterrupted, their hardened copper skin would have shattered the glass doors a long time ago.

The matter of the parasites was yet to be dealt with. The Antheri or the Metalides would find Jamie much faster than the marred could. He started to collect his things, sitting against a cubicle with an unlit fireball in his hands.

It had been fashioned out of the Florids sap and some paper he found lying around the office. A wildfire is just what he needed to distract the marred within the building to make an escape.

At the other end of the office floor was the isolated manager's room. Jamie considered locking himself in but shook the thought away. Staying here meant death.

It seemed like his only choice was to follow the lady in her descent. He'd have to act fast before his head start on the marred dissolved to nothing.

22

Shambling over to the window, Jamie got a better view of the untimely predicament he found himself in. The streets were flooded. An ocean of marred drowned all hope of survival. Some fought against each other, while others were clamoring to get inside.

They would be on top of him any minute now. He wouldn't be fast enough to hide before they noticed the rope, let alone getting onto the streets with such a large horde lingering below.

So what other option did Jamie have but to make a distraction?

There was no use in preserving a building nobody cared about if Jamie wouldn't be around to see it, and he was in desperate need of time. Jamie threw his bag back over his shoulders and coated the paper ball with sap, lighting the match after a few tries. He rolled the paper ball in his palm, feeling it squish beneath the pressure of his fingers.

Jamie took no joy in destroying things through his own efforts. He wanted to witness the world, not shape it. It felt wrong to alter the destiny of this building– wrong to tarnish the beautiful abominations behind the barricade.

But would nature not rebuild? Then there would be something new in place of the old. That was the only way to see new things, was it not? And was that not the very thing that Jamie lived for? To see new things. To experience life to its fullest after being unable to face it for so many years.

Winding up his throw, Jamie slammed the ball into the office furniture, quickly turning away as the flames started to grab hold. Darting to the window, Jamie reached for the rope with as much stretch as he could give without tumbling out of the window. The wind blew it closer but was just out of his reach.

Then he heard glass shatter.

With a whip of his head, Jamie glanced towards the entrance– towards the glass doors which were no longer there. Florids and Mechatollies overcame their differences and tumbled over the barricade, skittering away from the fire and into the offices. Skittering towards Jamie.

The rope began to swing away as the breeze settled. He couldn't wait any longer– Jamie had to go now. With a quick jump, Jamie perched onto the window, pushing away with his legs and reaching for the rope just before a Mechatolly could reach him. He began to fall, and the creature came along with him. This was surely how he was going to die, falling to his death.

Then he caught it. First his left hand– then the right. He slipped a foot down the rope before eventually catching himself by tangling his legs in the rope and stopping his descent.

Only his misfortunes weren't going to end there. It hadn't been a moment of peace before Jamie felt a weight slam onto his shoulder and tumble off his bag. The Mechatolly, which had boldly chased after him, was determined to take him with it, as the force of the collision ripped Jamie's hands away from the safety of the rope.

Beginning to fall head first into the mass, Jamie flailed his arms in an attempt to grab anything to once again stop his free fall. Yet again, he came to a dead stop– though not by catching onto anything.

Jamie was hanging upside down like a bat and could feel blood rush to his head. Managing to keep his bag securely on him, Jamie looked at his leg.

The rope tightened around his ankle, both saving and trapping him. Jamie started to feel dizzy, even after only a few seconds of dangling. Jamie glanced around, quickly trying to search for a way to escape the trap he had made for himself.

Although the simplest option would have been to break the glass next to him and reenter the building, it would be a shortsighted solution. Florids and Mechatollies were likely on the floor he was dangling next to, on their way up to the floor he had jumped from. Glass shattering would only get him swarmed by the horde he had just risked his life to avoid.

Jamie tried to reach for the rope but lacked the strength to pull himself upright. Had he not encountered the lady with the whip and been left exhausted from the counter, he might have pulled off such a feat. Granted, he wouldn't be in this situation to begin with if not for her. He slowly started to spin, looking for where the lady had escaped to. The building next to the one he was dangling from had a few broken windows, one of which was close to where he was hanging.

Using the glass wall next to him and what little strength he had left, Jamie started to swing himself like a pendulum. He got closer and closer to the shattered window until he eventually grabbed the broken glass itself. It was painful, but his gloves protected him from the brunt of the damage. Finally, he dragged himself onto the musty floor, quickly freeing his leg and watching as the rope swung back and thwacked against the other building.

Wanting to not spend any longer in the dangerous alloy zone, Jamie tried to stand but was stopped by his leg. He was struggling to keep weight on it for long. Walking would be difficult; running near impossible. The last thing Jamie wanted to do was stay in an unfamiliar building until the streets cleared. Let alone until his leg got better.

All of his food was stored at his base, a few buildings over. All of his medical supplies were there, too. With his left leg almost completely useless, he'd be unable to run away from or put up a proper fight against any danger. He had never been so helpless before, but hope was not lost. When one door closes, another would open– with all the marred that flooded onto the streets, the buildings were guaranteed to be mostly empty.

Starting to make his way up the stairs, Jamie listened for any indication that marred were nearby, though he heard none. He had caught a break.

Making his way up to the rooftop, which was just as empty as the building below, Jamie snuck a peek over the edge to look at the horde. There hadn't been much of a change from when he last looked. Escape would have to wait until morning, when the commotion calmed down. But for now, exhaustion overwhelmed Jamie. Attempting to maneuver from building to building would only send him plummeting to his death.

Now that he found himself in relative safety, his body seemed to grow heavier, as though he were a piece of lead thrown into water.

It felt as though weights had been tied to his eyelids and boulders strapped to his limbs. His knees buckled under the pressure, finally allowing Jamie a moment of rest. The ground of the roof was rough, yet warm and comforting.

This is where he would remain for several hours. His body eventually forced him awake as the pain in his leg grew, allowing him to escape his dreams. The moon was already high in the sky when he came to.

His gaze was pulled from the roof once he stood upright, his face illuminated by a raging fire. Jamie gasped. It was inconceivably large and still burning despite how long he had been sleeping. He could not even see the fire in its entirety from this angle.

Using the light from the fire, Jamie first went to survey his wounds. He dragged himself over to the edge of the rooftop, taking off his boot and rolling down his sock. It was red just above his boot; where the rope had tightened. The saving grace was his boot taking most of the pressure from the rope. He was lucky for the lack of extreme swelling. The pain was tolerable when he placed weight on it, a stroke of luck.

Jamie rolled the sock back over his ankle and slipped his boot back on. The rest seemed to do him well, as his arm had also somewhat recovered, though a nasty mark surely remained.

Allowing his legs to dangle off the ledge of the building, Jamie took a moment to survey the area. The view from up there was nice. The wind was softly coasting through the air, and the sky only held the moon and stars. He took his mask off, allowing himself a moment of relief.

The cool breeze felt pleasant on his haggard face, though the smoke from the fire was smothering. The fire had spread several floors above the one he was on and was a rather jarring sight. It would consume the whole building if it didn't rain soon. Some Mechatollies had trapped themselves inside, and Jamie would watch as they flung themselves out of the building to escape the fire.

A few Florids had been drawn out from the other structures but they weren't as keen to run into a burning building. Despite the fact that they had a greater sense of self-preservation than the Mechatollies, a lot of them would perish, regardless. Jamie dragged his attention along the streets, watching as numerous fights broke out among the Florids and the Mechatollies.

If the fire died down before he had to leave, Jamie would return inside to search for the copper remains of the Mechatollies. Next time he would have to be more careful. He really didn't want to run into that lady again. Just thinking about their encounter made his skin crawl.

Not that Jamie was trying to be cowardly, but he had no plans of going out of his way to harvest copper. He hoped that she had left the city already, or that the movements of the Florids and the Mechatollies had pushed her into hiding, but he wouldn't be counting on it.

She was skilled enough to get the jump on Jamie. More importantly, she was smart enough to wait until he had finished harvesting and his guard was down. Though if one wanted to survive in an alloy zone, they had to be smart and resourceful. He suspected that she must have had a lot of experience when it came to robbing people of their hard-earned copper.

In the meantime, he still had a day left until the convoy was supposed to drive past the city. He would probably spend that entire day avoiding the Florids and the Mechatollies as he tried to escape into the forest. This mission was a bust, and he was lucky to still have his life. Yet his failure didn't bother him much at the moment. For now, he had time to himself. A moment to admire the haunting beauty of a desolate city and the all-consuming flame.

The white-hot blaze was vibrant, and the smoke stained the sky, starting to blend in with the darkness of the night. He was close enough to feel the heat coming from it. From this distance, he saw almost every inch of the fire's ferocity. The destruction that *he* caused.

23

It had been almost a month and a half since the winter hiatus began and, subsequently, his encounter with the thief. He was making his way through a line, grabbing a tray of pre-planned food.

Decrepit but clearly well-loved decorations were strewn about the hall, highlighting the celebration. "I thought you loved New Year's." Jamie turned to look at Prost, who was standing in front of him.

"I was just thinking about the food. I'm starving." Jamie's gaze flicked towards the tables crammed with people but didn't linger.

"I know. Neil talked forever," Jamie giggled at Prost's remark as the two looked for an empty spot, which they eventually found and sat down at. Jamie began picking at his meal. The food was good, and he was hungry, but his mind was elsewhere. He was still mentally in his last expedition, occupied with the lady with the whip and the city he had burned.

Prost recognized the look but wasn't going to pry. "There's a lot more people this year." He changed the subject, looking around the crammed mess hall.

"There's been a lot of newcomers recently. Guess the winter is hitting the smaller towns hard," Jamie dismissed as he continued picking at his food.

"Don't you–" Prost stopped as he felt a hand brush against his shoulder. Neil had found them and decided that they had to join his escapades. He had a food tray himself, which was identical to everyone else's.

"What are you two doing, sneaking off all by yourselves?" He laughed with that big, friendly smile of his. "We're sitting outside. Why don't you join us?"

Immediately Prost was placed on guard, not responding to Neil's question. Jamie, however, was on good terms with Neil and completely obedient to his beck and call.

"Sure," Jamie was quick to say, placing his utensils down and following Neil outside. Prost had no choice but to follow, as Jamie tugged on Prost's sleeve a few times to encourage him to join them. They were sitting outside on a park bench a few yards away from the building. Taking a seat by Neil's side, Jamie started to listen to their conversation.

"Look at us. So many *Roses* you could call it a garden," Sicaren laughed, offering a small wave to Jamie. Everyone who one would expect was there: Sicaren, Natty, Ivette, and the new additions of Neil, Jamie, and Prost.

"Just because we're coworkers doesn't mean we have to be joined at the hip." Prost sat next to Ivette, casting a glare in Neil's direction, though Neil seemed unbothered. "You really have to keep calling us Roses? It's so childish. Just because Neil is into gardening doesn't mean he gets to name everything after them."

Ivette nudged Prost's elbow. "*Prost–* can't you be nice? I think it's great how close all of us are."

Neil switched the conversation to delay the inevitable fight that Prost would start. "How are the new batch of cars coming along, Natty?"

Rolling her eyes, Natty released a large, exasperated sigh. "Don't even get me started. Tires are spinning all over the place. Some of the axles are so rusted that I can barely turn the wheel. But the engines are working fine with the fuel Sicaren gave me. At least there's that."

"It's been of higher quality recently, hasn't it? Neil got me better ingredients. No need to ration copper any more," Sicaren chirped, happy to talk about the biofuel.

"With how much you talk about your recipes, I'm surprised the formula that makes Crawford's biofuel hasn't leaked to the whole world. Even Minerva wants a piece." Prost had stopped eating by this point, speaking between puffs of his recently lit petala. At least he had the courtesy of blowing the smoke away from the table. This was his third roll of the night– one was smoked before Neil's speech, and the second during.

"Is something the matter? You're snider than usual." Neil looked at Prost with concern and that familiar smile Prost hated so dearly. "It's like what Ivette said. We're all family here. There's no need to be so defensive."

Prost gripped the petala and nearly tore it in half at the mention of family. "You're right," was what he managed to say, muting the obscenities he was mentally throwing at Neil between huffs of petala. "I must be tired. I'm glad Sicaren is so talkative. Someone has to counterbalance Jamie, don't they?" Prost stood, an empty smile on his features.

"You're leaving?" Jamie questioned, standing halfway before Neil placed a hand on his arm. Quick to rise but soon to fall, Jamie was once again sitting. "I'll... take your tray inside."

Prost flicked his hand in a sort of gesture that both thanked Jamie but expressed his indifference to the fate of the food tray. The mood of the dinner shifted once Prost left. It felt like they could finally breathe again– both without the presence of petala or Prost. But things were just... different without him.

Everyone could feel it. There was a rift slowly growing within Neil's inner circle. Everyone knew the history between Prost and Neil. How things got to this point. Everyone, it seemed, except Jamie.

It wasn't that he was incapable of asking– or that he was too scared to. But could he really rely on any of them to give him a straight answer? They had all been personally involved with the feud for years now: everyone in the Pale Roses was implicated in one way or another.

A noise interrupted Jamie's train of thought. Neil, pulling him from his descent into Prost's madness. Just as he always did. Neil cleared his throat, interlacing his fingers as he waited for the table's attention.

"I think we deserve a drink. Who'll join me?"

24

2048, present day

For reasons beyond himself, Neil had insisted upon joining Jamie on one of his outings into the alloy zone. To Jamie, despite all of his love and admiration for Neil, he saw Neil as an old man whose days of adventure were over.

Someone who would slow him down.

Still, when Neil first made the request, Jamie said nothing to protest it. Which is how, in the first hunt after the winter break, Jamie was saddled with him.

"Have you ever... done this before?" Jamie questioned, looking at Neil's mask. The pair had nearly arrived at the city they would be investigating. Seemed like a good enough time to make small talk before they'd have to be quiet for nearly the rest of the trip.

The mask was much more ornate than his own. Obviously, more of a status symbol than a practical item. The small copper spikes which lined Neil's head seemed useless.

They were too small to puncture anything, maybe other than Neil's own hands. It was a crown of copper thorns. Perhaps it was fitting, for a man so heavily involved in the copper trade.

"No. Well– yes. But acting as a copper chaser? No." Upon closer inspection of Neil's mask, Jamie concluded that the mask was much too nice and impractical to be worn in a place like this.

The thorns looked as if they would snag. The metal seemed malleable. It was like using a cannon filled with cement in battle. Intimidating, sure, but nothing more.

Neil bore a hunting rifle. It was almost completely concealed within his coat, with a silencer to boot. The thing must have been expensive as all hell.

In the modern day, mundane era gear like that was the stuff of legends. Jamie had only heard about Neil's weapon of choice during the odd conversation with some of the other Roses.

"So why'd you come with?"

Neil shrugged slightly, readjusting the sling of the rifle. "Wanted to see how you stacked up against other copper chasers, I suppose."

Jamie rolled his eyes at the statement, which was hidden by his mask.

"Sure." He had only heard of performance evaluations in exasperated whispers. The adults of the mundane days made it sound even more treacherous than the fiercest of marred.

True to Neil's word, he did not do much during the expedition. Neil had little experience with the work of a copper chaser. It had been years since he had left the walls of Crawford. If not for his constant talking, it would have been as if Neil had never come at all.

This peace could not last forever, and end it soon would. It happened after all the copper had been bundled up. Jamie heard a noise which he so dreaded.

A snap; the crack of a whip. It was not loud, though it was undeniable. "What's the matter?" Neil questioned. He did not know what it was.

"It's her. She's *here*." Jamie glanced around and would soon find the lady who tormented him. She bore a grin, slowly approaching the pair like a shark.

"You brought a friend," she teased, looking at Neil with amusement. He was much too old to be an explorer; she surmised that much.

"What's your name?" Neil asked calmly.

He knew who this lady was. The whip she carried was quickly recognizable. He reached for the rifle, though Lila's gaze was sharp. Neil could see her ready her whip as his hand drew closer. He dropped his hand to his side, knowing that such a weapon would do him no good here.

The lady shook her head. "A man with manners? What are you playing at?" She paused a few meters in front of them. Long enough for her whip to stop them should they lunge at her.

"I know you want to take what's ours," Neil spoke on behalf of Jamie, who hid behind him. Despite his unsteady demeanor, Jamie's grip on the bag was rock solid.

"That's right," the lady confirmed.

"Then you could give us the courtesy of your name before we hand over our resources."

"I don't think you have much of a choice in the matter, old man." She retorted, slapping her whip against the ground to intimidate him.

Still, Neil persisted. He grabbed the bag from Jamie, walking towards the edge of the building. Then he held the bag over the edge. "Name."

This threat seemed to worry the lady. All she cared about was the copper, after all. "You wouldn't."

"But I would," Neil smirked, peeling one of his fingers away from the bag. It would be impossible to salvage if it hit the ground.

The marred would come to see the commotion and get the chunks lodged into their flesh, carrying the copper off into nowhere.

"You're bluffing."

"You can certainly find out." Another finger peeled away from the bag.

"Fine! Fine. Okay." The lady sighed, mentally diminished by the threat of losing her precious copper. "It's Lila."

"Good, then, Lila. I'm going to leave this bag here. Then my friend and I will take our leave, and you can have your copper. Sounds like a deal?"

Lila waved them away, seeming rather annoyed. It would be best not to test her patience. Neil grabbed Jamie, who was still possessed with fear, and fled the building with him in tow. They walked to their base in silence. It's not that Neil was mad. Jamie could tell that much.

In fact, Jamie could tell that Neil had gotten exactly what he wanted from that encounter. Something in those eyes– the web of Neil's mind that grew in intricacy with each passing moment– Jamie could tell Neil was pleased. That some part of his plan had fallen into place.

It was not until they were safely home that Jamie spoke. "Why did you ask for her name?" He questioned, sitting next to a dead campfire.

"You never know when it might be useful." Neil sat next to Jamie, placing his rifle by his side. Jamie's gaze lingered on the rifle. Why didn't he seize it when he had the chance– as Lila's focus was diverted onto Neil? Why could he not bring himself to act? *Why?*

Jamie could not meet Neil's eyes. He was ashamed of himself for freezing up during the confrontation. "Okay," he said simply.

"I'm nearly fifty, Jamie," Neil admitted. "I won't be here to protect you forever. There are countless people like Lila. People you'll have to fight off, be it through your strength or your wit."

Neil was right. Though they did not fight with words, Lila and Neil had a battle of their own. If Neil could not confuse Lila like he had with his odd questions and careful threats, she could have easily taken their heads off.

"I… I was scared, Neil." Jamie drew a shaky breath. Melancholy permeated the air. It was difficult to breathe.

"They can never hurt you more than you hurt yourself. What do you have to fear?" Neil asked with genuine intrigue.

Each second dragged on painfully. "I'm not sure. Death? Blindness?"

"Yet by allowing yourself to be consumed by your fear, the threat draws ever closer. What would have happened had I not been there? You would have waited for her to kill you, no doubt."

"No– no, I wouldn't have." Jamie protested, but knew that Neil was right.

"No matter who it is. A stranger. A foe. A *friend*," Neil said that final word with emphasis, leaning forward and resting his arms against his knees. "Why do you think I let her take the bag?"

"Because she would have killed us if we tried anything else."

"No," Neil spoke like a disappointed teacher who had just failed half the class. "Because there are sacrifices we need to make for

Crawford– sacrifices to be the best. Sometimes it means compromise. But once you give them a crumb, you must take it all back and more. You know what I mean, don't you? What you must do the next time you see her?"

Jamie swallowed his shame, gaze flicking between Neil and the dead fire between them. Lila wasn't just some robber. She had a presence– one that suppressed Jamie. One that he had encountered before. One he never wanted to fall victim to again.

"I do."

25

The expedition with Jamie seemed to have rekindled Neil's adventurous spirit, as the next time the convoy left, he joined them again. Of course, Prost accompanied him on this mini-voyage.

"It's been quite a while since we've left Crawford together, hasn't it?" Neil was looking out of the car window, resting his arm on it. It had been a while since he was on the open road, and Neil was mesmerized by how the world had changed.

"It's been at least a few years for me." Prost was watching Neil, who was sitting behind the driver's seat. Neil was smiling.

"We should go out more. We've been planning another expansion project for a while, after all. Wouldn't want to get left behind by the world because we were too scared to face it."

"Always the proactive one, aren't you?" Prost looked away from him, also looking out of the window. Instead of admiring the scenery, he watched the decrepit road signs zip by. "Once you figure something out, you won't let go. You and those hunches of yours."

Neil laughed. "Oh Prost, when did you become such a flatterer?"

"Suppose I'm in a good mood today. Enough to humor you."

The car jerked forward, slowing down quickly before coming to a complete stop. Neil, having committed most of the routes to memory, was confused by this. "Why have we stopped? The next checkpoint isn't for another hour at least."

Shrugging, the driver looked back at Neil. "Maybe there was some debris on the road. The first car up the line will radio in soon enough with an update, I'm sure."

Discontent with this answer, Neil leaned forward and reached for the radio on the center console. "Jones, can you see anything?" Despite the new vantage point, Neil still couldn't see much of anything beyond the car in front of them. There was always an uneasy silence whenever one was left in the dark and stuck on the open road– as if the forests were beginning to close in on the cars, hostile to the damage they were causing.

In the meantime, Prost was watching the trees instead of trying to figure out what was in front of them. This was typical, as Prost was always on the lookout for marred and other potential threats.

Jones shook his head, taking the walkie-talkie out of the cup holder. "What's going on up there?" There was a moment of silence before someone from the first car answered.

"Some robbers laid out spikes on the road. Say they're looking for something. Us and car two are going out to confront them," the radio announced as the car waited anxiously for an update. Their answer would come in the form of gunshots, a few firing off before the road returned to silence.

"What's–" Neil didn't have the time to finish asking his question before more gunshots rang out, this time from behind them. Jones looked into the rearview mirror as more robbers approached from the end of the line.

The walkie spurred to life again, this time from a driver in the last car. "They put spikes behind us!" The lady on the radio spoke frantically, being cut off as the sound of a car door was thrown open.

"Get out now!" A different voice commanded. Turning around, Neil watched as one of the robbers opened the car door of the woman speaking on the radio, pointing a gun at her. Another robber grabbed her, throwing her out of the car.

"Shit– that's Patricia's car!" Jones blurted, pulling his hands off the wheel and bringing them to his temples.

Prost didn't seem panicked, though he never did in these situations. That's why he joined the convoy in the first place: to protect Neil if something went awry. Prost readied his rifle, though he wasn't hasty to start his attack. "Both of you should run into the woods. I'll give you some cover, then follow after."

Neil glanced back at Prost, wanting to tell him to come with them but knowing that the best option would be for him to stay behind. "Stay out of trouble." Neil put his hand on the door's handle, checking to make sure it was safe before throwing the door open and running off. Prost peeked out of the backseat door, firing at the robbers behind them but was unable to hit a target before they scrambled out of view.

The robbers flattened themselves against one of the cars, which made them harder to hit but easier to avoid. They fired wildly at Neil and a few others who were running for cover, managing to pierce Neil's leg. Neil stumbled, falling face-first onto the ground as he placed weight on the shot leg. One of his men turned around, grabbing Neil's arm and dragging him into the safety of the trees.

Neil cursed, grabbing his wounded leg once he propped himself against a tree. Luckily his leg had only been grazed and was still usable, but he could feel a shock of pain shiver through his leg with each step he took. From this position behind the tree, Neil was unable to see the conflict, but was certainly able to hear it.

Gunshots rang through the air like missiles, disturbing the normally serene forest. The conflict was a desperate struggle. People jumped out of cars to get to better cover, only to be shot down before their feet ever hit the ground.

The attackers had, despite their sneak attack and taking advantage of the initial confusion, started to lose momentum. Slowly they were being pushed back, further and further down the line of cars. While many of the drivers were relieved, Neil couldn't help but be suspicious. Why attack such a well-armored convoy with so few people? Just to immediately disengage when the battle inevitably turned against them.

It was illogical.

The attackers started to retreat into dense trees for cover, though not all were able to make it to safety. Everything went quiet after the last attacker ducked behind the treeline, only the ringing in their ears to fill the gap.

Neil stood, making his way back to the road. It had been quiet for several minutes now. Believing that the fighting had ceased, Neil was caught off guard by a single gunshot that came from deeper in the forest on the other side of the road.

Another shot followed only a few short seconds after, yet none of Neil's people returned fire. Whoever had fired was far away from the road, leaving the survivors of the convoy as confused as Neil. *Who was still fighting?* Convinced that this was a sign of something ominous, Neil ran over to the cars as fast as he could.

His gaze darted from the ground to the cars to the trees. With a careful eye he scanned the bodies, hoping– praying– that Prost was not among them. To Neil's relief, Prost did not lie amongst the dead.

Something else troubled Neil. Among those still standing, Prost was also absent. With Prost's whereabouts unknown, Neil assumed the worst, looking over at the side of the forest where the two lone gunshots had emerged. In the heat of the moment, Neil forgot about all the contention between himself and Prost. He needed to know that Prost was okay. That his companion was *alive.*

Hearing the sound of a car's engine roar to life behind the brush, Neil ran towards it, ignoring the warnings of his people. Neil ran through the trees without care, bumping into branches and stumbling over loose roots. It was only a few seconds before Neil found a clue: a discarded gun. Upon closer inspection, Neil could clearly see a large pool of blood close to it.

A second gun, Prost's, wasn't even a foot away from the first. Blood was splattered on the gun and the trees. Yet there was no blood from the other side– no other bullets that would have shown some sort of resistance. It looked like his people hadn't put up a fight. The first thought in Neil's mind was that this was some sort of execution, not the continuation of battle.

Something was odd about the scene. Of course, the lack of bodies itself was suspect, but the blood was the most intriguing. Neil was no expert, but it didn't take a detective to notice that something was off. *Why was there only one pool of blood?* It was as if the second gunshot hadn't hit anything. Neil suspected that Prost or Jones might still be alive. It was possible that they kept one of them to obtain information. But for now it was all conjecture– one which came from a man who was paranoid of every slight anomaly.

But if Neil was right, it would only be a matter of time until one of his people was no longer of use and their attackers would dispose of him. Neil would have to act fast, but first he had to take care of those whose statuses weren't unknown– those who had perished. For now, Neil thought it best to return to the road and establish a new plan.

"What– what should we do?" The first driver watched Neil as he exited the forest. Others had already started to assess the damage done to the cars and gather up the spikes to get them out of the way. They'd have to start moving fast, as Florids and Mechatollies would soon gather in this place of bloodshed. Some Florids were already starting to pour out of the forest but were suppressed by eagle-eyed lookouts.

"This trip can't have been for nothing. We'll resupply in Minerva during the discussions and return on schedule. The dead should be taken back to Crawford now so they can be processed and their families informed. Then we'll give them a… proper burial, so they can be put to rest at home," Neil spoke with an unusual speed, which was around the pace at which most people spoke. He wasn't sure how to make heads or tails of the situation.

He had never been ambushed before, at least not since he established the trade routes. Was it his pride that made his defenses sloppy? Why did they attack this convoy and not the countless others that travel this route daily? Or was it rather that they were simply unlucky? Surely his convoy couldn't have been the easiest target. It was all very peculiar– too much so for his liking. He'd have to track their attackers down. This assault was unacceptable.

Someone must be punished.

26

Not many knew of Prost's death. Those who passed were given a dignified funeral and graves to rest in. There was a graveyard just outside the town walls, in what was likely a park before the end of the mundane era.

The funerals were held over the span of a week. By the time Neil had prepared the quant funeral for Prost, who had no family to speak of, Jamie returned.

Only five people attended his funeral.

Neil, who stood next to the headstone, wore a pensive look. Opposing him was Sicaren, the antithesis of Neil, who shamefully wore his emotions on his sleeve. Ivette, who was gently holding Sicaren's shoulders and had a similar sorrow about her. Natty was kneeling in front of the grave, mumbling something. It seemed like a prayer. And finally Jamie, who couldn't face the grave at all.

There were many vines behind the grave, growing along Crawford's outer wall. They reached for the sky. Jamie watched the leaves on them, which were dancing in the subtle breeze. It would look like Jamie was completely disinterested in the death of his friend if one were to only glance at him in passing.

"Who did this to him?" Sicaren asked between sobs, holding his face in his hands. Ivette tried to calm him down, but he was inconsolable.

Neil shook his head, looking at the grass. They didn't have a body to bury; the grass wasn't even overturned to pretend that there was one. "I… I don't know," he spoke with an unfamiliar heaviness. "We have leads. Nothing concrete."

Natty had stopped her prayers, looking up at everyone. Standing, she brushed the dirt off her knees, focusing on Neil. "Then what do you plan to do?"

"I will make it right." Neil's voice was confident as always, but the way he carried himself said otherwise.

Ivette remained unusually quiet, not asking any questions of her own. She would look at the others, but never spoke a word of condolences, only offering a shoulder to cry on.

The first to leave was Natty, who left to return to her workshop. She was shortly followed by Sicaren and Ivette, leaving only Neil and Jamie. For the first time, Neil showed the first hint of emotion.

Sadness.

"Prost always wore a ring," Jamie said suddenly, as if it were a thought that had just popped into his mind.

"Yes, he did."

"Why?"

"He was married."

"To who?"

Neil was silent for a while, as if he were thinking about the answer. "You've never met her."

"Did you?"

"Yes… I knew them before they were engaged. The wedding was… it was nice. I was his best man. I still remember finding the rings with him. They came in a matching set." Neil chuckled softly, thinking about the time they robbed the jewelry section of a museum to find rings for Prost and his wife.

"Then… what happened to her?"

Again, Neil fell silent. Memories seemed to flash through his mind, but would be gone before he could linger on them for long. "The same thing that happens to everyone else."

"Why didn't you bury them together?"

"We could never find her body," Neil's voice quivered when he started, before clearing his throat and trying to continue with poise. "Even in death, they weren't all that different, I suppose. Leaving this world without a trace."

Jamie had, for the first time, looked at the empty grave. The corner of his mouth twitched into a slight frown before reverting to its typically neutral state. Placing his hand on Jamie's shoulder, Neil began to gently lead Jamie away from the grave.

"We should do something. Too much sadness is bad for your health."

"When does the next convoy leave?"

Neil seemed a bit shocked by this response. "You– you want to go outside? Right now? Why take that chance?"

Jamie knew how to hold his own out there and, moreover, he did not want to be part of any discussions about Prost. "I'll be alright. Besides, it's how I clear my head. That's all. And, it comes with the bonus of being able to help you."

At first, Neil seemed suspicious of the statement. As he thought about it more, he seemed to be able to rationalize what Jamie had told him. "Still– I just… think you should hold off. At least until the next convoy comes around."

Jamie nodded, agreeing with Neil. "When is that, then?"

"Three weeks from now. But if you don't feel fully ready when it comes around, you tell me. I mean it. Last thing I'd want is to lose someone else."

"I always tell you everything, anyway," Jamie said nonchalantly. "Besides, if I get injured, I'd be out for the count for way longer. What do you take me for, some kind of novice?" Jamie asked, eliciting a small chuckle from Neil, even though Jamie hadn't meant for it to be a joke.

Seeing Neil relaxed had a similar effect on Jamie, who managed to crack a brief smile.

"I see your point," Neil admitted.

The two spoke for a while longer and eventually left the graveyard in higher spirits than they had entered with. Eventually they fell silent, passing through the different buildings inside Crawford's walls. It was louder than normal. Those who returned rejoiced, while the families of the dead attempted to hide their sorrows through the festivities.

Even the *Pale Roses* couldn't resist the distraction. But neither Neil nor Jamie would join. By the time they approached Jamie's apartment, the noise had mostly quieted.

"They wore the same shirts," Neil blurted before Jamie could start for the stairs.

"What was that?" Jamie lazily glanced over at Neil, tracing his fingers over his apartment key.

"The attackers. Yes– yes they… they all wore the same shirts now that I think about it. There was a logo and an acronym. It was…" Neil fell silent, thinking back to the attack. "I'll have to look at the bodies. I can find a clue there… I'm sure of it." There was something hidden within Neil's voice, something Jamie hadn't heard before. An untamed excitement for a puzzle he was slowly starting to piece together.

27

2049, present day

It had been several months since Jamie's last hunt. If it weren't for the attack on the convoy, he would have already been out there again. Jamie cursed those bandits. It was because of them that he was yet again confined to these walls. Neil had finally allowed him to return to the alloy zone after some apprehension, and he was finally free from the bustling city of Crawford. Jamie was exactly as he wanted to be–alone.

Alone except for one person. The thief with the whip, *Lila*, would certainly still be around. It was as if she knew where he was going to be. She must have been tracking the convoy somehow. At least there was the assurance that Jamie would be safe until he gathered copper. That was all she cared about.

Usually Jamie harvested copper at the first place he could find, but this time waited until he found somewhere defensible. A small clay studio near a public park would do well. It was decently far away from other structures, but had some good spots to hide. Climbing up the concrete wall, Jamie propelled himself onto the roof of the building and twisted his body around to look inside.

Instead of glass windows, a wire fence was installed to keep thieves out. More importantly, inside the art studio were five Mechatollies. There seemed to be a side room, so there was a good chance that more were hiding beyond where Jamie could see.

Jamie was already beginning to form a plan. Maybe she'd have to fight them to get to Jamie if she tried to steal the copper. That's a sight he'd like to see.

Before that, he'd have to lead them out of the studio so that he could actually collect the copper to make the trap. Picking the door open, Jamie started to creep around inside.

He snuck past the first five and pressed his ear against the side door, listening for any movement inside. Lacking a response, Jamie cracked the door open to check. It was a firing room, only having a kiln inside, excluding the two Mechatollies.

They looked how they always did: like statues. Fully opening the door, Jamie started to search for something to use as a distraction. Behind the two Mechatollies, a board with a few completed pieces sat on a messy table that was covered in a thick layer of dust.

One immediately stood out to Jamie, and he quickly snatched it off the board. It was a ball: small enough to fit in his hand but large enough to cause some damage and at least create a loud distraction. It was painted white, with a pink heart on it. Cute, but most importantly, practical.

Snagging a long string on his way out, Jamie looked for a good place to make noise while he tied the ball to the string. An aluminum canopy shaded the walkway from the art studio to some nearby buildings. The aluminum was heavily rusted and allowed the sun to poke through.

It would be durable enough to withstand a few hits from the ceramic ball if needed. Using the same route as he had before, Jamie scaled the building and tested the string's integrity before he threw it. Then he began to spin the makeshift flail.

Jamie spun the line faster and faster, finally letting the string go at its lowest point. The ceramic ball soared, only stopping because there was no more string to continue.

Flakes of aluminum and ceramic were shot into the air, but the ball remained intact and the string uncut. Jamie listened to the inside of the art studio and he started to reel in the ball again, making more noise as it was dragged along the uneven aluminum surface.

Sure enough, the Mechatollies had been alerted by the distraction, bursting forth from their metal shells to search for the source. By the time they had escaped, the ceramic ball was back in Jamie's hands.

Once all seven Mechatollies were accounted for, Jamie slinked over to the other side of the building and lowered himself to the ground in front of the entrance doors.

Once the doors were closed, he moved the art desks and some of the chairs in front of them to create an improvised barricade. Looking at the ceramic ball, he quietly thanked it before placing it on one of the desks. Then he started harvesting the copper as per his usual routine.

Though he wasn't allowed to finish, much as he predicted. Hearing the door being carefully pried open, Jamie nabbed the copper sack and ducked behind one of the tables.

It was the thief, Lila. She closed the doors behind her and quietly slithered past the barricade with ease. Jamie tucked himself further behind the table as she started looking around the room. Lila seemed confused. Of course she expected him to hear her, but she didn't expect Jamie to completely disappear.

"Boy," she called, though spoke quietly so as not to incur the wrath of the Mechatollies. "I don't have time for your games. That man isn't with you anymore, so just give it up before the monsters come." Lila looked around for Jamie, losing him in the clutter. "Don't make me wait. I saw you with the goods earlier! I know you have it on you, and I know you're still here. You can't stall forever."

It was clear that Lila was confident. While she was ready for a fight, her guard wasn't up as if she was preparing to go up against an equal. Regardless of what she thought of Jamie, she knew his habits well.

She had been following him for some time now, maybe long before their first encounter. Which meant she knew how Jamie worked and how he despised any form of noise. She thought that she could bully him.

Jamie slowly lowered the copper-filled sack into a crack in the wall, watching her while staying hidden behind the messy tables. This was about more than just survival for Jamie. This was about his ability to venture beyond the walls of Crawford– something he valued more than life itself.

If Lila continued to steal Jamie's loot, which she surely would, Jamie's position as a copper chaser could fall into jeopardy. He would resort to murder if it assured his freedom, just as he had in the past.

Lila's knuckles had gone white from clutching the whip. It seemed like she was upset from their past encounter. He snuck from table to table, quickly dashing behind obstacles as she made her rounds about the studio.

Jamie grabbed a piece of loose copper from the ground, bouncing it around in his hand as he gauged its weight. This would suffice. The thought of just shooting her and being done with it had crossed Jamie's mind as he continued to play this game of cat and mouse. But Jamie was quick to rule this option out. There was only one route of escape: through the barricade. But if Lila were dead, there would be nothing to distract the Mechatollies with.

The noise would only quicken their descent upon Jamie, after all. Once her back was turned for a few seconds, Jamie popped his head out from behind a table and whipped the copper chunk into the space a few feet behind her.

Almost as if by instinct, she spun around and cracked her whip at the copper. Copper chunks exploded from the point of impact, and a deep gash was left on the copper that remained. If it were him instead of that copper, his head would have been taken clean off. She stared at the copper for a while, agitated. "Quit messing around. You think I won't keep my word? I'll seriously kill you!"

Jamie looked at the door as the first Mechatolly arrived and began to slam against it, then several more followed after the first. He made the barricade weak since he knew someone was tailing him, but it was taking longer than he had hoped for the Mechatollies to get past it. While this forced him to stay in Lila's proximity for longer, this gave Jamie more time to ensure that she'd be unable to escape.

But Jamie had to be fast, nevertheless. He was crouched close to the door, and there was no way the Mechatollies wouldn't see him before getting to Lila. That's if they didn't all pile onto him first and totally ignore her.

Behind him there were some sinks, which were mostly filled with various debris from the Mechatollies and dead insects. Once the Mechatollies burst in, he could use it as a stepping stone to get on top of a row of cabinets next to it. First, he had to keep her occupied on the other side of the studio so she couldn't reach him with her whip.

Unwilling to fully commit to using a gun, Jamie found a slab of dried clay beneath a table and decided to use it in tandem with the clay ball. Jamie raised the slab above his head and threw it towards her. Lila cracked her whip at it, splitting it in half and causing it to lose momentum before it could hit its target. What she didn't expect, however, was a clay ball the size of a baseball to come hurtling at her immediately after. It hit her square in the face and knocked her back onto a stack of cardboard boxes. Bright red blood began to flow from her nose, and she hissed with annoyance, thrashing at the boxes as she pushed herself up.

Jamie had already dashed out of his hiding spot, propelling himself off the sink and diving onto the top of the cabinets. The shelves creaked and the contents inside rattled with the sudden jolt, though it stayed attached to the wall.

Lila was hot in pursuit, vaulting over a table and sprinting towards Jamie– then the doors flung open.

Mechatollies spilled over each other, crawling over and under the table in a coordinated assault against the first thing that moved: Lila. She was about to crack her whip at the cabinet but was stopped as the stampede of Mechatollies began to flood in. She looked between Jamie and the door; the color draining from her face.

That's when she realized– he *planned* this. She thought she had Jamie in the palm of her hand, when all this time she had it all backwards.

She turned, heading to the back of the room as the Mechatollies honed in on her, trying to buy more time as she searched for a way to escape. They were hot on her trail– she barely had time to jump onto a table and ascend higher onto another cabinet. Unlike the one Jamie took refuge on, this one was freestanding and the top was hardly above the extent of the Mechatollies' arms.

They banged against the cabinet, causing it to rock violently. She latched onto the chain-link fence, acting as a window behind her for dear life, kicking at the fingers of particularly tall Mechatollies.

Jamie watched as she struggled against the will of the Mechatollies, attempting to use her whip, only for it to be stolen from her. All the Mechatollies had gathered on the other side of the room, and once Jamie was sure he was in the clear, he began his descent from the cabinet.

Staying crouched, he efficiently returned to the crack in the wall to get back his sack of copper. Jamie watched as the rocking of the cabinet grew more extreme, along with her cursing. He vaulted over the table, running off and leaving Lila behind. He reasoned that if it were her, she would have done the same. Or maybe just killed him outright to be sure.

He would retreat from the scene, much as he usually did, though not from fear of being caught by the Mechatollies. Despite his growth, Jamie was still unable to face the real world: unable to face the consequences of his actions.

28

The ride home was by no means a pleasant one, and neither was the walk to Neil's office. Jamie's mind was preoccupied with the events of the mission. He had to take this to his grave and feared that he would be imprisoned by the civilized people of Crawford if they found out a murderer walked amongst them. They would never understand. But Neil would. Neil knew about Jamie's troubles with Lila. He even encouraged Jamie to do what he did.

Inevitably, she would have gotten Jamie killed. Did this not justify Jamie's action? To be preemptive in his attack to ensure not just his survival, but his ability to leave the walls? The opinions of Crawford's citizens meant little to Jamie if Neil cut his position because he couldn't bring back any copper.

Still, Jamie could not be sure of Neil's reaction. What if he imprisoned him within the walls– the fear that Jamie's mind kept returning to. The thought of captivity made his skin begin to prickle, and it was only soothed once he met with Neil. Jamie felt removed from the normal pleasantries of their conversation, anxious to both tell Neil what he had done and wanting to do everything in his power to avoid the subject.

"You seem different today." After only a few minutes, Neil finally brought up Jamie's sullen behavior. It wasn't difficult to spot by any means, especially for one as observant as Neil. It seemed, rather, that Neil was unsure of how to approach the subject. "Were you hurt?"

"No, I… it's nothing like that. I'm unharmed." Did Jamie *have* to admit to possibly murdering someone? Nobody would have to know. Then Jamie would never have to be punished. He could get away with it all. Murder in the alloy zones was normal. Neil had excused it in the past when they first met, after all.

But he couldn't keep a secret from Neil. Even if he tried, Neil was simply too good at reading people. The avoidance of the question only made Neil more suspicious and intrigued. "Then what…? Did you witness someone die? Did you… kill them?"

Jamie's head jolted upright, his eyes widening in surprise. The secret wasn't kept for long. Neil found out scarily fast. The reaction got a chuckle out of Neil, who was amused at such an obvious reaction. Jamie opened his mouth to speak but couldn't muster any words together.

"You should really get a better poker face, Jamie," Neil scoffed, grinning. "But it's not hard to piece together. You usually get straight to huffing over the troubles Lila gave you. Now you're just… quiet."

"You know I don't want to kill people, Neil. It's out of necessity." Jamie got defensive at the accusation. "It was an accident. Me or her."

"So it *was* Lila."

"Me or her," Jamie repeated with unusual sternness.

Neil fell silent, looking at Jamie with intense eyes. It wasn't anger, but rather a look of deep concentration. As if Neil were deciphering Jamie. "How did you do it? Could you have just scared her off?" These questions were neither meant to probe nor excuse Jamie. Neil had gone fishing, just as he always had.

Neil's gaze felt like that of a sweltering summer sun. There was no shade to take shelter under– no water to offer relief from the heat. "She was interfering with the job. I couldn't lose it." Jamie glared back, challenging Neil's gaze but never enough to overpower him. "Besides. *I* didn't kill her. It was the Mechatollies."

"But did you not bring them forth? Did you not secretly hope they would kill her for you?" Neil questioned, leaning onto the table in front of him and causing the leather in his seat to crumple uncomfortably loudly. He interlocked his fingers, resting his chin upon his clasped hands.

This was agonizing torture. Yet Jamie still did not know the answer to the question, even after mulling it over during the car ride to Crawford. "Do you have a point to make with this, or are you just trying to make me feel bad?"

The room fell into silence yet again while Neil continued to study Jamie's expression. It seemed like Neil had reached whatever conclusion he was working toward and shook his head once he finished the thought. He then leaned back in his chair, hooking his index finger under his chin. "I have a new mission for you, Jamie."

"Is this really a good time to bring that up?" Jamie's voice signified his confusion, but he listened intently, like a dog who overheard his master mention the word treat.

"It's a great time to bring it up. See, we've run into a bit of a problem. Someone's gone and stolen Sicaren's recipes, and I have it on good authority that they'll be selling them soon."

"You want me to steal it back from them?"

"Exactly."

Jamie went quiet for a moment, thinking about Neil's proposal. Make no mistake, Jamie was very good at getting into some place undetected. But those places usually didn't have humans residing in them. But if he got to venture into the alloy zone without the convoy, the end result would mean more chances to explore. That was all Neil needed to say to convince Jamie.

Neil picked up on Jamie's silence but continued, nevertheless.

"If our recipes get leaked, Crawford could be in danger. Our industries– undercut by thieves. Fuel is important to our economy, Jamie. And more distributors of our product would make our fuel sector unprofitable. We'd only be able to focus on our auto industry. That means fewer expeditions."

This was, of course, an exaggeration that Neil had engineered to coerce Jamie into agreeing with his plan. It would take a lot more than a few competitors to place Crawford's industries in danger. But what a few competitors could easily do was dethrone Neil as the second king. That was one thing Neil couldn't stand for.

"Yeah, I heard you," Jamie voiced, glancing back up to meet Neil's gaze. "When do I leave?"

29

Despite Jamie's abundance of experience with this type of mission from his time before Crawford, he couldn't help but feel anxious. It had been so long since then, and so many things could go wrong.

Jamie breathed in deeply, skulking around the approximate meeting place. It was deep in an alloy zone that was far away from any civilization– especially Crawford. The only reason they knew of the sale at all was because one of the buyer's people sold out the meeting in exchange for citizenship at Crawford.

They produced a copy of the contract between the buyers and the thief, along with one of Sicaren's recipes. It gave the enigma enough legitimacy to force Neil into sending Jamie to investigate and intervene if the claim held water.

It was a few hours before any sign of human activity occurred, and Jamie had begun to worry that he was in the wrong place– or that this entire operation was a fraud. A single man approached, carefully surveying the area though was unable to spot Jamie; at least, there was no indication that the man had seen him. A thick cloth binding wrapped around his face, just beneath his eyes, and draped down past his shoulders.

The man's long, brownish hair almost covered his eyes, but Jamie could clearly see how nervous he was– this was undoubtedly the seller he had been told about. As a second group began to emerge from the other side of the building, Jamie retreated and left the building to avoid being seen.

He would have to act fast, but Jamie already had a plan and was just waiting to spring it into action. Walking a few blocks over, Jamie pushed through a set of doors and entered an old mall. It was dark, but Jamie used a hand-cranked flashlight to lead the way.

The names on the stores meant nothing to him, and he couldn't recognize the valuables on display– this was an untouched fragment from the mundane days. But there was a good reason for that. Jamie slowly approached the edge of the floor, looking at the bottom of the escalator.

Dragging the beam of the flashlight from his feet to the bottom of the escalator revealed the copper mass that had been building, and further exploration revealed an army of Mechatollies. Jamie glanced behind him, towards the entrance and the faint light that poured into the mall's entrance.

Digging a hand into his jacket pocket, Jamie slipped a small bell out and raised it above his head. It chimed three times before Jamie placed it back into his pocket and began running back the way he came, now with a sizable following behind him.

Pushing through the doors of the mall, Jamie glanced back and, sure enough, at least a hundred Mechatollies were keeping pace behind him. He remained in a sprint, charging towards the meeting place he had left just five minutes prior.

The buildings zipped past Jamie in a blur, and Jamie imagined what this sight must have looked like to any onlookers. As he drew closer to the front door, Jamie prepared himself for the parkour he'd need to perform to avoid certain death. Even a momentary lapse in footing would give the copper horde behind him enough time to catch up to and kill him.

He inhaled sharply and nearly choked on the air, using the door handle as a foothold and propelling himself onto the roof of the building. The Mechatollies slammed against the door and after a few seconds managed to burst through it with their combined force.

Though their original intention was to pursue Jamie, the Mechatollies were distracted by the larger selection of prey inside and refocused onto the seller and the buyers. Jamie could hear the chaos and sighed in relief, not at their suffering, but that the plan had worked.

Pushing himself off the floor, Jamie wandered towards the side of the roof and dropped down, catching himself on the window to watch the battle unfold. The buyers had guns, and the seller had a small handgun and was using them effectively, though there were simply too many Mechatollies. Jamie's eyes wandered around, and he noticed a blur of someone escaping through a window on the other side.

Jamie blinked, trying to figure out if what he had seen was real. It was no more than a red flash that nobody else acknowledged. Nobody was wearing red, at least not based on what Jamie had seen earlier, so he dismissed it as a trick of the light and refocused on the battle ahead of him.

The seller had run out of bullets and turned towards the other exit, managing to burst through it after a few tries. The buyers were also beginning to make their way towards it, fending off the remaining Mechatollies. This wouldn't do. Jamie released the window and dropped down to the ground, chasing after the seller.

At first, Jamie had nothing but a general direction to go off of, but as he got further from the gunfight, he was able to pick up on the seller's frantically fleeing footsteps. This awareness went both ways, as the seller glanced back and saw Jamie in hot pursuit, picking up his pace in response.

The seller was fast. Jamie was faster.

The distance between them quickly narrowed– from fifty feet, to ten, then to just a hand's reach away. Jamie pounced, tackling the man to the ground as they slid a few feet forward before their momentum let up. Getting on top of the man, Jamie restrained his arms and made sure the seller was neutralized before beginning the interrogation.

"*Where is it?*" Jamie barked, speaking between labored breaths.

"My pocket– my left pocket! Just take it." The seller hissed, not fighting against Jamie's will as much as he had anticipated.

Jamie's hand slowly felt for the stranger's pocket and pulled a neatly rolled piece of paper from it but stopped once it was half removed. He sprang upright, whipping his gun out from its holster and aiming it down the street the two had just run from. There was a person at the other end of the alley– a man in dark red clothing.

This man clearly wasn't part of the buyer's group and disappeared as suddenly as he had arrived in a familiar red blur. He didn't stay long enough to allow Jamie a good look at him. With a glance, Jamie returned his gaze to the seller, whose neck was lodged beneath his right foot. A part of him wanted to kill the seller, but a more vocal part told him not to.

Jamie was told to make this look like an accident, and his cover had been thoroughly blown. As such, he was unsure whether to put a bullet in the man's head and ensure his silence, or let him go, knowing that this would make two witnesses to his crimes.

The seller strained under Jamie's gaze, swallowing back the lump in his throat and hoping that Jamie would make up his mind soon. Jamie exhaled sharply, taking his foot off the seller's neck before bolting towards the opposite end of the alley, away from the stranger in red.

It was only a few minutes before the buyers found the seller, but Jamie and the recipes were already long gone.

30

The debriefing of Jamie's mission didn't last for long. There wasn't much to say because Jamie downplayed the severity of his failure, fearing what Neil would do if he were to find out. Thankfully for Jamie, there was something else on Neil's mind.

"Word's come from our informants," Neil said dismissively, changing topics, which he was clearly waiting to talk about since Jamie arrived. "It's time to take our revenge, Jamie."

"You really found them? Are– are you sure it's them?" Jamie could hardly contain himself. His woes had seemingly washed away upon hearing the news. They had found Prost's killers. Though it had been a month since Prost's death, it was all Jamie could think about. He wanted to see the faces of the people who committed the crime.

Neil nodded, interlocking his fingers. "They seem to be mostly self-sufficient or at least reclusive. One of their people did business with Minerva while you were gone. Then we followed them back." Neil took out a map, pointing to a plane hangar a few miles off the main road. "They live in the Pasko Aviation Museum. It used to be a hangar for the military, a long time ago."

"What do you think happened to the planes?" Jamie started to study the map, looking at the nearby cities and towns. Pieces of tape with a red X drawn on them were placed over the abandoned and dangerous locations. He had seen the map a couple of times before, having gone to some of the crossed-out cities to harvest copper.

"Well, last I heard there still aren't any planes in working condition. At least not ones that operate. Too expensive and loud."

"Too expensive and loud… you know what that reminds me of?" Jamie looked up at Neil, smiling softly.

"Cars are actually a feasible venture– *you know.* And much safer than a plane. I doubt we'll return to the skies any time soon. Too many marred, and not enough people." Neil crossed his arms, leaning back in the chair with a playful expression. "And since when did you start talking like Prost?"

Jamie shrugged. "Anything I need to know?"

"Their leader has been gone for several days. She was meant to go to a conference with other smaller settlements in the area."

"She was *meant* to? What happened? Did she not go?"

Neil looked up at Jamie, caught off guard by his persistence with this line of questioning. "Ah, no. She did. It seems like she's still there. It's probably some unionization meeting. It's really nothing interesting, but sure is time-consuming. Either way, we're sure that she's still at the conference. Which means that Pasko isn't working at full capacity. Their guards might be dropped since their marshall isn't there to supervise. It'd be best to strike before she gets back. Then they'll be none the wiser and flounder without their leader."

"Then… what's the plan?"

"You'll go by yourself through the west, then leave the road to approach the south side of the museum." Neil traced his finger along the lines on the map, pointing out the roads that Jamie would follow. Neil paused, glancing up at Jamie before continuing. "Then you should… set fire to the place."

"You know I'll do it, Neil." Jamie took a breath and paused before asking his last question of the meeting. "It's all just… been going well, more than usual for us. You're sure that these are the right people?"

"Without a doubt." Neil placed a hand on his chest to emphasize his sincerity, leaning on the desk. "I would never do something so extreme if I wasn't *absolutely* sure."

31

There was a special emphasis on the secrecy of the mission Jamie was about to partake in. Even greater importance than his previous job, which, at least to Jamie, seemed more morally reprehensible than what he was doing now. At least this expedition could be seen as revenge for the murder of Crawford's citizens.

This job was a personal one. Pasko slaughtered Prost. They ambushed the convoy; they were heartless and executed the people Neil called his neighbors. This infuriated Neil, and it was the duty of his most trusted subordinate, who was still living, to deliver that pain onto their enemies. It was Jamie's duty.

So that is how Jamie found himself on a battered bike, making his way a few hundred miles from Crawford to an unfamiliar place. At first, he was hesitant to take on such a job for Neil. It was not as though Jamie didn't trust him, but it felt like he was starting to become Neil's hitman, rather than his copper chaser. Of course, there was no resistance that could go untamed. Neil, with his quick wit and undying charisma, had convinced Jamie to take part in his plot to destroy Pasko.

The trip itself would take several days, weather permitting. But the weather was never particularly nice around Crawford, especially as one went further north, as he was. It could take a week.

Rain, crumbling back roads, trees, and Florid vines climbed over fences and poured onto the streets. Jamie could already feel that getting his bike to Pasko in one piece would be quite an arduous process. Each turn of the bike's pedals caused a groan and creak in retaliation. Much to Jamie's despair, the bike never seemed to recover from its old age, despite all of Natty's efforts.

The ride ultimately went better than Jamie had suspected. Staving off a cold for the five days' travel, he only had to make a few quick repairs and a single tire change. And when he finally reached his goal, Jamie rejoiced at the sight: a metal pole which was erected from the ground. Its sign was discarded nearby, but it was easy to find as the sign prevented any grass from growing under it. Taking out his knife and hacking away at some thick vines, Jamie could just make out the weathered words.

Pas.o Avi…on Mus..um, 1 mil.

It was enough for Jamie to recognize. Really, if the town was trying to hide it, they should have taken down the metal pole or removed the sign altogether, but Jamie wouldn't look a gift horse in the mouth. This was a well-deserved break after the long journey.

Happily jumping back onto his bike, Jamie continued down the road until he got a bit closer. He approached the museum slowly, keeping an eye out for any patrols which might have been protecting the main structure– he heard some signs of human activity, but they seemed restricted behind a chain-link fence.

The sun had yet to set, so he'd try to get a good look at the commune before jumping the fence and beginning his plan. He wouldn't have to do anything fancy this time at least; no excessive plans to sneak his way in. Glancing at the back of his bike, Jamie reminded himself of the two canisters of Sicaren's special fuel. The corner of his lip twitched, and Jamie released a deep exhale, looking to the roots of the trees in front of him.

He found himself at a crossroads, and Jamie didn't like the destination of either. A part of him wanted to fulfill Neil's request and get revenge, and another part feared the man he was quickly becoming. He was no better than those bandits who murdered and destroyed as they pleased. The only consolation was that this was personal.

For a man who was used to doing nothing more than taking orders and not considering the motivations behind them, this was beginning to take quite a toll on him. For now, Jamie distracted himself by keeping his eyes glued to the forest floor; he was cautious of any traps that Pasko might have set up. Jamie kept a tight grip on the bicycle's handlebars, as if ready to speed off at a moment's notice. Not as if that would be possible, given the densely packed trees.

A shiver crawled down his neck and wriggled down his spine. Jamie went to look behind him, only to find that he couldn't move his head at all. Yanking his knife out from its holster, Jamie tried to cut at whatever grabbed him, taking wild slashes at the air. Although he had certainly managed to cut through something, the mysterious force would take his knife before he could do any more damage. His hand became numb, and the sensation quickly began to spread throughout the rest of his arm.

First, a small spike of pain, then nothing. The bicycle dropped beside him as his feet were lifted a few inches above the ground. Jamie's eyes were unable to focus on anything, and his pounding heart was trying to rip itself from his chest. It felt as though he were reduced to a small insect, caught in a spider's web– then he realized what had caught him.

It was such an unusual trap that only someone with intimate knowledge of an Antherus would be able to induce this stage of the parasite. A Medusa. Sicaren had talked about it enough for him to know its effects by heart. The paralysis, the engulfing, and finally, being pulled up into the bell– the coffin.

This was a jarring feeling for Jamie. Watching as the ground slowly escaped him, unable to do a thing about it. Yet it somehow felt familiar, as Jamie was not unused to being powerless. He only wondered who had engineered the trap.

Jamie thought that this was what dying felt like. One's soul slowly slinking away from their body, flying to the heavens. He wasn't dead yet, but he would be soon. He would fall asleep and awake as a Florid.

No wonder Sicaren always told him to be careful around those things. He was completely helpless against them. Only a few seconds were allotted to him before he was completely trapped. He was folded up into the small bell that lazily hung from a sturdy branch.

Even as he felt his skin press against the slimy interior of the prison, he was still unable to differentiate the film from the surroundings. If not for the mild visual distortion and blurring, Jamie could have believed that he was floating.

Then he felt something hit his face. Like a mist of vapor, filling the sack. "*This is it,*" Jamie thought to himself. This was how he became one of the marred that he dedicated his entire life to studying. His scattered thoughts became clouded; his eyes heavy.

It would be several hours until that portion of the woods saw any more action, as a pair were doing a final patrol before night. First, they saw the bicycle which sat beneath the trap the town set, then they saw Jamie trapped above it. One grabbed the bike while the other disarmed the Medusa which held him. He fell fifteen feet into the patroller's arms, who nearly dropped him, but not quite.

"Damn. She's good," the first remarked, surveying the state of the bike. "It's like Leslie's got a crystal ball or something."

"I bet she's got a strategist tucked away somewhere. Probably's got Ann hacking away at plans. No way she's got the foresight to pull something like this off." The second fumbled around Jamie's body before managing to hold him properly and stand upright. "You recognize him?"

The one with the bike moved closer to the second one. "That's definitely him. Not a mask you forget quickly. Especially not after what he pulled. She'll be pleased."

"Then let's get inside. It's fucking freezing."

32

Jamie was awakened by the harsh morning light and the rough rope rubbing into his wrists. During the night he had been brought into a room with a single, barred window, and had been restrained to a chair. The chair seemed to be more rust than metal. Even with the feeling in his fingertips dampened, Jamie could feel flakes of rust fall from the chair like petals falling from a wilted flower.

This slumber of Jamie's could have been eternal. It was the best he had had in years. No nightmares, no memories. Just rest. And how nice it would have been, never having to reawaken and face what would follow. Yet life would go on without a care for Jamie's woes.

"Morning, stranger." The lady in the chair spoke as she noticed him begin to stir. She looked at Jamie as one would a rabid dog: pitifully and with disgust. "You're lucky I'm here instead of my wife. She would have left you for the Florids to take. Thanks to my good graces, you'll feel better soon."

She paused, crossing her arms and waiting to see if Jamie would say anything. His lack of response caused her mild annoyance, which she did not vocalize. "I know you're from Crawford, and I know you've come to kill us. In a half-hour a man will come visit you. If you want a chance at leaving, I suggest you tell him what you know." The lady calmly got up from her chair and quietly left the room, leaving Jamie to his thoughts.

Jamie released a heavy breath, rolling his head before finally tipping it backwards to see the rest of the room behind him. Predictably, there was nothing of use to aid his escape. For now, Jamie began rubbing the rope around his wrists against the rusted chair. He could feel flakes of rusted metal from the chair peel away, and the sharp surface was digging into the binding.

It would take a while, but this was the best shot Jamie had at escaping. Unfortunately, the escape attempt came to a grinding halt as he heard footsteps approaching the door. Jamie sat up quickly and glared at the door, watching a man emerging from the dimly lit corridor. He had a pleasant smile; it made Jamie nervous. People who were too cheery should be kept at arm's length, as Neil always told him.

"Hello," the man said, sitting down where the lady once had. Although Jamie was certain that they had never met before, something about him seemed familiar. "Slept well?"

"Enough with the pleasantries. I'm not going to tell you anything, so you might as well kill me already." Jamie was studying the man, as the familiarity was gnawing at the back of his mind like a fly he just couldn't ignore.

"We aren't going to hurt you, Jamie." Jamie frowned, but the man continued on, nonetheless. "My name is Colt, and despite our history, I trust our leader's judgement that you could help us."

"You're that seller, aren't you? The one who stole our recipes. How do you know my name?" Jamie threw his guess out and was surprised when Colt tilted his head in affirmation of his statement.

"I wouldn't say we stole it." Colt shrugged. "And it's not your name I would be worried about. It's about what we know about you– and Crawford– that *you* don't know. That's really what you should be worried about."

"Why now? When you knew that Crawford was on your backs– knew that we were coming. *Why?*" Jamie furrowed his brow, and a pit began to form at the bottom of his stomach. He was avoiding the obvious conclusion that this had always been a trap.

"I think you know. Now, if you want any more than that, won't you hear our plea first?"

"You killed the people of Crawford. You killed Prost. Why would I do anything you say?"

"Because things aren't what they seem, Jamie."

"*Don't call me that.*" Jamie snapped, though Colt kept his composure despite the aggression.

"I think there's someone you should meet." Colt stood, leaving his chair and going toward the door. Jamie said nothing in protest and watched with an annoyed glare as Colt began to twist the handle open.

There was someone standing outside. Jamie wasn't sure for how long this person had been listening in on their conversation, but it had certainly been for a while. He stepped into the doorframe like some sort of hero making a grand entrance. It was unmistakable who stood before him– Jamie's scowl melted away and shock painted his features.

It was a dead man.

It was Prost.

33

A deep, suffocating silence permeated the room, with the three displaying distinct expressions. "Could you leave us, Colt?" Colt nodded his head and left upon Prost's request, gently closing the door behind him. "Your tricks get old, Jamie. Sneaking in? We could have seen that coming with our eyes closed." Prost lamented, locking the door behind him.

"What's going on?" Jamie blurted out as soon as the door locked, his expression of shock morphing into one of concern.

Prost approached Jamie hesitantly, trying to explain the situation to him without scaring him off. Of course, he couldn't say everything outright. It wouldn't make sense to Jamie, and would only alienate him further– he had this sort of unhealthy dependency on Neil that Prost had to be wary of. "I left of my own free will," Prost began.

"Of your own will…? But you– you were shot! We thought you were dead– no, they dragged your body away. And why are you and that… *Colt* guy so close?"

"*Jamie*– please, just hear me out. I'll explain, but you have to trust me."

The room fell quiet for a while as Jamie considered his options. Although his loyalty to Neil was fierce, his desire for freedom was greater. And now, Neil couldn't protect him. "Fine. Would you just untie me first?" Prost nodded and began to undo the knots on the rope as he started the story from the beginning.

Prost's abandonment of Neil had started long before his betrayal. What kept him was a mix of addiction, depression, and guilt. But Prost wasn't always this way.

He was once somewhat normal.

In fact– he was *happy.* Happy until the loss of his dear wife. Many years ago she had left on an expedition and never came back to him. She was everything to him, and she was gone.

There were many chances for Prost to leave. Chances for him to escape Neil, the man who he thought had killed his wife. Maybe not by his own hands, but it was his fault, nonetheless. And that is what Prost had thought for a great many years. That was until he met Leslie.

She approached him one day. It was nearly a year after Jamie had joined them and two since his wife's death. "Prospector," she whispered to him. It was a moniker he hadn't heard in years. "We must find somewhere private."

Prost looked at the stranger with great concern. "How do you know that name?" He questioned, his voice shivering slightly. Only two people knew that name. Neil and his late wife, Silvia.

"I know the person who gave it to you. That is how. The name's Leslie." She put her hand out for a shake, but Prost didn't accept the offer.

"What do you mean– how do you know her?" Prost grabbed her shoulders, nearly shaking her off her feet.

If Leslie had not been warned about Prost's instability, perhaps she would have been frightened. She placed a hand on Prost's arm, trying to calm him down. "She is my leader. She is waiting for you. Awaiting the moment until you can be reunited."

"She's– she's *alive? She's really alive?*" Prost's eyes widened slightly upon hearing the news. He glanced around. There weren't many people, but enough that someone would take notice of their conversation. "Let's– yes. Let's talk. Somewhere private."

Once they had locked themselves into a private room, Leslie told Prost everything she knew. How his wife had been set up. How she escaped. Then, how she created a community to one day reclaim what she had lost. Her old life, the safety that came with it, her friends, and her husband. Prost.

If it were up to Prost, he would have left right that second. To hell with the consequences. If it meant seeing Silvia even a second earlier, he would have done it.

Leslie practically had to lock him inside the room to keep him from doing something so drastic. He had to lie low. Stop stirring trouble. At least until they could enact their plan. First, Prost would have to escape.

The chance to do so would come two years after his first meeting with Leslie. When Neil and he were leaving for a meeting with the first and third kings. It was supposed to be a clean escape. Her group would toss some people around and give Neil a fright. Then Prost would make his escape during the chaos.

Things never go as well as people plan, the staged kidnapping being no exception. At first, everything seemed to be going well. Sure, some of Leslie's fighters were a bit trigger-happy, but what's a good show if not for the performers? Slinking back to his side of the car, Prost threw the door open and barreled towards the forest.

Running in a straight line, Prost looked for a small X which had been painted on the root of a tree. He continued to run in a line once he spotted it, shortly after running into two people and a car.

It was Leslie and Patricia, one of the drivers.

The two women were talking as Patricia took out the radio, which had once been in the car. She opened up the back and handed over a small, black disk. It was a tracker.

Background checks were nearly impossible in such a world. With enough time, having a spy slip through the cracks was just a waiting game. "Are we waiting for someone?" Prost asked, anxiously adjusting his grip on the gun.

"Yeah. You," Patricia mumbled, crossing her arms.

Leslie scoffed at Patricia's remark. "Let's go."

"You're not going anywhere," a voice sounded, running up from behind the trees. "Step away from them before I shoot." The three glanced at the man who had followed Prost. The man who pointed a handgun at Leslie's head was a stranger to all but Patricia. Jones was a kind man. He cared for Patricia, helping her secure a spot as a driver despite never having met her before her arrival in Crawford.

Without Jones's help, Prost's escape would have been nearly impossible to complete. Gently raising her hands, Patricia slowly started to approach her friend, Jones. "Woah, woah woah… Jonsie. Look, I'm– we're okay. See? Just calm–"

"Calm down? What the hell are you doing out here? I thought they nabbed you! Who's this lady? Ain't she with them?" Jones was uneasy, glancing at Patricia as she approached. He seemed on edge, even in her presence.

"That's right, she is. But Prost managed to stop her before she could take off. Come on, he has a gun. Just let him handle it."

"I just– I don't–" Jones would have been reassured by Patricia's heartfelt words. Yet something irked him. It was their eyes. The way Prost and Leslie looked at him, their gazes were the same. One of pity. Of sorrow.

"Jones, you're scaring me. Give me the gun before you hurt someone you'll regret." Patricia gently lifted the gun from Jones' hand, taking it before he could regain his bearings. He didn't resist– he still trusted her, even beyond his confusion. It was a trust poorly placed.

She moved her hand only a few inches over, lifting it under his chin. Before he could even realize that the gun had been turned against him, Jones was dead. Blood painted the leaves red, exploding from his head like confetti. Patricia barely flinched at the noise. She fired a second shot into the trees, finally done with Jones's gun.

Not a word was exchanged between those who remained as Patricia dropped the gun to the floor. She was clearly looking at Jones; her eyes had met his even as the light left them.

Yet she wasn't *seeing* him. With a steady hand, Patricia would wipe a speck of blood from her face, crouching down to the space behind Jones's body.

With a single sweeping motion, Patricia hooked her arms under Jones's armpits and lifted his limp body. She dragged him to the back of the car and loaded him into the trunk, as if he were loading regular cargo and not a corpse.

Nobody said anything.

What was there to say?

People got messy in war.

When Prost had finished explaining, Jamie looked at him for a long while. Weary– doubtful, but nonetheless wanted to place his faith in Prost. Jamie owed him that much as a friend. "Then what about selling off Sicaren's recipes? Was that all just another setup?"

"We had to keep Neil occupied– make him feel like he was making progress to keep him in the dark about the real plan. We just hadn't planned on… well, you. Shit, luring an army of the marred to our facade? Didn't know you could come up with something like that."

"I guess we're both full of surprises." Prost bobbled his head, acknowledging the usual series of events that led them to meet again. Not that he wasn't anticipating it. "Why have a big… shootout? Why not leave quietly or… or fake your death in an alloy zone?"

"We needed something that was more than you could handle. You think there aren't others? People Neil employed who did such horrible things, not even we were allowed to know about them. He'll call upon them again soon."

Jamie's gaze sharpened. He felt no more informed than before Prost began explaining. "Who?"

"You'll find out soon. I need to know that I can trust you first. That you won't run off to Neil once we let you free and tell him everything you found here."

"None of this makes me trust you any more than before, you know that?"

Prost sighed. "Yeah, I do."

"So, what now?"

"You can leave, or you can stay," Prost said, as if he were asking Jamie whether he preferred tea or coffee.

"Just like that?"

"Just like that."

Jamie fell silent, dwelling on this turn of events. Prost was watching him with a sharp eye, knowing that this was one type of freedom that Jamie wasn't used to. It was difficult for Jamie to commit to anything, let alone something of this magnitude.

While Jamie wanted to trust Prost, and more than anything to see this dispute resolved so he could return to his uncomplicated life, another part of him didn't want to help.

He wanted to bury his head in the sand, so that maybe he could return to being a copper chaser. Return to unadulterated freedom. But it was clear that he was a boulder on top of a mountain, already set in motion.

The momentum was inevitable; it was just a matter of how hard he'd hit the ground. Prost could recognize Jamie's internal turmoil and stood upright, pulling him from his thoughts.

"I'll let you think it over. You're free to stay as long as you'd like. But a word of advice? Don't let anyone know you're from Crawford– especially not that you're the Bluejay. Colt might have forgiven you, but I wouldn't test the waters."

34

To most, Silvia was nothing more than a ghost. A copper chaser who could not survive the alloy zones. One body buried amongst a pile of others who thought they could surmount the dangers of the marred. The eventual fate of all the greedy fools who traded in copper. Eventually, the Mechatollies would reclaim what they had lost– they always did.

Even many of those in Pasko did not know her name. They did not know her face, nor her voice. If one were to ask, they'd simply cast a confused look before returning to what they were doing before. Blissfully unaware that she lived so close. In the roof she had dwelled, confined for more years than she could count.

But this was how she had to live in order to survive. Only a few could be trusted. Jamie and the rest of the community were not among those who were. Prost and Leslie, Silvia's messenger and the puppet leader of Pasko, were the only two. Not even Ann knew. It was to keep them safe and to remove as many variables from her master plan as she could.

Prost would visit Silvia every day, even when she discouraged him. Disappearing for too long was rather suspicious, after all. There was only one point of access to Silvia's dwelling. A single panel which hadn't been bolted down. It sat atop a locked storage closet, one that was out of the way from most people's daily activities.

It was early evening when Prost decided to visit Silvia. With a bit of effort, he lifted himself into the attic and rolled onto the floor, shutting the entrance behind him. "Your plan. You're sure it's airtight?" Prost asked quickly.

"Someone's fired up, aren't they?" Silvia pulled her gaze away from the maps on her desk and looked over at Prost. "From the second Neil's convoy drove on that road and we rescued you. Why? Don't tell me you have cold feet."

"It's not that– just… what if Neil gets impatient and sends all of his soldiers?"

"I thought you'd know our dear friend better than that, dear." Silvia smiled fondly. "He's not the type. Too busy trying to steal the first king's throne to do anything that would waste resources– god forbid, taint his spotless reputation. It's all going as we had planned, and your friend is safe in our care. Neil has no other confidants who could harm us now. Not without a full-scale attack."

Prost sighed. "I guess I'm just nervous. But I trust you."

"Will your friend from Crawford be joining the mission?" Silvia questioned, thinking about how to cleanly rid themselves of Jamie if he went rogue. Not that this was her preferred route, anyway.

"He's on the fence about it, but he'll come around. I know he will. Once he realizes that Neil will lose, he'll jump ship. He cares too much about leaving the walls. If he doesn't need Neil for that, he won't risk his life for him. I know it."

Silvia quirked a brow at Prost's final statement, though decided that ignorance is bliss and didn't push for additional details. If she didn't know, she wouldn't feel obligated to tell her people. They were just as hungry for revenge as she was, and she didn't need to be accused of harboring one of the horrible people they all hated before their advance on Crawford. At least until her plan was completed, this was one variable that she wanted to avoid. "Will you bring him to Myra's encampment?"

"You think that would help?"

"You know she doesn't work without payment, and her troops are already beginning to mobilize. That means our dear Napoleon's fingerprints will be all over the place. If you really want to pull the boy away from Neil, he'll need to see this himself. I can't guarantee it'll work completely, but it'll start a rift between them. I'm sure."

"Neil always hated that name," Prost chuckled. "Comparing him to a failed king? Did you ever really like him?"

"I did. I liked the man in the cubicle next to me. I liked the guy who backed me up at work when our boss gave us shit. But he never should have been called a king. He's a man, just like the rest of us. Just like Napoleon. He thought he was a wolf when he was a sheep. He pushed people off cliffs. He pushed *me*. And that's why he needs to… be gone."

"If that's what you think, then I'll do it." Prost stood, pressing a kiss onto her forehead. Silvia returned the kiss before Prost could pull away and smiled at the way he got flustered like a teenager when she kissed him.

"Will you be returning to your friend soon?"

"He needs time. Living beneath someone's thumb is the only life he's ever known– I think he's scared to bite the hand that's kept him fed. He's just a well-trained soldier. A bird parroting the words of his master. But I know he can change."

"Birds can be retrained, Prost. We'll show him there's another way." Silvia lifted Prost's gaze, speaking in a warm but firm tone. "Give him another master, if we have to. Just make sure he doesn't destroy all that we've built." She turned back to the table, looking at a picture that had been ingrained in her mind. A picture of the woman Silvia most despised. "The dominoes are going to start falling, Prost. Just bring him where we need him."

35

It had been nearly two days since Jamie had been taken in by Pasko. Night had fallen again, but he wasn't within the confines of Pasko's perimeter. Prost had taken him just after supper– Jamie wasn't sure why but didn't ask any questions.

They walked through broken paths and dense forests for several hours before the distant light of civilization bled through a crack in the trees.

"What is this place?" Jamie whispered; it wasn't that he was unused to this kind of trek, though this wasn't a spur-of-the-moment evening stroll, either. The few questions he did ask throughout their journey were met with silence or short, unhelpful answers.

"A camp. We're going to attack this place within the next few days," Prost finally said.

"Well… why?" Jamie carefully left the treeline, though there seemed to be no danger present. A few feet from it was a hefty wall made of various junk; it wasn't so dissimilar from some sections of Crawford's walls. It wouldn't be very hard for even an average person to scale.

"There's someone inside that needs killing." Prost placed his hands on the wall and climbed it quickly. This clearly wasn't his first time.

"Killing?" Jamie knew that if Prost wanted someone dead, then there was a very good reason for that. Rarely was Prost forced to rely on force when dealing with someone; usually he could intimidate them into fleeing. So whoever this was, they were clearly special.

"Why don't you join me up here and I'll show you." Prost pulled a monocular from his jacket, waving it in front of Jamie– though just out of reach.

Jamie scoffed at the display. "I'm not a dog. You can't just wave a treat in front of me and expect a trick. We've been walking for hours." Jamie placed his hands on his hips, expecting a reply. No words were spoken, though they didn't have to be. The slight raise of Prost's eyebrows and the slight pull-back of the monocular was enough to change Jamie's mind. He grumbled, though joined Prost on top of the wall in two seconds flat.

"Give me that," Jamie said hurriedly, snatching the monocular from Prost's hand.

"This was a winery back in the day– and before us is the vineyard. What remains of it, anyway. Not sure what it was called then, but I know what people call it now. *The moat of metal*," Prost said the title with an unusual cadence, over-enunciating the words. "Look at the interior wall– pure brick. It's protecting that little commune from the trap of their own design."

The monocular was easy to use. Jamie brought it to his eye and only had to wait for his vision to adapt to the pitch-black abyss of the moat.

Even with the moon– it was like the moat was absorbing the light. And an endless pit, one Jamie knew they wouldn't be able to cross. It wasn't the lack of light alone that made the moat of metal impenetrable.

There was something on the brick wall that protected the winery– something moving. Not quite alive, not quite dead. A monstrosity that even Jamie had difficulty fathoming. Jamie was struggling to make out what exactly the creature was, focusing on the glimmer that reflected off discolorations on the brick. *Copper?*

"What *is* that?"

"Hell on Earth."

"I'm serious." Jamie complained, though his brain had finally made sense of the creature on the wall. Prost was still wrong, of course. This was something far worse than hell-spawn. These were Mechatollies– dozens of them.

The wall that surrounded the winery had been layered with copper– years' worth. Some Mechatollies were stuck in the copper: fused with the wall. The very defense mechanism that they relied upon to protect their feeble, rotting bodies was the very same mechanism that ensnared them. Layer upon layer– until the copper was too thick to escape from.

The wall was a band of despair. Even the dead minds of those creatures seemed to be aware that this wall was their coffin. In this copper, their own armor and salvation, so too came their undoing.

One near the ground had an arm outstretched, its jaw lazily agape and seemingly unable to close it. A few seemed content, looking at others on the wall with a distant fondness. Two reached out towards each other. Only a few inches separated their reunion– that distance would never be closed.

A few were still cocooned, though others were awake. Some could only move what was above their torsos, while others could only move a single arm and their eyes. What they all had in common was their attempts to travel upward– towards the noise of people inside and the light which poured out from the winery.

They were like moths to a flame, so determined to reach a goal that they effectively killed any chance of ever reaching it.

Jamie thought that this was perhaps the worst the moat had to offer, but he couldn't have been further from the truth. As his gaze trailed down the wall, he noticed Mechatollies that were further from it and had yet to be imprisoned.

There were hundreds more dotting the rows of extinct grapevines. Most of them were cocooned. Some were swatting at the dead brush, looking for prey that they would never find.

"Plus there's a… few dozen skilled marksmen inside. They'd have no problem shooting at you if they saw you running around in there," Prost added, as if the impossibility of crossing wasn't already apparent.

"So then what? Why bring me all the way out here just to show me this? Not that I mind the view." Jamie continued to look around the moat of metal, inspecting the Mechatollies tethered to the wall.

"Because I need to know you're up for a mission. Thought if you knew what kind of war zone you were walking into, it would help." Prost reached for a petala; one that wasn't there. He settled for a petal of a Florid, shoving the flower into his mouth.

"Mission?" Jamie half scoffed, interrupting it with a smile of bewilderment. "You want me to kill this mystery man for you?"

"No, there'd be others. And it's woman. Mystery woman."

"Look, Prost. You know we're friends." Jamie lowered the monocular and looked over at him. "But killing? I'm not a hitman. Besides, a bullet's not really my style."

"I'd be willing to bet there are explosives inside that camp of theirs. We could blow a hole through the wall. The noise alone would lure the Mechatollies inside. Let them do all the work. It has your name written all over it."

Jamie rolled his eyes, raising the monocular again and returning his gaze to the wall. This time, he was searching for weak points. "You still haven't told me who it is you're after. This mystery woman. What'd she do to you?"

"She was hired to kill someone very dear to me. Sent after my wife. I think you know who ordered the hit."

Jamie bit his tongue, closing his eyes and pressing the monocular against his forehead. There were so many questions brewing in his mind– really, he just wanted to know: *why*? But the logistics of a feud that started long before he met the people of Crawford didn't concern him. Prost waited patiently for an answer that would disappoint him. "I don't want to be part of your… revenge plot, Prost. Neil's my friend. I know he hurt you, and I'm not… dismissing that fact. But I can't do what you're asking of me."

The pace of their speaking slowed to a crawl, each word deliberate– not a word out of place, in fear that they might misrepresent their thoughts and intentions.

"Do you remember New Year's? The day before Neil recruited you. And you told me you'd get me something as thanks for saving your life. Do you remember what I asked for?"

Jamie searched his memory for that night. His eyes widened with realization. "A favor."

Prost nodded slowly. "What we've started is too big to stop. Even if we were to walk away, the idea wouldn't die. Neil's victims would find their way back to each other. This woman has brought so much pain to so many people, and Neil was her benefactor. Those people want justice. And… I think you'll see why, but first you need to join us. Just this one mission– and if you still believe in Neil, you can return to Crawford."

The wind began to pick up. It was overpowering– dampening their words and spreading them across the moat of metal. Jamie looked back towards the moat. It was a leech, draining the temporary peace Jamie had found. He wished he had never seen the amalgamation on the wall– never seen that living grave.

"I will honor my promise to you. Besides, if this is too big to stop, I might as well ride the wave instead of being swept up by the tide."

36

2042, seven years earlier

The copper chaser knew that her time was drawing to a close. As was the case with many who took on that role, yet none ever expected their demise. Hidden robbers, bear traps, starvation, *infection.* Nobody ever saw it coming because they had been so used to surviving– what was to make that expedition any worse?

But even for a copper chaser, the way Silvia's last mission for Crawford went was anything but normal. First it was her saw– the metal snapped clean off the plastic handle at the bend. She should have suspected something was awry at that, but kept working faithfully with her remaining tools.

Next was after she had finally collected all the copper she could carry. Silvia had only walked a few steps away from the collection site before the bottom of her bag ripped open, causing all the copper chunks to clatter against the floor.

Unable to believe her misfortune, Silvia was forced to abandon all of her work as Mechatollies had started to descend upon her, attracted by the noise. While she managed to keep her distance, more were joining the chase.

"Where are they all coming from?" Silvia thought to herself as she dodged away from some shambling Mechatollies that had gotten in front of her.

Even the Florids had started to join the horde's ranks, creating an ensemble of screeching and chittering. The commotion only drew in more marred from the buildings, with a few particularly brave Mechatollies hurling themselves out of windows to reach Silvia faster. She heard their copper shells crack as they hit the ground; their bodies, once full of vigor, lay motionless.

All the chaos was only attracting more problems. Silvia couldn't run forever, either due to exhaustion or because she would end up cornered by two hordes of marred. If Silvia were to have any chance of surviving this mess, she'd have to make a choking point.

Her prayers would soon be answered, as she was running closer and closer to a graveyard. Once Silvia got over the steel gates, she'd finally be given some room to breathe. She could see the neglected headstones– was just barely able to make out the features of an angel on a mausoleum. It was as if her guardian angel had come down from heaven to protect her.

Of course, vaulting over a fence was no difficult task. If her horrible landing was to be ignored, anyway. Silvia felt the weight of her haste the second her foot hit the ground. She gasped in shock as she pulled her knee up to her chest and clutched her ankle. Silvia tried to squeeze her ankle as tightly as she could, and a pained groan escaped her throat. Anything to dull the throbbing pain of a twisted ankle.

Alas, Silvia wasn't given as much time to dwell on her shortcomings. Mechatollies slammed against the fence, hounding it, desperate to make it fall. Yet unflinching, the fence remained. *For now.*

With a heavy wobble, Silvia rose back to her feet and grabbed her handgun. Some Mechatollies had started to climb over their companions, staking themselves on the decorative spear heads which lined the fence. Silvia's handgun zipped up towards the most persistent of the bunch. She took a steady aim, then pulled the trigger.

But there was nothing. Not a shot, not even a sound that was loud enough to overcome the clanging of metal. Though she persisted, the result remained the same. Lowering her handgun to get a better look at it, Leslie released the magazine, checking the ammunition. Although nothing was visibly different, bullets wouldn't refuse to fire without cause.

"Damn it!" She hissed, reloading the gun and replacing it with a hunting knife. Silvia thought about the third mishap, and possibly the most egregious of them all. The snapping of a saw, then the tearing of her bag? Coincidence, maybe. But duds in her magazine? Silvia would be a fool not to recognize the pattern. Someone had tampered with her things. *Sabotaged* her.

Silvia prepared herself to pick off the stragglers who were managing to throw themselves over the fence. Sure, killing them manually would be harder, but that's the hand that Silvia was dealt. The hand *someone else* dealt her. As she hobbled to the first Mechatolly, who had taken a much worse fall than herself, she made a vow to plant a knife in the back of those who betrayed her, just as they had done to her.

As if practicing, Silvia slammed her knife into the nape of the Mechatolly in front of her, dragging the knife down its spine. The Mechatolly strained, but soon fell limp. With the first of many now dead, Silvia looked at the wall of metal that clamored before her. The fight would not be an easy one, but she refused to become part of the metallic choir.

But her willpower could only take her so far, and there was no denying that Silvia was exhausted. Her muscles ached. She could not tame her trembling hands and squeaking joints. Yet her pain amounted to something: she was safe, at least for now. The onslaught of Mechatollies had ceased, although many still remained beyond the graveyard fences. It was funny in a way. A place of death became a refuge for life.

A rustle behind her caused Silvia's ear to twitch. Fearful that a marred had managed to breach the wall and had snuck up behind her, she spun on her heels to face the source of the noise. Gripping the knife in her hand, Silvia's eyes darted around the graveyard. Yet it seemed almost empty. It wasn't until her second pass through the graveyard that she had noticed something amiss.

A lady was draped over the angel on the mausoleum, a smirk on her face. It seemed as though she was waiting for Silvia to notice her. Silvia recognized the lady in an instant. Her arrogant mask, which covered only half of her face. The pervasive eyes which seemed to penetrate the stone-cold expressions of even the best poker players.

Yanking her gun out of its holster, Silvia's gaze narrowed upon her. "Myra– how did you get here? Is this your doing?" Silvia spat out the words, struggling to control the tremors in her hands as she attempted to steady the gun.

Yet Myra seemed to find Silvia's plight amusing: the fear, the desperation. "Did what?" It was clear from the look in Myra's eyes that she found delight in watching Silvia flounder. And it was even more so, considering that she had a large hand in what had happened to Silvia.

"Don't play your games with me," Silvia demanded. "I already know how you are. Just admit it."

"No games?" Myra chuckled, swinging herself over the angel and hooking her legs around its waist. It was a fitting position for Myra; she was dangling from the angel like a bat– like the bloodsucking fiend she was. She was inverted from the angel– just as her morals were anything but holy. "You gonna shoot me? Come on, take your best shot. If you can, I'll answer. But if I win, you do as I say."

Frowning, Silvia's grip on the gun tightened until her knuckles became white. This was clearly a taunt, as both parties knew more than well that Silvia couldn't hit Myra, even if she wanted to. Her movements had grown sloppy– slow– in her exhaustion. Silvia had no chance of winning Myra's game. Even if Silvia tried to resist, the iron on Myra's hip would make short work of her.

"What's the matter? Too scared to play your hand?" Myra laughed, pulling herself upright before jumping back down. She was always one for theatrics.

"You're too eager to play yours." Silvia backed away slowly as Myra approached her. One step forward, one step back. "Is this because of your exile? Or has someone *motivated* you to do this to me?" Silvia demanded.

"Exile? Who said anything about that? But since we're bringing that up, I forgive you for not even coming to my defence when they thrust me out of Crawford's gates like some sort of rabid dog." Myra feigned sadness like an inexperienced actress.

"The second king didn't want you and now you're bitter, but I had nothing to do with it. That whole mess was *your* fault. You would never have been stable enough for him." Silvia glanced behind her at the ever-approaching fence. Desperate arms reached out for her through the gaps. Myra was blocking all other routes away– the only path Silvia had was closer to the fence. "You've always been *insane*!"

"It's funny because the king *does* want me– need me, even. He's always needed other people to do his dirty work. Shame you couldn't keep up. But you know how it is! That secretive king of ours. He even called us one of the same. Even if you don't think so. That's what he'll tell the people, anyway. That those pathetic little morals of yours aren't so different from mine."

"I'm nothing like you. I don't kill people. Not for *fun*."

"Ah, that's right." Myra snickered, watching as Silvia ran out of room to walk away from her. Not unless she wanted to be torn apart by the destructive mob of metal bodies behind her. "That's what got you into this whole mess, isn't it? But after this, nobody will think you're as righteous as you say you are. If you go quietly, we may just leave your reputation intact. Leave you a nice little legacy to be remembered by."

Silvia slowly dropped her hand, which held her gun, and let it rest by her side. This was but a ruse, and when Myra had dropped her guard at the impression that she had bested Silvia, Silvia lunged towards Myra, knife still in her other hand. Despite the sudden attack, Myra was better prepared for combat than Silvia was. After all, Silvia had just been chased halfway around the city and was suffering from a twisted ankle.

Myra snaked out of the way, pushing Silvia as she passed, which caused her to lose balance and fall to the ground. "Has the exhaustion made you sloppy? Or is it just your old age?" Myra mocked, looking at Silvia writhe on the ground; now covered in grass and leaves.

Huffing, Silvia looked back at Myra, thinking of what to do. Of how to survive her. "What do you think of Russian roulette then, hm?" Myra held her gun up to her face, observing the craftsmanship of the gun which might take either of their lives.

Yes, this was a gun fitting to kill someone great like herself. It bore the same flower which the Florids grew and was Myra's prized possession. Spinning the chamber a few times, Myra waited as it came to a complete stop, watching as Silvia's expression sank with each click.

"Stop dragging this out. Shoot me," Silvia demanded. Although it may have seemed like a plea for mercy, Silvia's request was a strategic one. Myra wasn't the type to get things over quickly. She inflicted fear and pain on her victims long before she killed them. Even in the direst of situations, Myra would still play with her food.

Yet what she lacked was tact. Something Silvia had in excess. It was a gamble, but Silvia needed to bait Myra. Just as Silvia predicted, Myra didn't shoot her. Instead, Myra made a small hum, as if considering. "Get up. Slowly. Wouldn't want to hurt that ankle of yours any further, would we?"

Silvia grumbled, slowly getting up. She had scooped up a handful of dirt, though it was much too hard to be of use. "*All I have to do is get close enough,*" Silvia thought to herself, dropping the knife at Myra's command. "*Then I can blind Myra... no, no. That's a horrible idea. I'd just get myself shot.*"

"So, let's go on a walk, Silvia," Myra sang the words. "I've always wanted to be an archaeologist. Well, not really. But we're going to try it out today. I want you to go inside that structure." Myra pointed to the mausoleum with her gun, then nudged Silvia's shoulder to turn her in that direction.

"You're gonna make me a grave robber?" Silvia frowned but didn't protest Myra's orders. There are only so many times a person can poke a beehive before they get stung.

"No. Consider this an act of goodwill. You'll get your own grave. That's quite a luxury these days. I probably won't even get one. Maybe your husband won't, either." Myra pushed the end of the gun into Silvia's back, pressuring her to continue moving forward. "Kick the door down."

"I can't. Not with–"

"Didn't you hear me? I said, kick it down, or I'll break off your foot and do it for you." Myra watched Silvia rack her brain over the instructions. She could hardly place any weight on the foot as it was, let alone kick a thick wooden door down. Yet the door clearly wasn't very structurally sound. Years of damage and neglect were apparent.

Silvia looked up at the angel that adorned the mausoleum. It seemed to be looking down at them, observing them with little regard. That's when Silvia remembered that there was no such thing as God–no such thing as a guardian angel watching over her. If there were, she could have grown to be old, fat, and happy. But she was none of those things, and now she was going to die. But if there were no God to judge her, why did she have to play by the rules? Silvia swore that if she were given another chance, there was nothing she wouldn't do to get revenge against that crooked king and his vile lapdog.

The idea of eternal slumber within the crypt crossed her mind. She never expected her death to be so… *slow*. To have to wait for so long until she would finally be killed. Although discontent with the idea of death, it would certainly make a better place than to rot in the streets. Or worse yet, join the ranks of the marred. So with what remained of her strength, Silvia smashed her shoulder into the door.

With a pop and an uncooperative groan, a large crack had formed along the left door, starting from where she struck it. Another blow of equal force would be enough to warp the door, allowing Silvia to finally push it open. "What now?" Silvia rushed out the words, short of breath from the small act.

She didn't look back at Myra, looking into the crypt. There were stairs leading down, but what exactly lay at the bottom was impossible to see. The bottom of the crypt was completely devoid of light, despite the door being open. Where the light shone was a different story. Vines overtook the stone and cement interior, growing in and around the walls.

"Now you go inside," Myra said, pragmatic about the whole thing.

"Why? Aren't you going to kill me?"

"Mh. I decided you should just starve. My trigger finger feels a bit weak today. You can go inside now." Myra chirped.

Turning her head, Silvia stared at Myra; an exhausted look in her eyes. She threw the dirt in Myra's face, but it didn't blind her, as Silvia had hoped. Rather, Myra found the action absurd, maybe even comical. Myra wiped a speck of dirt off her face, looking at the slightly muddy stain on her finger.

She scoffed, followed by laughter. "What was that?" Myra asked herself, flicking the dirt away. Then she looked back up at Silvia, uttering the last words she would ever hear. "You should have accepted his deal, Silvia." Myra smirked, looking at Silvia's expression. Deciding that she had tortured Silvia enough, she placed a hand on Silvia's shoulder.

With that same hand, she thrust her body into Silvia, causing her to go crashing down the stairs. Myra watched as Silvia's body tumbled into the abyss. After a few seconds of her falling, Myra heard a splash as Silvia had reached the bottom of the crypt. After that splash, there was nothing.

No thrashing or gasping; just silence. Silvia had met her end, and Myra almost envied her. Silvia had a nice grave, albeit a nameless and watery one. Something which even all of Myra's riches wouldn't be able to secure.

37

2049, present day

The change was subtle, but Jamie could notice it all the same. The air in Pasko was thicker. People talked differently– looked at their neighbors differently. It wasn't suspicion; at least for now, they were all united by a common goal: tearing down the Crawford that ruined them. They were going to mobilize soon.

Jamie was overlooking the canteen from a perch that circled the room. He saw people at their calmest: as they ate. Saw who talked with whom– saw as their movements changed. This is when he felt most normal. Observing.

"We need you," Prost said, walking up behind Jamie. He leaned against the railing, as Jamie did.

"Why do you always want my help just after dinner?" Jamie sighed, pulling away from the railing.

Prost smiled, draping his arm over Jamie's shoulders. "Can't have my little helper working on an empty stomach, can I?"

"Oh, stop it." Jamie rolled his eyes, shrugging Prost's arm off. Prost gestured for Jamie to follow and led him outside the hangar. There were a few people in the old parking lot and a handful of bikes.

The furthest away was Leslie, the leader of Pasko. She was talking with the other two, though Jamie couldn't hear it from the entrance of the museum. Colt was there as well and stood next to a lady Jamie had only seen in passing. Leslie was the first to notice Jamie and Prost approaching and waved them over.

"I'm glad you're here," Leslie acknowledged. "We all mostly know each other. Everyone, this is Jamie. Prost recommended that he join us, and I expect you to accept him. Jamie, you've already met Colt. This is Lucy," Leslie gestured to the other lady, though she didn't seem pleased to meet Jamie.

"We've been planning this for ages now, and we're bringing in some stranger at the last second? It wasn't even a week ago that we had him in handcuffs," Lucy protested.

"We all start somewhere, don't we, Lucy?" Colt nudged, bringing up something from the past that seemed to calm Lucy, if slightly. Jamie imagined that she might not have been so dissimilar to him. "If Prost says we can trust him, then that's good enough for me."

Jamie nodded towards Colt in thanks. It wasn't so long ago that Jamie had a gun pointed at Colt's head, after all.

"The moat of metal has allowed the mercenaries to remain virtually untouchable for years," Leslie interrupted Jamie's thoughts, beginning her speech. "Trying to breach the compound through there would be nothing short of suicidal. Which is why… we're going to enter through the main entrance."

"Have you lost your *mind*?" Lucy blurted. "Their sentries would tear us apart the second we leave the treeline."

"Which is why we're going to make sure they never see us. Or– more accurately, you." Leslie leaned on the bike on her left. "We've struck a deal with one of the people who has access to Myra's camp. Let's say he's… discontent with how she operates. His only requirement is that this doesn't get traced back to him, and he'll smuggle us in. He's parked an hour away. Any questions?"

"How'd you find this guy?" Colt piped up, crossing his arms. "What if this is just a trap?"

"He came to us not long before Jamie did. The plan changed once he presented his offer. I promise it's safer this way." Leslie sighed, thinking about the second part of the question. "How can we know anyone's true intentions? But he found us. Could have brought her legion and burnt this place to the ground before we even saw their faces. He didn't. So unless you want to try crossing the moat, this is the best we've got."

This seemed to satisfy the group, so Leslie continued with the rest of her plan.

"We're only going after Myra. If the others get in your way, then you have my permission to defend yourself. But avoiding a firefight is going to be better for us. Myself, Prost, and Lucy will hunt her down. Colt and Jamie will look for evidence of her connection to Neil. We know it's there– we just have to get our hands on it."

"What about your wife?" Lucy asked as the speech came to a lull.

"What about Ann?" Leslie replied, as Jamie recalled the woman whom he had first met when he was tied up. He had heard in retrospect that she was Ann, though he hadn't interacted with her further.

"She's not coming?"

"I won't put her in danger. She's the only other person whom people trust as our leader, and the revolution needs someone to guide it. Should anything… happen to me during our hunt." Leslie stood upright, mounting the bicycle. "Let's not keep our smuggler waiting. Come on."

38

Something about the smuggler felt familiar to Jamie. Perhaps it was the way he carried himself, confident and self-assured as he leaned against the car. As if nothing could hurt him, even in the alloy zone. Perhaps it was the way he dressed: dark clothing with hints of red beneath his jacket.

"I appreciate you doing this," Leslie thanked the smuggler as she hid her bicycle in the shrubbery.

"I'm not doing this for you. That lady's crazy. I would leave if I could, but I imagine you would see why I couldn't– not while she's still around."

Jamie was quick to hide the bike, refocusing his attention on the smuggler. Everything about him stood out. Maybe it was just Jamie's paranoia, but something about him was different. Not in a malicious way, just *something abnormal.* His mask, for instance. It was metal– like his own. It even had the same leather straps and a neckpiece. It was painted black, save for the faded yellow metal plates used for the eye sockets– clearly added later as a repair piece.

"Well, I appreciate it all the same."

The smuggler nodded. His gaze passed over everyone Leslie brought with her. It seemed to hold on Jamie for a moment longer, before returning to Leslie.

"You brought more than we agreed upon," he commented.

"I figured it wouldn't be a problem," Leslie countered, to which the smuggler sighed.

"It's going to be a tight squeeze. Hope you're friendly." The smuggler walked to the back of the car and opened the trunk. He fiddled with something on the floor before popping a false panel out of place, revealing a hidden compartment. Then he gestured for them to get inside.

Leslie was the first in, then Lucy and Colt, followed by Prost. Jamie was about to raise his foot and crawl inside before a hand latched onto his arm, stopping him. He glanced back at the smuggler, looking into the pinprick-sized holes of the yellow metal.

"There's no room for you back there. The weight will cause the car to sag. Join me in the front." The smuggler pulled Jamie away from the trunk, closing the false floor and shutting the hatch. He walked to the passenger-side door and pulled the seat back. There was a space large enough to lay down underneath it, but it was small.

Jamie shuffled inside and was quickly locked in when the smuggler pulled the seat back over the entrance. He could hear the smuggler walk to the other side of the car, open the car door, and start the engine. After a bit of wriggling, Jamie was able to find a small hole to look through and pressed his face against it, cautiously watching the smuggler as he began to drive the car towards the winery.

The drive was slow. Surprisingly calm, in fact. The roads weren't smooth, though they weren't bumpy either. A melodic tune gently drifted through the car; the smuggler was something of a singer. For a moment, Jamie had forgotten what it was they were doing and fell asleep.

The voices of several people woke him up. The car was parked; the music had ceased. Jamie blinked harshly as he regained his senses, once again pressing his face against the peephole and looking out. The window was rolled down, and the smuggler was talking to a burly woman whose face he could barely see.

Flashlights shone into the car, agitating the smuggler.

"Watch it!" The smuggler hissed, which prompted a distant and docile apology from the inspector. They were checking the car for something. Jamie's heart began to race; he should have forced himself awake. He was completely defenseless here.

"Are you bringing anything in?" The gate officer by the window asked the smuggler.

"What type of dumbass question is that? We all know you check the car, anyway." The smuggler laughed, but it was clear he was annoyed.

"Them's the breaks, Herron. Myra's got rules," she explained in a bored tone. "Things to say, notes to take."

"I've been driving for hours. There's nothing I would like more than to go to bed. So no. No, I am not bringing anything in."

"All you had to say. Find anything?" The gate officer called to the inspectors, which elicited a few grumbles in reply. "Alright, open her up."

Jamie could hear a pair of boots approaching the car and open the door. They shone their lights around. First, the front seat– feeling around and opening the glove box. Jamie winced, pulling away as the light brushed over the tiny peephole. Then the inspector checked the back seats. Then it was the trunk.

Someone moved inside. They could tell the inspector was getting close. Jamie could feel the movement of someone as they began to panic, then someone holding them down. He held his breath, listening as the inspector brushed their hand along the trunk. The smuggler, Herron, never flinched.

The inspector near the trunk whispered something anxiously, drawing the attention of the gate officer near the window. She left Herron's side and walked towards the trunk. Jamie could hear the incoherent mumbling of alarmed whispers. Then a pair of angry footsteps began to walk back to the driver's side.

"You're a liar, Herron. Myra's gonna hear of this," she spoke quietly, not wanting the others to overhear. "Then we'll finally be rid of you."

Herron scoffed, and Jamie was sure there was a smug grin behind that mask of his. "It's a gift."

Jamie's hand reached for the gun on his hip, carefully slipping it out of the holster as he watched the stare-down between the two. He raised the gun to his chest, ready for the betrayal they should have seen coming. The gate officer fumbled with something out of Jamie's sight– a gun– he was sure.

"You expect me to believe that?" She snarled. "For who?" Jamie winced, his eyes closed as the gate officer lifted her arm up. He expected a shot, or maybe a whistle to alert the sentries. What he heard was anything but. "A bag of petala? You ain't got enough to share, and this is too much for one person."

Jamie cracked one eye open, looking through the peephole. It wasn't a gun in her hand, but a small plastic bag of petala. Questions immediately began to flood his mind. Was this Prost's? It couldn't have been– Herron seemed much too comfortable throughout the discussion. Then why would he have left the petala? Just to distract the inspectors?

"You're right. There's no way that could satisfy all of Myra's legion. But I think it's just the right amount for the inspectors." Herron grinned, and this made the gate officer go quiet.

She lowered her hand, stuffing the bag into her jacket. "Maybe you're not half bad. Alright. Take your catnap." She waved for the gates to be opened, and not a moment later, the car was off. They drove about 200 feet before reaching the compound and another 100 before Herron shut the car off.

First, he let Jamie out, then the rest of the group from the trunk. It was dark everywhere. They were behind one of the buildings and were finally able to breathe in fresh air. Jamie sat against the building, leaning his head back and looking at the sky. It must have been around midnight. Leslie shook Herron's hand.

"You did well," she told him.

"Just make sure you don't start shooting until I'm out of here."

"Gladly," Leslie watched as Herron climbed back into the car. He waited a few minutes before returning the way he had come. Then she approached her posse, who had regained their bearings by this point. "We all know our assignments. The three of us will find a place to hole up in for three hours, then we'll head for Myra. In the meantime, Colt and Jamie will get to work. Clear?"

They nodded in silent acknowledgement as the group dispersed into the winery. Colt and Jamie split up; sneaking around was safer when the only person you had to worry about was yourself.

39

Jamie started wandering the complex. He walked past the machinery and slipped into the shadows, sneaking past the mercenaries that were still awake. While there weren't many patrols within the winery, several small groups were loitering around and conversing with each other. It made sneaking around harder, though it was nothing Jamie wasn't used to, and it helped that they weren't actively looking for him.

There was one more gathering of people, which worried Jamie. This wasn't a social group, like the other two. Instead, it seemed like they were guarding something in another building, which looked more like a venue or a barn than for winemaking. Intrigued, Jamie started to slink towards it, approaching from the back of the building.

While there were no doors, there were plenty of windows. First he looked through, trying to see if there was anyone inside. While it lacked any people, something else caught Jamie's eye. *Cars.* Lots of them.

Although Jamie was used to seeing a lot of cars in Crawford, that was an outlier simply because that's what the city specialized in. But to see so many of them– cars that had barely a speck of dirt on their paint– was unusual, even by Crawford's standards. There seemed to be about half a dozen vehicles just inside the barn, but there were other, more worn cars outside.

Jamming his knife into the bottom of a window, Jamie released the latch and pulled the window up, enough for him to slip through. Once Jamie got inside, he quietly closed the window behind him before leaving to investigate the cars. He opened the driver's side door of the car closest to him and felt the seat. The craftsmanship wasn't half bad– the mercenaries must have had to pay a hefty fee for all of these. But a question was nagging at Jamie's mind.

"Why buy all these cars and let them collect dust in a barn?"

There was a part of Jamie that knew the answer to this question. It started with the question itself: started with its inherent flaws. The mercenaries didn't *buy* these cars. They were payment. But Jamie didn't want to believe that.

There must have been a reason. Anything– Jamie would have accepted anything. Jamie owed everything to Neil; he didn't want the good times to end. And no matter how much Jamie wanted to deny it, he didn't want to hurt a friend, despite all the suffering he knew Neil had helped cause.

It was strange. Irrational. A thought pattern a stranger would rightly call immoral. But Jamie was a man with few friends. Jamie needed Neil. So despite the mountain of evidence in front of him, Jamie remained a fence-sitter.

He didn't excuse what Neil had done, but Jamie knew that the things he had done on his own weren't much worse– at least Neil didn't commit atrocities with his own hands. Those people died fast. They weren't subjected to a swarm of Mechatollies– not like the kind he unleashed upon Pasko's pseudo trade deal. The path Neil was guiding Jamie down was going to lead him exactly where it had led Neil: to destruction.

Confronting Neil forced Jamie to confront himself. To judge Neil was to force Jamie to judge his own actions. Of course, Neil had put Jamie up to them– but Jamie could have stopped it at any time. Was it his selfishness that drove him to do what Neil asked every time? Desire? Fear?

It didn't matter now.

The cars took up most of the barn's floor space, but hanging from the ceiling Jamie spotted a few dusty tassels of faded white ribbon. As his eyes traced the ribbons, Jamie's eyes fell on a platform that overlooked the cars.

Making his way up to the second floor, Jamie cautiously looked at the perch he had seen from the ground. It was a large, open-air room, taking up a quarter of the space available before dropping off. Although it was clearly an intentional design choice, Jamie was still perplexed by it. The room must have been a bar of some kind, but was transformed into a war room.

There were maps everywhere, most of them being around settlements that had fallen under peculiar circumstances. Other than the large maps plastered around the room and left on the tables, nothing was laid about that would be useful to Jamie. The bar table had some cabinets on either side to support it, separated by an empty space. The cabinets were tucked away from view, unless one was standing behind the table.

The cabinets were unlocked, but tragically, mostly empty. The bottom-left cabinet contained a lockbox, which Jamie couldn't help but try to break into. Carefully lifting the box from the cabinet, Jamie set it on the bar table and took a few lock-picking tools out of his jacket pocket. As Jamie started to unlock the box, he heard the door to the barn open.

Cursing his misfortune, Jamie stopped to focus on the noise. It was two people, likely the guards from earlier. He heard them walk deeper into the barn, then turn around. They weren't leaving for the exits; rather; they were going up to the stairs. There was nowhere to hide. They were going to find him.

Ripping the lock pick out of the safe, Jamie bolted towards the railings at the end of the perch. He hid the lockbox under a map, jumping to the other side of the railing and reaching for the closest support beam, nearly an eight-foot gap. In a desperate leap of faith, Jamie reached for the beam and managed to catch it by the tips of his fingers.

Painfully pulling himself up, Jamie hid behind a vertical beam and lay flat against a horizontal one. He watched as the two guards made a path towards exactly where he had once stood. One of them bent down in search of the lockbox that he had hidden only moments ago.

The first guard spoke in a panic. "Wait– where is it? The lockbox, Herron said it was in here. Is there a different cabinet somewhere?" He stood, frantically looking around. Jamie winced, pressing his body into the beam to flatten himself further. The man's gaze passed over him but didn't acknowledge Jamie's presence; he had been overlooked in the man's panic. The first guard lacked a flashlight, and the second seemed to be less enthusiastic about searching.

"I bet that Beth girl took it. Probably already took it to Myra. You know how badly she'd been trying to warm up to her ever since she was sent here. First with that contraption and remote car of hers, and now sneaking the lockbox to Myra. Her and that Herron boy are nothing but trouble," the second guard scoffed, turning back to the stairs. "Come on, let's go. I'm going to have a *word* with our little competitor."

The two guards had left just as soon as they came, but Jamie had a feeling that they would be back soon. After all, once this Beth character revealed that she had, in fact, not taken the lockbox, the pair would likely be back for answers. Getting up from the beam, Jamie waited until the door to the barn had closed to make his return jump.

Once the lockbox had been picked open, Jamie searched through the files that were hidden within. Contained inside were pictures, transcripts, manuals, and even blueprints for the jar trap that released the Metalides on Valerie. Lacking the time to properly go through all the papers, Jamie quickly sorted through the pictures, watching the faces as they went by.

Most of the people he recognized– they were all from Pasko, and Jamie suspected the same of the faces he didn't recognize. The photos were fuzzy and clearly taken in a rush, but jarring nonetheless. Ann and Leslie were in the two pictures of lower quality, and were clipped onto a sheet of paper with instructions to give to the mercenaries. But there were two more pictures. One of Prost, and one of himself.

40

The photograph was alarming. Of course, any photo of himself would have terrified Jamie. But this photo wasn't like Ann's or Leslie's. It was similar to Prost's in its deliberateness.

In fact, Jamie recognized the exact place from which it had been taken. The winter of 2047, during the New Year's party, just in front of the dining hall.

Jamie could even see Sicaren's shoulder and Neil's arm wrapped around him. Prost's photo only featured himself; his back turned, but head facing towards the camera. A look of annoyance was directed at whoever was behind the camera, and a lit roll of petala was between his fingers.

Only one question was on Jamie's mind: how did Myra get these?

More importantly, how did she get her hands on the other information listed on this ledger? The contents of the paper to which it was clipped horrified Jamie, even more than the sight of that photo. On it was his name, address, occupation, a physical description, and a notes section, which contained two handwritten notes.

In an unloving and brutish flare of the pen, the first note wrote: *keep an eye out for him. He'll wander to places he shouldn't.*

Jamie would have laughed at the irony if he wasn't so distressed by everything else he had read. But the second note confused Jamie more than anything else. In the same handwriting as the first, it said: *Avoid killing as per the client's request.*

The only file that had such a note was his own; the other three were fair game– kill, torture– nothing was off limits. But why would Myra's employer care about Jamie?

He wasn't anyone; the details of his work were only shared amongst a very small, trusted group of people. Mostly the Pale Roses. He glanced towards the edge of the balcony, but his mind had fixated on the room of cars beneath him.

Obviously, these two items were connected, and somewhere deep in Jamie's mind, he knew how. Before he could admit the truth, he was again stopped by the opening of a door. He shoved his own papers into his coat and threw the lockbox back into the cabinet. Then he fled the scene again.

For a second time, the footsteps approached the second floor, and for a second time Jamie threw himself off the balcony. Jamie avoided tempting fate by not jumping to the support beam and instead dangled from the edge of the perch. Using the wall for support, he listened as the two guards rummaged around in the cabinets.

Finally, the first guard found it, much to the annoyance of the second guard. "You goddamn idiot!" He hissed. "Did you forget your left from right again, huh?"

"But– I'm sure he said that it was in the bottom left cabinet. And I *checked* the bottom left cabinet."

"Well, *maybe*, did you even *consider* that Herron meant the bottom left from the side of the rest of the room? Or maybe you're so braindead you can't even pay attention to simple directions?" The second guard scoffed in annoyance. "Now I chewed out Beth for no damn reason! You make me feel bad for making the new girl cry. Now I have to *apologize*," the second guard said dramatically, again starting to leave without the first guard.

The first guard scrambled up, hastily following the second. "Wait– I'm sorry! Wait for me." Jamie listened to their bickering and pleading until the door was finally closed again, attempting to pull himself up before simply dropping to the floor. He had at least learned to fall quietly, but his arms had started to tire after having to hold on for so long.

Leslie was yet to be found, so Jamie couldn't stop his search yet. Sucking his teeth, Jamie shook his arms out before leaving the barn the same way he had entered. There were too many buildings to search by himself; it would take longer than the night allowed, and that was if he could avoid being caught before dawn.

The two guards had mentioned delivering the lockbox to Myra. If Jamie were to follow them, he would likely be led straight to her; if not, then maybe her room. Clues to Leslie's whereabouts were likely to be hidden there.

Although the guards had a head start on Jamie, they weren't difficult to spot. The awkwardly shaped lockbox made it difficult to carry, and Jamie could see the man who was lugging it around from his place in the shadows.

The pair caught some points and laughter as they walked– or rather, waddled– past other mercenaries. Despite having to take the long route to stay out of sight and into the shadows, Jamie had been able to keep up and spotted them entering an unassuming building. They then left five minutes later and disappeared into the bustle of the mercenaries who were yet to turn in for the night.

Jamie's gaze fell on the trio's hidden outpost within the mercenaries' camp and contemplated returning to inform them of all that he had learned. But the nagging of Jamie's need for answers drowned out any voice of reason within his mind.

If he were to leave the building out of his sight, he could lose the chance to confront Myra and interrogate her on all that had happened to him– on why she was keeping his life from returning to the routine he was so comfortable with, even when he knew that Myra couldn't possibly be the root of all his misfortune.

Jamie wanted someone to blame, and he found his straw man.

Feelings of suppressed anger welled up within Jamie. He was only stuck here because he needed to wrap up the loose ends with Pasko, which he had already failed to do. But now Jamie had to ensure Prost's safe return to Crawford– something that the very man he came here to save wouldn't tolerate the notion of.

Prost had some sort of connection with Pasko that Jamie couldn't wrap his head around– a connection that Jamie was incapable of making. Jamie was jealous of that connection, and those feelings clouded his judgment; the confusion only made it worse.

He didn't know these people; he didn't understand why they were risking their lives for each other. Jamie didn't know why they were fighting or why he was forced to be a pawn in a game that started long before he became aware of his participation. Jamie didn't even fully understand where these paths would end. Nobody could tell him that, not even Myra.

Again Jamie crept up to the building, finding a window to enter from and infiltrating the premises. Landing in the room, Jamie looked around cautiously. It was dark– too much for him to make anything out. He searched for the door, carefully opening it to reveal a hallway.

There were several doors throughout the hallway, and the one at the very end had been cracked open ever so slightly. Jamie could hear a woman faintly humming from a nearby room.

Room 130.

Pulling his gun from its holster, Jamie slowly approached the room at the end of the hall and was unable to see anyone in the other rooms that he passed.

Jamie peeked through the crack in the door. The woman was alone in an unassuming room where no one else could hide. He aimed his gun at the woman's center mass and pushed his way past the room.

"You're Myra, aren't you?" The woman's back was turned to Jamie, and she didn't move from her seat on the bed to acknowledge his presence.

Then he heard a small click of a button.

The door slammed behind him, and there was a sharp hiss of gas as the room began to fill with an off-white fog. Jamie jumped at the barrage of noise before a sharp wave of nausea overtook him.

Myra had jumped up from her place on the bed, turning on her heel and rushing towards him. Her face was obscured by a gas mask, protecting her from the toxic fumes.

Jamie fired a shot before being overwhelmed by Myra's collision, managing to graze her shoulder but ultimately having his gun taken from him. She cast the gun to the other side of the room, and before Jamie could reach for a second weapon, she grappled his arm, dragging him down to the floor and locking his arm between her legs.

There was a brief struggle as Jamie attempted to free himself from Myra's grip, though he was ultimately unable to fight past the dizziness and Myra restrained him with a pair of handcuffs. Once

Jamie was secured to a radiator, Myra clicked the button a second time. The hissing of air stopped, and the door unlocked.

Myra pried the gas mask from her face, sat down on the chair and gulped down a breath of mostly fresh air. It burned her throat on the way down, but the discomfort wasn't enough to suppress her twisted thrill.

"Poor little Swallow," she started, pushing herself off the bed and sitting in front of a gasping Jamie. "Swam so far just to drown in shallow water."

"Why is this happening?" Jamie's words slurred together while he spoke. It was exhausting to do anything. Even the simple act of focusing on Myra was difficult.

She was clearly taller than him, stronger, too– even without the gas poisoning his lungs. Her hair was short and puffy. The general silhouette was easy to keep track of, but her face eluded him.

"I knew someone was sneaking around my stuff when those dolts returned empty-handed. They're stupid, not blind." Myra pulled Jamie's head forward, releasing the clasps on his mask and letting it hang from his neck so that she could see his face. "It's really nothing personal, Bluejay. We all get paid just the same. So I can't have you messing things up, you understand, don't you? I need money like I need oxygen– like you need adventure."

"Where does the road end?" Jamie blurted out in what was almost a cry.

This reaction was one Myra hadn't accounted for and one that she had never experienced before. It took several seconds before Myra could muster a response. "What?"

"When the dust settles." Jamie swallowed back what felt like a lump of sand in his throat. "Where will we be at the end of our struggles– at the end of this road?"

Myra was quiet as she processed Jamie's words, before a quiet scoff escaped her throat and a faint smile pressed on her face. She ripped the piece of tape off his mask, revealing the faded painting of a blue jay. "Silly bird." Myra leaned closer to Jamie, her lips almost touching his ear. "There is no end, even if they snip your wings, and you continue on despite it all. All roads lead deeper in. They all go nowhere."

Then she pulled away without another word, knowing that this riddle would cause Jamie more suffering than any amount of physical torture. So Myra departed, blowing out the only candle that had kept the room illuminated.

Jamie was alone– more alone than he had ever been. And he was no closer to figuring out where this road would lead.

41

2047, two years earlier

Myra was an odd lady. She enjoyed the thrill of a hunt. She liked watching as panic set into her prey. Her amusement was fed as they scurried around blind, running deeper and deeper into a maze of her design. And just when her prey is about to escape, she blocks their path with an equally impenetrable wall.

"One of these cups is poisoned, while the other is clean." Myra splayed her hands out, gesturing to the two cups in front of her with an excited grin. She was in a room not so dissimilar to the one she would later trap Jamie in, though without any of the fancy mechanisms that Beth had designed.

On the other side of the table, a man by the name of Mr. Sabot, a debtor of hers, was hastily glancing between the two cups. "What if they're both poisoned?"

"A mercenary should never break her word. Else, who would hire her?" Myra bobbled her head, as if the fact were obvious.

"You drink first. We're… we're not going at the same time. "I want to see the bottom of your cup first."

"Of course. Then we'll know within just a few minutes. Isn't it thrilling? I bet you've never taken a chance like this before. Just don't start panicking if you lose."

"Gamblers don't lose." Mr. Sabot straightened his posture, feigning confidence.

"Oh, that I know, Mr. Sabot. That I know more than anything." Myra smiled, gesturing again to the cups. "Well? Take your pick. There's no delaying the inevitable."

Mr. Sabot mulled over the two options, silently wondering how he had gotten himself into a private room with the north's most notorious mercenary.

His misfortune started a few hours ago, but really Mr. Sabot had been in a downward spiral for years. It started with gambling, a vice he really hadn't overcome from the days before the parasites.

But one day Mr. Sabot bit off more than he could chew and picked the losing of the two fighters in a brawl between marred. This was common in alloy zones that had been partially secured– enough for people to move in, but not enough for any sort of order to take place.

Really, he should have known better than to place his bets on a Florid going up against a Mechatolly. Florids lost those duels more than they won them– but that's what made betting on the Florids so appealing. All the *copper* one could win from the people who played it safe and bet on the Mechatolly.

Gladiator-style fighting between marred were all the rage, and Mr. Sabot couldn't help but join in the fun.

Then he bet what he couldn't lose.

Had he known Myra to be the kingpin of that particular operation, he never would have been so reckless with his money. But that was all in the past now. He managed to get by for almost a year by forking over the minimum payments, but that wouldn't last for much longer, especially not with the interest rates Myra placed on Mr. Sabot's loan.

That's when Mr. Sabot decided to take matters into his own hands. Arming himself with knives and duct tape for armor, Mr. Sabot snuck towards the Moat of Metal.

He thought he was quiet; he thought that all the Mechatollies were sound asleep. But if that were the case, he wouldn't be sitting across from Myra like he was now.

After he was discovered because of a Mechatolly's agitated screech, Mr. Sabot had been scooped from the Moat of Metal and his life had been spared. But Myra's mercenaries weren't going to release him as easily as they had caught him. He found himself sitting in an empty, windowless room, with only a short coffee table in front of him.

Now lacking weapons, Mr. Sabot debated trying to make a run for it. A quick pull on the door would show that such efforts were futile. Mr. Sabot whined, slumping over the desk.

With his spirits crushed, he waited for the inevitable. He wondered what would happen to him. If his body would be thrown out, or if he would be added to the Moat of Metal's numbers.

Swinging the door open with a push of her hips, Myra interrupted Mr. Sabot's dark spiral. She wore a smile, looking down at him as if he were a scrawny, lost dog in the rain who had come to her front door for shelter.

She was holding a platter, on which two intricate cups sat atop. "Why did you come here, Mr. Sabot?" She asked, placing the platter on the coffee table.

"You… remember me?" Mr. Sabot was taken aback, glancing over Myra. An iron was on her hip, but other than that she seemed unarmed.

"I remember everyone who owes me money," she said pragmatically.

Mr. Sabot quickly bowed his head, clasping his hands together. "Please, please! You charge too much interest. I… I can't keep up with the payments."

"So instead, you come to kill me?" Myra snickered at Mr. Sabot's logic. "I appreciate your boldness, but that often overlaps with idiocy. So, were you being bold, or an idiot?"

"I–" Mr. Sabot stopped groveling, as if having an epiphany. "I… I'm bold." He looked up at her hesitantly, as if trying to figure out if his answer was correct.

"Maybe you are right. Not long ago usury was quite the crime, you know? Maybe you have been sent to be my executioner, and not the other way around. A man, quite similar to you, taught me that. But he was a bit more impressive in the intellect department. In fact, he made the game we're about to play."

"Game…?" Mr. Sabot questioned, glancing around the room.

"Yes, a game. But I've added a little twist of my own. Herron's version is too boring. It's perfect for a gambler, like yourself."

A game of chance? Now that was something Mr. Sabot could get behind. It would certainly give him better chances than trying to kill Myra and all of her mercenaries. "Then what are the stakes?"

"It's simple. If you win, consider your debt forgiven. I'll even add in some extra copper to get you on your feet, as a reward."

"And… if you win?"

Myra's smile twisted, thrilled by the question. "Then you die. And all your possessions will be mine."

"I don't think–"

"You agreed to the terms when you snuck into my camp with the notion that you could kill me. Or we could not play the game, and you can leave feet first." The room fell still, and Myra tilted her head, goading Mr. Sabot for a response. He nodded quickly.

Myra then took out an empty vial from her jacket pocket and placed it next to the cups. That's when Myra explained to Mr. Sabot about the poison, and they had arrived at the present moment.

With a quivering hand hovering between the two cups, Mr. Sabot swallowed back the lump in his throat.

This was the curse of a gambler.

To take larger and larger gambits until one had made a bet they really shouldn't have. The pair continued to sit in silence as Mr. Sabot's gaze jumped from one cup to the next.

"This one." Mr. Sabot croaked, pointing to the cup on his right. "I want you to drink this one."

"I thought you would never make your choice." Myra scoffed, an amused smile on her lips. As her fingers wrapped around the cup, Mr. Sabot blurted out an objection.

"Wait! Wait, I– I think you should drink from the other one. Yes, yes. Not that one," Myra sighed, starting to get annoyed by his stalling. Still, she raised no objections, raising the other cup to her lips.

Swallowing the contents of the cup within a few large gulps, she flipped the cup upside down and placed it back on the platter. Mr. Sabot watched as Myra wiped her lips with the back of her hand in satisfaction. She stared back. "Your turn." She pointed towards the unchosen cup expectantly.

There was no turning back now. No trick Mr. Sabot could pull, no cards to count or hesitations to take advantage of.

So he reached his hands out towards the cup, tightly closing his eyes. All that mattered was Mr. Sabot and the cup, as the world around him hid behind his eyelids. He felt as the hard aluminum cup found its way to his mouth, before slowly accepting his fate and drinking the water within.

Before he could drink even half of the cup, a loud pop rang through the room, then a sharp stab penetrated his chest. The cup slipped from Mr. Sabot's hands as he looked down at his chest.

Blood spurted from a small hole in the center of his torso. Not a sound escaped his lips. He looked up at Myra, betrayal and regret filling his eyes.

A gun sat firmly in her hands– the one which was once latched to her hip. A tight, unbothered smile pursed her lips. Smoke still rose from the barrel from which the shot had come.

In a moment, he was dead.

Mr. Sabot's eyes rolled back in his skull; his head hit the floor with a loud crack.

"You're such a brute," Herron commented, looking upon Mr. Sabot's lifeless body with disdain. He had been waiting outside for the game to finish and opened the door when he heard the shot.

"Did I not follow your recipe?" Myra remarked, picking up Mr. Sabot's cup and finishing what was left of its contents. Once it was empty, she flipped the cup upside down, placing it next to the others.

"At least I actually would have put poison in the cups. You gave him hope for nothing."

"You speak as if you don't do the exact same thing. The only thing that changes is you hiding the life-saving charcoal in the sugar cubes. We're both cheaters, Herron. The only difference is that you poison both, and I none."

"The difference is that you shot him. Look at the mess you made," Herron glanced at the blood which painted the walls. It had started to seep into the wooden flooring. The blood was certain to stain.

“Good thing I have so many men at my disposal, then,” Myra remarked, picking up the platter and walking out of the room, as if Mr. Sabot’s death meant nothing to her.

When life is but a metric of the monetary gains to be made from it, a man like Sabot, who had nothing to offer, was worth the same as an ant. Neither had a speck of copper to their name and thus couldn’t afford to take up any of Myra’s consciousness.

42

2049, present day

"He's gonna be pissed." Myra laughed, casually chatting with some of her workers. They were sitting around a campfire, waiting for the sun to rise. It had been several hours since Leslie's rescue team had infiltrated Myra's camp. Although Myra suspected that there were more than just Jamie, she decided not to pursue them. After all, she had two of their comrades. In Myra's mind, there was no way the rats would challenge her after discovering that fact.

"I didn't even hear him scream. What did you do to him?" One of her people asked, a twisted grin on their face.

"Nothing he won't recover from. The details might make you hurl." Myra crossed her arms smugly as impressed nods spread across the group. She couldn't tell them what she really did, which was nothing.

She couldn't do much to Neil's workers, especially not one she had been specifically told not to harm. The man was powerful, too powerful for even someone like her to get on his bad side. In the end, Myra radioed Neil, informing him that Jamie had wormed his way into her camp but was safe in her care. She did, however, make it abundantly clear that she wasn't going to babysit– especially not when she knew there would be others.

"He passed out before I could get very far. Lucky bastard."

A few chuckles erupted from the group, agreeing with her sentiment. "You think he's with that group the king paid us to deal with? Maybe we can use him," one of them suggested.

"You've got some brains in you, after all. I think Herron's gonna be out of a job soon."

The group laughed, but a pessimist interrupted them. "What if there's more?"

Myra paused, considering their words. "What if?" She repeated, cupping a hand over her mouth. "What do you suggest?

Mobilizing? Using that boy as bait? Continuing as normal?" Myra asked in a rhetorical manner, staring into the fire.

"We could look for them," a scruffy ex-soldier to her right suggested.

"Pests will always come running when they smell food. Once they notice their friend's gone, they'll slip up and come looking for him." Again the group laughed.

"You said it, boss!" They cheered, much to Myra's amusement. Standing, she looked over at the strip of road leading out of the winery, thinking about what Jamie had said earlier. The road seemed shorter than usual. She released a quiet sigh, brushing off her knees and standing upright.

"We'll sweep the winery in pairs. Understood? The party's gonna start any second now." Myra picked up her gun and gestured for the scruffy ex-soldier to follow her. They walked away from the campfire, heading toward the dorms.

"How many do you think there are?" The ex-soldier raised a gun, carefully advancing down the hallway.

"What we should be more concerned about is how they got inside in the first place." Myra similarly unholstered her gun, pushing against the doors as they walked past to make sure none of them were left unlocked. It was quiet.

The ex-soldier grunted. "Where are we going?"

"There's more to their operation than meets the eye– I know it. We need to secure a package within my dorm." Myra slowed as she approached the door, pressing a hand against it. Still locked– good. "Stand guard out here," she commanded.

With a turn of the handle, Myra opened the door, raising her weapon and investigating the room. Her movements were steady and calculated. She swept the room: one corner, then the next, until she got a good view of everything. Then she glanced towards her bed, aiming her gun at the mattress. She continued her slow advance, raising the sheet with the muzzle and looking underneath. Clear.

Myra glanced towards the dresser as she straightened. She yanked the door open, stepping back as she trained her gun on her clothes. Empty. Knowing that there were rats in her home made Myra uneasy. She breathed a sigh of relief, closing the door behind her.

The bed was stiff as she sat down, but it was the only comfort Myra had. It was quiet. That disturbed her more than anything: the eerie stillness of life before death. Before war. She wanted to start fighting now. She hated waiting; hated feeling that she was no longer in control.

The gun slid back into its holster, and all was normal. If the rats were waiting, they were going to strike either just before or after the guards rotated. The anticipation was going to kill her.

Myra walked back to her dresser, checking the lockbox. It was still secure. "See anything out there?" She called to the ex-soldier, but after a second of waiting, heard nothing in response.

A frown creased her lips. "Answer when I talk to you, asshole." She turned toward the door and yanked it open.

What greeted her on the other side was the end of a gun. Myra felt a chill run down her spine as she stared down the barrel. The man holding it was one she knew well. One she hadn't seen in many years. Prost.

Even beneath the mask, Myra could tell that he was smiling. Prost enjoyed this. "Morning, sunshine. Why don't you go back inside? My friends and I would love to have a little chat."

She looked behind him. The ex-soldier was lying on the ground, unconscious. Scattered around his body was the rest of those little nightmares, crowding the hallway. The *rats* found food.

"You'll regret this. You should have just let her go– continued on with your life like the rest of us," Myra hissed. Her poisonous stare glazed over the rest of Pasko's posse. "You're dead men walking. All of you!" Myra's voice rose but was quickly cut off as Prost shoved her inside, clasping a hand over her mouth.

The remainder of them followed Prost inside, locking the doors behind them. They were going to have Myra to themselves for a while. Now was their chance to bleed her of all the information she had on Crawford and the second king.

43

"Neil's gonna be here soon. He'll come looking for that boy you lost. And he'll come looking for me. What do you think he'll do if he finds me dead?"

"Oh, I don't think he's going to do much of anything." Prost pulled up a chair as Leslie bound Myra's hand to the bedpost. "In fact, I think he's going to be ecstatic. He's had less work for you now that Crawford's brimming with people. We're doing him a favor."

Myra huffed but was interrupted by Leslie. "We know your ledgers are around here somewhere. Save us all a bit of time and tell us where they are. Maybe we'll let you live."

That got a laugh out of Myra. "We all know you're not letting me live. Not unless my boys come in here and mess up your plan. Just get it over with, or go."

"She's right," Colt chimed. He had rejoined the group before the hunt began and was watching the hallway with Lucy. "Jamie might know something. Let's just slit her throat and go look for him. Each minute we don't spend looking for him is a minute wasted. Napoleon gets closer with every second. Once he is, the entire legion will descend upon us."

Prost sighed, glancing between Colt and Myra. "Neil won't find her in time, even if he shows up now. You should know why we're doing this before we kill you."

"I already know why. Because I tried to kill that punk wife of yours and failed." Myra pulled against her restraints, looking at Prost with a scowl.

"That's only half the reason why."

"Then enlighten me, your holiness," Myra said with bitterness.

"Because you're just like Neil. You've spilled gallons of blood just for drops of fuel. People like you are the reason it's taken us so long to return to the right path."

Myra scoffed. "I don't remember you complaining about my methods when Crawford was in its infancy. You became soft. You all did. And you couldn't handle what I did for us. What I did to make sure Crawford survived those first few years."

"And now you're rotting it from the inside," Prost stood, glancing at Leslie. It was time; they could all feel it.

"Wait– come on. Let's work something out," Myra blurted, feeling a hand press against the side of her face to hold her still. A scream ripped from her throat as cool steel slid across it. She was gone in seconds, the once off-white sheets stained a deep crimson red as a torrent poured from her neck.

"Someone might have heard that." Prost stood up, brushing past Colt as Leslie wiped her bloodied hand on the sheets.

"What about Jamie?" Colt asked, confused. He followed Prost, glancing around and checking for any mercenaries that might have come running; his gun was at the ready. Leslie quickly dragged the ex-soldier's limp body into the room as Lucy grabbed the small lock box inside the dresser.

"Have faith in our leader's plan. You'll see him again."

This coldness shocked Colt, though there was a good reason for it. Prost knew that Myra would keep Jamie safe; else, he would already be dead. In either case, there was no reason to search for him. They needed Neil to find him and bring him back to Crawford.

Of course, there was no way of knowing certainly that Jamie would come back with what they needed– if he would come back at all. But Prost trusted Jamie would– after everything he told Jamie– after everything Jamie had seen? It was practically a given.

There were always contingencies, regardless.

"Let's hurry. They're already searching for us and sooner or later, they're going to notice their leader is missing." Prost glanced back. Lucy and Leslie rejoined the pair and swapped hands: Leslie carried the lock box as Lucy watched their flank with a gun at the ready.

They began to run, only slowing as they approached a corner. The exit was getting closer; once they were outside and in the dark, finding them was going to be much harder. There was one final turn– then they would be at the exit door. Then they would–

The door opened. Prost froze, pressing his back against the wall. The others could hear it too. Lucy turned back the way they had come; there was another exit. There *had* to be.

Leslie followed, then Colt and Prost. They scurried away, hurrying to the other end of the building. Prost trained his gun at the end of the hallway, his hand too unsteady to do anything more than fire off a few warning shots. They had enough of a lead on the mercenaries to avoid the pair– for now.

A few turns later and Prost was nearly at the exit again, not far behind the rest of the group. He turned the final corner, nearly slamming into Colt, but managed to stop himself just before the collision.

That's when he heard it. The noise he was beginning to despise.

Footsteps.

The mercenaries, marching ever nearer without realizing how close to danger they had gotten.

They were closing in. Even if the group were to turn back around, they would just end up running back into the previous pair. Hiding in Myra's room was too much of a risk. The mercenaries were bound to check the rooms– Prost could already hear them making the checks.

Slipping past them was also out of the question: one was always stationed in the hall and standing guard as the other performed the sweep.

They were going to have to fight.

It seemed that Leslie had already reached this conclusion. She angled her body towards the bend in the wall, preparing to jump out and shoot the mercenary stationed outside before they could return fire. Leslie raised her left hand and steadied her breathing, waiting for a break in the footsteps as they investigated the next room.

Like a rabbit, Leslie jumped out from behind the wall. Both of her hands clutched the gun as she fired off a shot, nailing the mercenary's center mass. The mercenary toppled over, but Leslie stayed where she was. Not a second later did she fire off a second shot as another body hit the floor. Then she began to run.

The rest didn't hesitate to join her, sprinting towards the exit. Bullets followed after them as the second pair of mercenaries were drawn to the noise. A bullet hit its target: Prost. He tumbled down and flew forward, traveling a few feet before his body came to a stop. His hand shot towards his leg, compressing the wound as blood began to spill from it.

Colt and Lucy turned around as Leslie jumped into the nearest car. The pair turned heel, running back for Prost. Colt wedged himself under Prost's arm and lifted him upright as Lucy shut the door, locking it. It wasn't going to last long; the mercenaries were already slamming against it, and there were more that would soon descend upon them.

It was going to have to do.

Lucy rejoined Prost and Colt, helping him walk as they rushed towards the car. The engine roared to life as Colt swung the door open and threw Prost inside, climbing in after him. Lucy didn't have a moment to close the door behind them as Leslie took off, speeding past the mercenaries and narrowly avoiding a collision.

They drove past the other cars, drove past Napoleon, through the gate and down the hill. Bullets rained down on the car. They hid behind the steel frame, praying that the bullets were not strong enough to pierce the metal. Leslie kept her eyes down the road as the car continued to speed up.

"Brace!" She screamed as the car slammed through the final gate, speeding down the rickety path.

44

Jamie was shrouded in darkness. His skin burned, his muscles ached, and his lungs fought against each draw of air he took, keeping him delirious for some time. Not that he could escape from his bindings, even if he wasn't. Sometimes he would hear gunshots, then return to slumber, then wake up again to find the battle continuing to rage on. He was in a daze, focusing only on the cuffs that were cutting into his skin.

The door to the room creaked open, a slow, careful opening. As if the person were carefully inspecting the inside to see if the room was safe or not. Jamie heard a gasp come from the entrance of the room, then the quick pattering of feet rushing towards him. Then he felt two gentle hands fall onto his arms– these weren't Myra's, Jamie was certain.

"Jamie– you're– what happened?" A voice he wasn't expecting to hear spoke to him, and Jamie half wondered if it were a trick of his mind. Neil was the one who found him. Neil reached for Jamie, his hand brushing against the clammy skin of his face. Though it rejected his touch; the frigidity caused Neil's fingers to reel away.

"Everything went wrong." Jamie forced the sentence out through clenched teeth, but could feel himself relaxing now that he was moderately safe. His voice was tired, but Neil heard something within it– a strange emotion, buried beneath exhaustion and blood. It was desperation. Even the words of a dying man didn't carry the fear that Jamie's did.

Neil froze up, noticing a piece of paper beside Jamie. It said two words: *you're welcome.* The sign made Neil's blood boil, but now wasn't the time to go chasing tails. "I'm going to get you out of here, okay?" Neil glanced around the room, looking for a key.

A messy tray sat atop a nightstand; a ring of keys sat beside it. Neil started to test every key until one finally unlocked the cuffs. He saw how Jamie's fingers trembled and twitched like worms caked in salt. While he had heard idle chatter about heating the Mechatolly's ichor and aerosolizing it, Neil never could have imagined how potent the toxin truly was. It left a gentle wheeze with each breath Jamie took, and Neil could only hope that the symptoms would subside.

Leaving the other cuff clasped around his wrist, Neil forced Jamie's arm over his shoulder and pulled him upright with great effort. Neil trudged forward as though he were walking through quicksand; Jamie was akin to a sack of lead that was only pulling him down faster. But Neil would never let go of Jamie; he was too important to Neil for him to simply toss Jamie aside, like a valueless heirloom that Neil alone treasured.

Gunfire continued to prattle on, but that didn't seem to alert Jamie. His head was slumped over, but was able to continue walking. "We're nearly there. Okay? And we'll get to go home. Just a little longer– just hold on, Jamie." Jamie mumbled something of an affirmation in reply, but it was impossible to make sense of what he said.

Despite how much gunfire there was within the winery, it was mostly concentrated in a single building. A set of footsteps ran towards Neil and Jamie, helping him load Jamie into a car. Neil got in the back seat with Jamie, while the other person got into the driver's seat. "The others– they're still here."

"It's okay– we don't have to worry about them. We need to get back to Crawford," Neil reassured, clicking Jamie's seatbelt. Turning his head towards the driver, he snapped at them. Jamie could hear the anxiety in Neil's voice, as if the words were eagerly jumping out of his throat despite his best attempts to suppress them. "What are you waiting for– *go*!"

The car lurched forward, taking a sharp left turn before speeding off. They drove in a straight line as the sound of gunfire slowly grew quieter. Neil's hands never left Jamie, shaking him awake and looking for injuries. It was a panic that he had never displayed to anyone before. He *couldn't* lose Jamie. Not after everything else that had happened.

But this couldn't slow the persistent decay of Jamie's ability to stay awake. Jamie could feel the old canvas seats and the seat belt that was digging into his neck, yet at the same time he couldn't. It was as if he were floating. Like nothing really existed. His mind was in a race against itself, yet at the same time everything felt nauseatingly slow. Neil watched as all his efforts to keep Jamie conscious stopped working. Pulling away from the limp body, Neil looked on in horror.

Lifting his hand, Neil moved two fingers towards Jamie's neck and hesitantly checked his pulse. Neil pressed his forehead onto Jamie's shoulder, burying his face between Jamie and the seat to hide the wetness that began to form in his eyes. Jamie's pulse was slow, but his heart was still beating. Neil was usually a man who was as sturdy and stable as a great tree, but not even a tree can remain unflinching in the face of a storm.

"He alive?" The driver looked at them through the rearview mirror.

"Yes. Just take us home."

45

There was nothing. More accurately, Jamie *felt* nothing; it was dark, quiet. He couldn't feel a wisp of air on his face or a speck of ground beneath his feet. He tried to move his fingers, to make a sound– even just to open his eyes– yet it all produced a similar result: *nothing*.

Then, just as Jamie had resigned himself to the silence and his mind began to calm, *he began to feel everything*. A bone-chilling night in a winter that would make even a penguin shiver. The howl of the wind and the far-off rustling of trees; a soft hum of electricity from a dying streetlamp. Jamie would feel that he was now standing upright and buckled under the crushing pressure of gravity as he stood against it.

For a while it felt as though Jamie were in a storm, as each sound and every touch felt amplified tenfold. But soon the wind would quiet, and the leaves along with it. The frigid air seemed to warm slightly, but it was still cold. The surge of sensations made Jamie nauseous, and the world seemed to spin around him, though that too would subside after just a few minutes.

Once Jamie had steadied himself, he slowly began to open his eyes, attempting to figure out where he was and how he might have gotten there. First, he saw a house– a *really* nice house. One with a well-maintained lawn not grown half an inch above the soil with a perfectly trimmed rosebush to pair. There was even a pristine white picket fence to match: not a splinter of wood was out of place nor any blemish on the white paint.

The street was dark except for a single lit streetlamp: the lamp directly above Jamie's head. He looked up at it, surprised to see a lack of rust and an intact plastic cover over the lightbulb. His eyes scrunched shut as he looked up at the lamp, which let nothing hide beneath the searing spotlight. This place frightened him. It terrified him because it was so normal… so *mundane*. With that thought, the realization of what this place was finally dawned on Jamie.

This wasn't some regular town. *This was Silverton.* But it wasn't the town he remembered. No, this was the Silverton from the mundane days– before the marred made the town what he remembered. And while, yes, it was cold outside; the heat was on and people were comfortable. Jamie wasn't sure how he had gotten there, but honestly, he didn't care.

His mind only thought of one thing: his home. He ran to it, darting from street to street as the streetlamps lit up when he ran beneath them. Would his family be there? Would he even recognize them? *Would they recognize him?*

The door was unlocked. Jamie ran through the tailor shop and darted up the stairs; he could hear the running of water and the faint noise of a TV coming from the living room. The lights were on; they must have been home!

Yet they weren't.

Jamie had gone back, but nobody was waiting for him. Nobody would ever be home. A shot of crippling loneliness shot through Jamie, and he could do nothing but crumple onto the carpet in front of the TV. He remembered the hours his family spent watching it together. The distant memories as they attempted to recreate the crafts from the art shows they watched.

The smell of glue; the sting of glitter as it got into his eyes and everywhere else in the house. Jamie could still see a few purple and pink sparkles on the off-cream carpet, which was slightly yellow. He remembered all the time he had spent on this carpet, sitting cross-legged as Sam braided his hair behind him.

He remembered the joy, which was eventually cut short as his parents demanded they go to bed. But he remembered how they would tuck him and Sam into bed each night. Jamie remembered that their father would kiss their foreheads as their mother watched from the doorway. Then they would close the doors to their rooms, and the siblings would eventually fall asleep.

Jamie hadn't realized that he had missed it. He hardly remembered this in the first place, but now he wanted nothing more than to relish the memories. Would he still have this connection if he hadn't become a copper chaser? It wouldn't have been the same, of course. Jamie knew that. But maybe he would still have had a family to come back to.

It wasn't that his family had disappeared from his home. Maybe it was that Jamie had pushed them out into the cold.

Jamie pushed the thought away as he buried his face into the carpet, gripping the fabric as it tensed beneath his fingers. He wanted to cry, but knew he didn't deserve to. This was all his fault. So Jamie held in his emotions, breathing through the slightly unclean carpet of his childhood home.

It had been about an hour, or at least, what Jamie assumed to be an hour, before he would leave the house. Jamie suspected that the rest of the houses would be just as empty as his own and wasn't in the mood to check. His eyes still stung, and it worsened when he stepped back outside into the chilly air. The surroundings hadn't changed, and the single working streetlamp remained consistent from before.

He looked up at the sky, but a thick fog obscured the stars. At times like these, Jamie could only really calm himself by immersing himself in his surroundings, but this was one place he didn't want to ground himself in. The forest bordering the town would offer relative safety, seeing as there were no marred to be worried about.

Jamie set off and would soon reach the perimeter of town, reaching where the wall once stood. Though there was no evidence of it at this point, Jamie was so familiar with the lay of the fence that he knew exactly where it should have been. It felt weird– being able to just walk in and out of town as he pleased.

It was as if he would be walking through a wall, even if it wasn't *technically there*. With a deep breath, Jamie took a step beyond where the wall should have been. His surroundings began to warp and melt like hot plastic. He could hear the wind whip around and slash at his face; hear the trees and houses as they crumpled like paper.

With a blink, it was all over, and Jamie was back where he started; his senses were no longer being assaulted. He looked around. The freshly cut lawn. The fence. The streetlamp just above him. At first glance, everything was as it had been when he started. Just one thing had changed.

A second streetlamp was alight. It was to the left of Jamie and maybe fifty feet away. But that wasn't what surprised Jamie the most. A girl in a ruffly white dress. She glowed like a beacon on an unforgiving ocean. He wanted to call out for her, but knew he didn't need to. She wouldn't run. Not from him.

"I've missed you, Jamie," the young girl chirped in a cheerful voice. She wasn't older than sixteen. Her hair was black and short; a big, innocent grin on her face showed off the gap between her front teeth.

Despite not having seen her in years, Jamie instantly knew who it was. "Amanda?"

"You came back," she stated calmly. Her demeanor was odd; not excited, not sad. Simply neutral. It was an emotion she rarely showed, even when she was alive. She was a rambunctious child.

"No, you… can't. Amanda is dead. Why are you here?"

"That's because you are, too." She slowly nodded, prancing towards him. His companion wore socks which were, again, white. Each step seemed like a lofty one, as if she were no longer bound by gravity. Yet at the same time, she couldn't get much farther than a normal jump before being rubber-banded back to the ground.

Jamie's eyes widened slightly and his mouth fell slightly ajar. He watched as Amanda began to approach him, a new streetlight lighting up as she walked under it while the ones passed shut off. They reacted to her in the same way as they did to him. "I'm… what?"

"Don't be scared." She started skipping around him. The stone path beneath her feet must have been ice cold, yet she didn't once flinch. "Because now we can play together forever! No more marred, no more parasites. We don't have to starve or freeze. Everything is as it should be."

"No… no, I– I can't be dead."

"I was the same way when I first died. But this place is really great! No monsters lurking in the shadows. No shadows for them to even hide in! We never have to look over our shoulders. Never again."

Jamie's hands reached for his mouth, looking at his companion in horror. "This isn't– it's not real."

His companion rolled her eyes, stopping in front of Jamie. "What's wrong? Is there someone you're gonna miss? All you have to do is wait. All roads lead here."

"I'm in hell," Jamie announced, much to his companion's annoyance. Her face twitched, the unnoticeable smile on her face contorting into a frown.

"*What?*" She spat the word out.

"The mundane days? Where I can't leave this forsaken town? *Where nothing is as it should be*. I'd rather be thrown into the inferno."

"But you have *me*," she pouted, much like a child. Really, she hadn't changed at all from how he remembered her.

The thought of spending the rest of eternity with such a person in this disgustingly perfect town sickened him. Before she died, she betrayed him. She offered him up for death, and now, ten years later, she wanted to go back to the happy childhood memories they shared. Worse yet was where they were. How could he be confined to such a stifling place for the rest of time?

He didn't want to stay here.

But what could he do? Nobody could come back from death. No, not even the Mechatollies or the Florids were capable of that. Jamie was dead, just as she had said. Returning once more to the floor, Jamie's knees fell down with a bang. They did not hurt for long.

In this momentary lapse, Jamie thought back to his time on Earth. His life was short and chaotic. Most people would hesitate to call it much of a life at all. It was full of regret– of places he had yet to go; things he had yet to experience.

He gripped his hair, trying to cover his eyes; trying to hide. His silent heart strummed back to life, ripping through his chest as though it were trying to escape. His mind ached; his stomach churned. This was all wrong.

What a life he had lived! He murdered, he stole, he lied. And here he was, wondering what it all meant.

"If I could do it again." Relinquishing his hands from his head, Jamie looked up at his companion. His cheeks were flushed; his eyes burned. His voice fluttered and throbbed. He sounded as if he were desperately choking back tears, yet unable to imprison them at all.

Skeptically, she crossed her arms and sat down next to Jamie. "What do you mean?"

"I should have… I should have lived a different life. Should not have… shied away from the world."

The companion crouched down next to him, tilting her head. "I thought you saw all that the world had to offer?"

"I did. Of course I did. But… isn't life about the people you meet, too?" Jamie stopped himself, unable to say anything else. Once again he found his lips to be sewn shut. "I did a… pretty lousy job."

Jamie could hear Amanda sigh as she took a few steps away from him. "How am I supposed to play with a depressed adult? You've changed." She was quiet for a moment before continuing. "Go back to the edge of town. You'll find answers there. But should you decide to return, I'll be waiting."

Without a word, Jamie would stand, understanding what Amanda meant and determined to get out of this place. He had taken only a few steps before Amanda spoke one final time. "And, Jamie… I'm sorry."

Jamie glanced behind him, but Amanda had disappeared. His mind was left to brew on those two final words. Amanda was just a child; as was he. Neither of them deserved what happened to them on that day. She wanted to survive, just like he did, and saw only one way to do so.

He forgave her. He forgave himself.

Before long, Jamie was once again at the edge of town. But instead of just the forest and the invisible barrier, there was someone standing a few feet beyond the border. It wasn't Amanda; this was a young boy. This was Jamie the night before he was taken by the cultists.

"Look to the stars…" the boy hummed, staring directly into Jamie's soul.

"... and you'll always know where you are," Jamie finished the boy's sentence. Yes, Jamie remembered it now. John, the injured cultist whose place he took among the group. John was the one who taught Jamie many things: how to pick locks, squeeze into tiny places: everything one would need to know in their line of work.

These were his last words before succumbing to his illness. The last words he spoke after asking Jamie to take his life.

Look to the stars and you'll always know where you are.

John knew Jamie struggled to keep himself grounded, and even in his final moments, John wanted to help him. Jamie wanted to forget that night. Forget that phrase; forget the kind words of his captors. Yet it had once again returned to him. Even though he had only known Jamie for a short while, John could recognize that look in his eyes. The eyes of someone who had seen far too much; one who looked for hope in such a destructive and unforgiving world.

"What would Amanda say if she saw us now?" The boy asked after a brief pause, a somber tone carrying in his voice.

"What do you mean?"

"You're like them. The ones who killed her. Amanda would be upset," the boy became very serious, and he disregarded his melancholic undertones. His form snapped, twisting and turning like a tree branch that was growing much too fast.

"No… that's not fair. This is what we have to do to survive. The people who died were… accidents. It wasn't *murder*," Jamie parroted Neil's comforting words, but the boy didn't seem content with the answer.

"You know what that is, Jamie," the boy's words began to boom, echoing across the entire town. "You know it exactly. A fairytale that Neil told us to keep us pacified. Keep us submissive. But that's all it is. *A fairytale*."

"Stop it–" Jamie hissed, shielding his face as the boy's form began to rapidly outgrow him.

"You'd march off a cliff if he told you, and you'd do it with a smile. Do it whether he gave you a lousy excuse or not. You'd lie. Lie to me. Make up some story that it was only because you wanted new experiences. You're a liar, just like everyone else!"

"That's not true!" Jamie protested.

"You thought you were free, but you were just a bird caught in a large cage," the boy hissed, much like Jamie. "And you locked *me* up too. Just so you wouldn't have to hear it. But now I'm *free*. Us both, soon."

"Then what? You want me to throw everything away? To destroy my life over pride?"

"I want you to *admit* it. Admit that we're just Neil's playthings."

The pair stared at each other with equal intensity. They didn't need to share words to communicate what the other was thinking; they knew each other too well to need to. Jamie took a step forward beyond the border.

His surroundings once again melted, but this time it was not unpleasant. He was not returned to where he had started. Jamie was freed.

46

One week later

The thing about Neil was that he had a tendency to overdramatize things. Maybe it was just so he could justifiably plan for the worst-case scenario, or just so he could feel in control.

Despite that, Neil was probably the most relieved of all of them when Jamie was finally able to get treatment.

Neil wasn't the patient type. But he found it in himself to wait for Jamie's examination to finish and for him to go home before speaking to the doctor. "How bad is it, really?"

The doctor sighed, taking her gloves off and sitting down. They sat in her examination room, where she cleaned Jamie's wounds. "You think I lied, or something? He'll live." The doctor clicked her tongue. "He's fine. A few scratches from the fight and some rubbing on the wrists. But we'll have to see the long-term effects of that toxin he inhaled."

Neil nodded, tapping his thumbs together. "What's the worst that could happen to him?"

"Well, his lungs could collapse, and with the equipment I have here, he'd probably die. But that's not remotely likely to happen. With the right medication and rest, he'll be fine."

"Good. That's good. Thank you, doctor."

"Of course, Neil." She smiled softly, standing up and starting to clean the room. "Just tell him to come in for a checkup in a week's time. But come in right away if something feels off."

"Sure, sure. I'll make sure that he got to his apartment alright." Neil stood, leaving the doctor to her work. He waved to his people as he brushed past, but didn't stay long enough for a chat.

If not for one particularly persistent individual, he would have made it to Jamie's apartment in record time. "I really don't have time to talk, Pat," Neil grumbled, continuing to push past the unathletic driver.

"Wait– Neil– it's… hold on!" Pat finally got a good grip on Neil's arm, forcing him to stop. "I was chatting with the guys in car two. And– well, I drew the short stick." Pat was referring to the second car that had come with them to Myra's camp. It was mostly soldiers; even the driver could fight.

"What are you getting at?" Neil snapped.

"Well… we hear a lot of stuff on the road, you know? Anyway, those mercenaries have kinda… *dispersed*." Neil looked at Pat with a look that told him he needed to stop stalling. "We picked one of them up, and they were talking about the assailants. And… well, one of the people they described– I mean, it sounds ridiculous," Pat laughed, glancing away and holding his neck with his hand. "They said it was Prost."

Neil froze, gaze narrowing onto Pat. "How would they be sure?"

"Well," Pat trailed off. "You're right. I– I don't… I was just so sure. The merc was right next to him. I mean, they– he sounded exactly like I remember Prost. The hair, the clothes– the way he held himself, how he looked. I guess I just…"

This finally got Neil's attention, stopping any struggle he was once putting up. What was Prost doing there? Neil's head began to spin. Why would he be fighting with Myra?

What was going on?

Neil placed a hand over his mouth and began to spin wild conspiracies in his mind.

Was Prost working with Pasko? What if he had turned Jamie against him?

Jamie was gone for a while. Neil thought that he had been imprisoned, but what if he had stayed with the raiders *willingly*? Neil glanced towards Jamie's apartment.

A gentle yet firm hand rested on Pat's shoulder. "You know that can't be true, Pat. We're all mourning, I get it. But he's dead and we need to let him go."

"You're right," Pat conceded.

"Let's keep this between us, okay? No point in starting rumors." Neil squeezed Pat's shoulder and turned away. Just as quickly as the conversation had started, it was over. Neil continued making his way towards Jamie's residence, thinking of ways to broach the topic without causing alarm.

Knocking on the door, Neil waited for Jamie to answer. He hadn't seen Jamie anywhere on the streets, but there were quite a few people, seeing that the workday was over. After a short wait, Jamie opened the door. He looked as if he were just about to go to sleep, but was interrupted by Neil's knocking.

"I hope I haven't come at a bad time," Neil apologized.

"No, no. I was just getting ready. Was there… something you needed?"

"Well, no. Just thought you might want some company."

"I'm really tired, Neil. Can we talk in the morning?" Jamie turned to close the door, but Neil held it open. It was as if he were desperate to speak to Jamie before he slept– like everything would be different once Jamie woke up.

"Just for a few minutes. The doctor and I talked. And you should hear it."

With a begrudging sigh, Jamie released the door and allowed Neil to come in. "So, what is it?" He sat down, sinking into the chair.

Neil glanced around Jamie's apartment. This was the first time he had been in there since Jamie moved into it. There were hundreds of little knick-knacks strewn about. Everything came from what Jamie had scavenged in the alloy zones.

A careful step was needed to avoid trampling anything, but Neil would eventually make his way to a seat next to him.

"Right. Yes, the doctor. Check in with her at the end of the week. And, uhm… any shortness of breath, check in."

"Okay?" Jamie lowered his hand, looking at Neil skeptically.

"I brought some canned beans. Thought you'd like a quick meal," Neil fumbled with his words, struggling to say something of meaning. He had never been one for idle chatter.

"No… something about a lung that threatens to shrivel up like a raisin. It's somehow… made me lose my appetite." Jamie complained, resting his head against his wrist. "Why are you really here, Neil?" He asked in a bored tone.

Neil felt as though he had no choice but to answer Jamie's question, so, begrudgingly, he would. "You're good at what you do, Jamie. And we've worked together through thick and thin. But…" Neil paused, carefully considering how to word his next sentence. "I want you to know that I'm here for you– that I care about you. And, if that's as a friend or as your boss, then I'll be it."

Taken aback by Neil's unusually caring words, Jamie couldn't help but look surprised. "Where's this coming from?"

"You were with them for quite a while. And, what happened at Myra's camp…" Neil faltered, starting to rub his fingers against each other. "I don't know what you saw, or what they told you. Just remember who they *are.* Liars– thieves, tricksters. But know, nothing's changed, despite what they have told you. I'm still the same; everyone and everything you know, it's just as how you left it."

Despite Neil's speech being an attempt to dismiss anything which would sway Jamie into disloyalty, his words had the opposite effect. Jamie's eyes narrowed, but only slightly.

Even that minor twitch was enough for Neil to recognize that something was wrong. He'd have to come up with a new plan. An herbicide which would decimate the seed of doubt before it could blossom into a flower of betrayal.

Maybe Neil thought that he was the only one in the room with these ideas, but the exact same things were going through Jamie's mind.

Neil was scared. Jamie could *feel* it. And Neil wasn't the type to go where the current took him; to let loose loyalties fly.

"He doesn't trust me," the thought zipped through Jamie's head like a bullet. There was no way to regain Neil's trust, at least, not to how it was before– not fast enough to keep Neil from acting on his paranoia.

"Yes… I know. After all, they're the reason any of this happened to me," Jamie swiftly came up with an excuse, seeing Neil's nervousness. Neil wasn't the type to show his emotions. He would have been a great card player. So even smaller ticks of unease told a lot. Jamie concluded one thing: something large was lurking beneath the surface. Something which made even Neil lose his mask of control.

But it didn't matter now. This careful game of pushing and pulling between them? It was all bullshit, because they both knew they were playing it.

Jamie made his choice by not telling Neil about Prost immediately, and by how Neil's visit was going, his attempts to calm Neil had been failing.

Deep down, Jamie knew that he had been made.

47

2050, present day

Maybe it was a coincidence. Maybe it was fate's twisted sense of irony. Either way, both Jamie and Neil found themselves in front of Prost's vacant grave. They had taken care to avoid each other– at least, Jamie had been.

The pair said few words to each other this time. Jamie was too busy fussing over the grave, wondering what his own would look like. How ironic it was; so few people had a marked place to rest upon their passing, and here they were, looking upon the grave of someone who was very much still alive.

The graveyard was uncomfortably silent for them both. Despite everything that had come up, they wanted what once was. It felt like the only thing there was to talk about was something that would further sour their relationship.

Neil turned to leave, before freezing a few paces away from where he had started. He turned back, looking at the headstone. "I wish we… had a name to bury him with."

"What do you mean?" Jamie turned to look at Neil.

"He never told us when we met him all those years ago. He never gave us a name." Neil thought back to when he was a much younger man, not long after the marred showed up. He dove into the depths of his memory, back to the sunny days when he met Prost twenty-odd years ago.

Neil wasn't a particularly fit man. Back when his life could still be called *normal*, the most exercise he did was running to the break room so he could get a coffee with some creamer before his coworkers. Not that the marred cared. Normal life, jobs, safety– all they cared for was multiplying their ranks.

When the marred first appeared in the city, one far away from Crawford, Neil found himself trapped in a dense office with his coworkers. Only a few managed to survive.

Most of them Neil had long forgotten the faces of. But there were two that he remembered. Silvia and Geoff, his prick of a boss. The three of them were in Geoff's office when the marred devoured the place they once called work. January 20th, 2030.

"I'm sure you two know why I brought you both here," Geoff said from his big, overbearing chair. It was much nicer than the one Silvia and Neil used. Even the two chairs that sat in front of his desk were nicer than the average employee's chair. But Geoff didn't allow the two to sit. Only those who deserved to sit got to, according to him. Like his golfing buddies, or really anyone above him in the company.

"Sir, I think–" Neil tried to explain, though was stopped by Geoff's sleazy voice. Neil couldn't stand the sound of it.

"You think. *You think*, do you? That's news to me. You two have any idea what you've done, ey?" Geoff opened one of his desk drawers, slamming a manila folder in front of them. "Because that would require just half a brain cell to realize, which I don't think the two of you put together have. Silvia, explain it to me. What do you *think* happened?" Geoff turned away from the two, drifting his chair a half foot away to grab his coffee. Geoff was special. He got his own coffee machine, provided by the company. But Geoff didn't deserve it. Not in Neil's eyes, or anybody who worked beneath him.

"There were– there were some... unfortunate and unpredictable market crashes, sir. Due to backlash with a clinical trial–" Silvia was cut off as Geoff interrupted once again. It drove Neil insane. He was trying to keep his calm, digging his nails into the palm of his hands to distract himself. It wasn't working.

"Yeah, yeah. Railroad company spilled some chemicals and whatever other shit nobody cares about into some bog. The clinical company says that it had important cargo on that rail which set them back years in research and millions of dollars. You know who else got set back millions of dollars? *Our client*. Because you bozos thought that a fucking *clinical* research company was a good investment."

"Well– sir, even high-profile companies were putting their investments in. They were working on something worthwhile. The people would have loved it; it could have made millions– billions, even!" Neil added, but Geoff would hear no excuses.

"You know when else those triple-A companies were going wild? Before the market crash in 2007, so let's use our *thinking* skills a bit more, Neil." Geoff turned away to get some more coffee, but turned back to continue his rant. "And you know what else I saw? You invested last year, in 2029. Even though they only went public *last month*." Geoff spat as he spoke, and little specks of water fell onto his desk. "So you wanted early access tickets, is that it? Hoping to land on the company that would reinvent the phone, but it turned out to be a phony. They probably didn't even have cargo on that train; they were just trying to avoid a suit. And you fell for it."

"They– they weren't *fake*. Silvia and I saw for ourselves. I mean– they were working on a serum which inhibited cell growth, every hospital in the world would have been using it. We saw it work before our very eyes! A small, dying sprout grew into a healthy sapling in minutes. And they were about to move onto animal testing in our sister city with lower regulations. I mean– the applications were limitless!"

"And I'm sure they would have made a lot of money. Then you would have received fat holiday bonuses. That is, if their *serum* wasn't lost to the damn leeches!" Geoff scoffed, starting to drink his coffee. The two watched as he drank, not yet dismissed from his office. He was drinking for another minute before finally setting the cup down on the desk. Geoff loudly sighed, as if bored by the exchange. "You're fired."

"We're– *what?!*" Silvia blurted, losing her poised stance and resting her hands on the table.

"Why?" Neil also stepped forward, caught off guard by the sudden termination. They had both been great employees and made millions for the company. One mistake, even though it was undeniably significant, neither believed to be a large enough offense for such a reaction. "We're– we're invaluable to this company! Silvia negotiated more deals with even the worst of clients than everyone else on this floor *combined.* And my eye for numbers has found us countless diamonds in the rough. This isn't fair, Geoff!"

"Life ain't fair, kiddo," Geoff stated simply, as if making a comment on the weather rather than altering the lives of two people.

"We– we could sue you! Wrongful termination isn't something that'll go unnoticed. We deserve a warning– not to lose our jobs!" Neil's outburst was starting to turn the heads of the workers next to Geoff's office, even with the door closed.

Geoff dramatically rolled his eyes. "Fine. Neil Ervines: misuse of company time, unable to work in a team, creating a hostile work environment through excessive competitive drive, disobedience. Silvia Oakes: abuse of employee perks, excessive conversing with coworkers– also known as *gossiping*– and encouraging employees to leave work despite projects being incomplete. But of course, the list goes on for both."

"That was one time– and it was already seven!" Silvia blurted. That wasn't fair– none of it was. Geoff was never a particularly kind manager, always setting unreasonable deadlines for his team. It's just that Silvia didn't want to see her coworkers suffer because of it.

They both knew Geoff was grasping at straws for each infraction he listed. Waving a hand in front of his face, Geoff refused to hear anything else from the two. "I want you both out of my office and your desks cleared by end of day, or I'll have security drag you out."

"Just please–" Silvia started, though stopped as she watched Geoff pick up the phone on his desk and start to dial security. Neil had already turned to leave while Geoff was waiting for security to pick up, but Silvia remained where she was. "We'll make it up to you– work overtime, anything."

"Someone has to take responsibility, and those people are you."

"Your guys sure got here quick." Neil commented, pushing the door open and glancing back at Geoff.

"What are you talking about? They haven't even picked up yet," Geoff scoffed, annoyed at Neil's obvious attempt to trick him. But the commotion was certainly not quiet, and wouldn't go unrecognized by Geoff for long. After a few seconds, he looked up to see what was happening. The smugness left Geoff's features, replaced by confusion and a smidge of anger at the interruption to his power trio. "See what's happening," he demanded.

Neil scoffed. "You're not my boss anymore. Why should I–" then he looked back at where he last saw the security. A pair of guards and a lady they didn't recognize were outside the offices, next to the elevators. It seemed as though a lady, one of their coworkers, had collapsed in front of the elevators. From this distance and the way she was moving, Neil guessed that she must have been seizing.

One of the interns, bless her heart, got up from her desk and went to check on the three. Neil couldn't hear what she said, as she was too far away for any words to be audible. One of the security guards snapped his head towards her, causing her to jump back in surprise. Then, without any warning, he jumped up and sprinted towards her, tackling her to the ground.

This caused a number of workers to get out of their seats, some to get a better view, others to step back in fear of what they saw. A few rushed towards the intern to try to get the security guard off her, but the added noise only caused the other guard and the stranger to become attracted to the commotion.

Neil shut the door, looking back at Silvia and Geoff, who were also invested in the scene.

"What the hell was that?" Silvia asked, now looking through the glass panes that showed the rest of the office and the ensuing panic.

"I'm calling the police," said Geoff, as he hung up the phone with the unreachable security team and typed in the new number.

"What are we gonna do? They're attacking everyone." Neil joined Silvia, continuing to watch. Some of their coworkers pushed past the commotion and escaped to the elevators, while others huddled in the corners of the office. Some even stayed in their cubicles.

"Hello this is– yes, I'm– how did you know?" Neil's and Silvia's attention turned to Geoff as he started to speak with the operator, prattling on about the building address and where his office was. "Well then, you know I need police over here. If people are distracted, we lose money! What do you mean there's no police available? Don't you know who… you're sending the *fire department*?!" Geoff was almost brought to a shout, ready to smash his phone against the desk. "How could there be no police available? What do I pay my taxes for! So they can sit around all day?"

Glancing at each other, Neil and Silvia scoffed at how absurd he sounded. Silvia approached Geoff, snatching the phone out of his hand and starting to talk to the operator instead, much to Geoff's disbelief. Although Geoff started to throw a tantrum, Silvia ignored him. "Please excuse him. What should we do while we wait for the fire department to arrive? Mhm… Alright. Thanks." Then she hung up, calm as ever.

"What did they say?" Neil asked, turning away from the window. The crazed security guards and the stranger had moved on to other targets.

Moving away from the phone, Silvia drew the blinds on the office window. "Don't engage. Don't let them see you. Just wait for help to arrive and defend yourself only if you have no other choice."

48

2030, twenty years earlier

"Can we really just… leave them out there? I mean– they're our coworkers." Neil frowned, troubled by the morality of their actions.

"You're right. You two should go out. Sounds great," Geoff chimed in.

"We can't go out and save them. But if they come, we should let them in." Silvia dismissed, trying to remain cold about the whole thing.

This plan would soon be tested, as banging sounded from the door only a few moments later. "Please– please, please! Let me in!" Their coworker cried.

Neil, the closest to the door, was about to open up the office for their distressed coworker, but was abruptly stopped. "Don't you *dare* open that door!" Geoff demanded, causing Neil to stop and look back at his former boss. Geoff had taken a signed golf club off the wall, pointing it at Neil. "I'll knock your head off if you open that door!"

Silvia's eyes narrowed at Geoff, put off by his actions. "What are you thinking? Why the hell are you doing this?" Silvia scoffed, crossing her arms.

"I swear I'll break this door down if you don't let me in!" Their coworker jiggled the door handle, shaking the entire door.

Neil let go of the door handle, slightly raising his hands in surrender. As much as he'd like to help his coworker, he didn't want to find out if Geoff would use his golf club against him.

Before anyone could say anything else, they heard the sound of a scream and bodies hitting the floor. All three peeked out through the blinds, watching as one of the security guards wrestled with their coworker.

The three didn't watch for long. Neil and Silvia looked at each other in horror. Even Geoff seemed rattled, though whether that was from fear or shame was yet to be seen. But there was undoubtedly a subtle look of pride, as if he had successfully defended his territory and not just condemned another human to death.

Perhaps their coworker would have stayed down after the security guard left. But after he was free of her grasp, he saw that twisted man staring at him from behind the curtain. Something inside of their coworker snapped; after years of mistreatment, he had had enough.

Rage swelled within him, even as he lay on the ground, gasping for air. Their coworker rolled onto his side, reaching for one of the cubicles. From it he grabbed a crystal paperweight.

Their coworker fell to his knees in front of the window, raising his hands above his head and smashing the rock into the window.

Yet again, Geoff's smug expression faded as cracks started to form on the glass. The loud noise drew the stranger away from her pursuit of their coworkers and towards Geoff's office.

She stood next to the coworker as the glass shattered, spilling into the office without a moment's hesitation. Stepping through the blinds, she pounced on the first person she saw: Geoff.

In what looked like a reflexive motion, Geoff swung the golf club at her head, causing the stranger to fall to the ground. She didn't scream; no; it sounded like she was clicking her tongue at him. But it was much too fast and inhumane to sound like a clicking tongue.

To Neil, it almost sounded like a grasshopper. A very angry one. About to hit her for the second time, Geoff stopped as he noticed his precious gold club was now bent.

Cursing, Geoff threw the club at the stranger. Despite likely sustaining a concussion, the lady still seemed determined as ever to continue her assault. She grabbed his leg, lunging towards him and chomping down on his heel. Geoff squealed. A high-pitched scream, which would have put most opera singers to shame.

Neil heard more footsteps approaching, likely the other two security guards. Grabbing Silvia's hand, he started to sprint out of Geoff's office. The two security guards were hot in pursuit of Silvia and Neil, chasing after them as they weaved in between cubicles. It was chaos. Their coworkers were on the floor– dead and dying. Some were upright, wandering around the office and attacking the few people that still remained.

More of their coworkers joined the chase. Although they were fast, the pair managed to just barely stay ahead, making more distance with each sharp corner they turned.

Silvia was just a few steps ahead of Neil and barreled towards the glass door where the chaos began. There were elevators to their right, but Silvia took a sharp left turn, darting towards the emergency exit.

They both got inside the stairwell as the closest coworkers began to reach the door, and with both of their weights combined, Silvia and Neil managed to lock the crazed pursuers out. The security guards leaned on the doors, then bashed against them with barbaric swings and animal-like strength.

Ultimately, nothing they tried worked, and the security guards became disinterested in the pair in the stairwell. Neil and Silvia waited a little while longer after the noise had stopped to ease up on the door.

They both took a moment to catch their breath, relieved that the guards and their coworkers had finally left.

Although they both enjoyed the moment of calm, another problem quickly became apparent. Staying in the stairwell wasn't an option. Eventually, they'd have to leave and either return to their office or flee to a different floor.

"How… how are we gonna get out of here?" Neil asked, looking up at the stairs above. It's possible that none of the floors above theirs had been affected yet, considering the lack of noise.

"I don't know. I don't want to be stuck here and wait for the fire department anymore. We should leave the building. We could wait outside." Silvia stood, offering her hand to Neil. "Let's leave before they come back."

Standing, Neil started to walk down to the first floor with Silvia. "I just… I don't understand why they would attack the whole office. Do you think they got fired too? Wanted to exact revenge?"

"Like our coworker after he got locked out?" Silvia shook her head, shrugging. "But why attack that poor intern instead of coming straight for Geoff?"

"Crazy people do crazy things, I guess."

"I guess. But who was that lady then? Was she from a different floor?" Silvia pushed on the emergency exit door, which opened on the ground floor into the lobby.

There were some people walking about. It seemed almost normal. There were papers carelessly tossed onto the floor, plants knocked over, and porcelain scattered on the ground.

What was even more peculiar about the mess was that nobody was moving to pick it up. No, instead most of them were just idling about in the lobby. But not all of them were passive. A few saw the emergency escape door open. They snarled, making a similar rattle as the lady in Geoff's office did.

Suddenly the door was fully swung open, the receptionist jumping into the doorway. Her mouth was agape, as if trying to do an impression of Edvard Munch's *The Scream*.

Both of them jumped back, running away from the wailing receptionist. "Downstairs– downstairs!" Silvia blurted, bolting down the stairs two steps at a time. Neil sprinted after her, more of their enraged colleagues pouring into the stairwell and chasing after them.

Silvia got down first, holding the door open and yelling for Neil to hurry. Neil almost slid through the door, landing on his stomach while Silvia slammed the door shut. It locked behind her. She clutched her employee access card, backing away from the door as more bodies rammed into it.

"What the *hell*!" Neil sat up, watching as the door remained unflinching, even as more weight was piled onto it. "There's *more* of them?"

"They're going to break this door down. How'd you get to work this morning?"

"I– I took the train. Why?" Neil was thrown off by the question.

"I rode my bike." Silvia started to get further from the door, slinking deeper into the employee garage.

"Please tell me you mean bicycle." Neil started to follow in Silvia's footsteps. Backing slowly away from the door as if it were a snake. Once they got a bit further, they turned their backs to it and began to run.

Silvia threw her helmet on, got onto her motorcycle and gestured for Neil to get on behind her. His feet barely left the ground before Silvia revved the engine and burned rubber as she rode towards the entrance. Neil looked over her shoulder, watching as the gate started to rise. The attackers from the lobby were beginning to pursue them.

With each step they took, the gate seemed to rise slower and slower until the receptionist's hand nearly grabbed Neil's dress shirt and pulled him into the mob.

The bike lurched forward just before they were caught, and the shutters nearly took the pair's heads off– but it was now or never. The sun hit their faces, and Neil never thought he would be so relieved to leave work.

People were running, a mix of evaders and pursuers. A few others had the same idea as Silvia and Neil, trying to drive their cars through the hectic streets. The less capable drivers and the cowardly were the first to wreck. Either crashing into people or swerving to avoid them, totalling their cars in the process.

Silvia was neither. She weaved past the chaos, swerving out of the reach of people trying to grab them and carefully avoiding the debris on the road. Silvia seemed to know where she was going, avoiding the city center and driving to the outskirts of town. Neil saw all sorts of people as they drove past.

People in hazmat gear that had been sent to clean the train crash, people in suits, uniformed students, and so many others he just couldn't keep track of. As the buildings got shorter in their escape from the commercial district, the types of people on the street changed, but their aggression stayed all the same.

Silvia skirted past all of them without any hesitation, making fewer hostile jerks of her bike as the debris on the road lessened. The number of those who were unable to escape the densely packed districts spiked dramatically.

The pair got as far as Silvia's single tank of gas would take them. Once the fuel was gone, Silvia walked the bike with them, and they continued their journey on foot.

They walked for several days, seeing many people drive past, but none of whom would stop to help them. Their destination was a nursing home far away from the town; it was where Neil had sent his mother when he was unable to care for her. But now even that seemed like a far-off dream.

They were starving. But a glimmer of hope presented itself to the resilient. A car had crashed into a road sign, obscuring it from those who drove past.

When Silvia and Neil went to check the wreckage, they found the car devoid of people and there were no supplies they could make use of– it had already all been taken. But the sign was a glimmer of hope.

It pointed towards a small village a few miles to the northwest. The pair managed to reach the entrance to the village before sundown.

Although seemingly empty, Neil heard the sound of a fight coming from deeper in, near the heart of the village. Silvia left her motorcycle propped up against one of the houses as they both followed the source of the commotion.

What they saw confused them. A man with a pickaxe, fighting against a group of five strange creatures. They looked human, but clearly couldn't have been. Their movements reminded the pair of how their coworkers and the other city dwellers acted during their escape.

But they were so mutated– so deformed– that the possibility of those creatures once being human seemed unfathomable. Vines grew from their skin as they did from dirt– colorful pops of flowers sprouting from the vines as if nothing were wrong with this.

While Neil was daydreaming, Silvia picked up the lid of a trash can and rushed over to help the stranger. Using the top as a shield,

Silvia barreled through a trio of the odd-looking people, toppling them over in her wake.

If he had not been so busy fighting, perhaps the man with the pickaxe would have looked perplexed at her appearance.

Watching Silvia so fearlessly charge in to help a stranger inspired Neil. Quickly he looked around for something to use as a weapon. In one of the yards, there was a baseball bat and a glove a few meters away. Neil snatched the bat, going to join the fight, but was distracted by a much bigger threat.

A bug. It looked like a giant, green, flying shield beetle– it scared Neil more than the crazed humans. He started to blindly swing at the bug, forgetting all of his childhood baseball training in the face of danger. The bugs, which seemed to multiply as more and more appeared from seemingly nowhere, were smitten down through Neil's efforts.

After battling against the creatures and exterminating the bugs, the three stood victorious– and exhausted. The stranger with the pickaxe had killed the five attackers, while Silvia used the trash lid to keep the creatures from overwhelming him. Neil was preoccupied with swatting at bugs the entire fight.

It was a few minutes before they spoke to one another, and Silvia was the first to speak. "What's– what are you doing here?"

Despite the stranger likely fighting against the creatures for much longer than Silvia and Neil did, he seemed to recover faster than they did. The man was clearly athletic and vastly stronger than the pair. "I'm… from the mines." He lazily gestured to his pickaxe.

"Well… what's your name?" She further questioned.

The man seemed to think about his answer. "I'm the Prospector."

"*The Prospector*?" Neil quirked a brow. "Sounds like a title."

The stranger looked at Neil, who was lying flat on his back on the ground next to him. "My name. It's the prospector. I'm the prospector."

"I think… I'm gonna give you a nickname, the Prospector." Silvia thought for a moment. "How does Prost sound?"

The stranger, Prost, nodded at the proposal. Neil didn't seem completely onboard with the idea. Although he was tempted to call them both crazy, he decided to mildly question them instead. "How'd you get *Prost* from *the Prospector*?"

"Well, if you get rid of half the word, you're left with Prost. And that sounds much cooler than *the Prospector*." Silvia smiled, proud of her work. "I learned it from the word scramble games in the newspapers they put in the break room."

Neil scoffed. "How come Geoff gave me demerits for wasting company time and not *you*?"

Silvia shrugged before laughing at the absurdity of the situation.

49

2050, present day

Crawford was beginning to turn into a war zone. It had started ever since Jamie returned: first, there were a few more guards in each rotation. Then a few stationed atop the wall. A few times, Jamie had caught people with rifles coming in and out of the unused floors of taller buildings.

Observation was a skill he had been endlessly thankful for whenever he went out to the alloy zones, but now, all Jamie wished for was the blessing of obliviousness. He wished that he had never been dragged into this war. Or at least, that it could pass by without bringing him closer to the eye of the storm.

Though it seemed like this was where it was heading. Someone had been keeping an eye on Jamie. He wasn't sure when it started, but the specifics didn't matter. Not now, anyway. A blip in the corner of his eyes, a shifting shadow, the outline of a distant person he had seen a few too many times.

Maybe it was just paranoia. He had seen too much of himself in Prost recently– including that signature fear of others he had struggled to shake in Crawford. But Jamie knew it wasn't paranoia, just as Prost did. There was only one person in Crawford he knew of who would be tailing him.

Ivette.

She was skilled. Skilled enough to train excellent soldiers while still hiding plenty of secrets and techniques for herself. Besides, Neil wasn't going to trust just anyone with stalking Jamie. Not because he couldn't find someone with enough skill, but because he feared rumors. Rumors that his kingdom was beginning to crack. That he was going to slip in the rankings.

Rumors that Neil was inferior.

All because he couldn't keep a few people in check and would lose everything he had worked for so long to build. In a stable kingdom, what type of great monarch had to trail his own people? His inner ring, at that. It was a scandal, no matter how one spun it.

Not that the rankings ever mattered to Jamie. If Ivette caught wind that Jamie was scheming to defect from Crawford, she was going to put a stop to it. Be it telling Neil or interfering herself.

There was a convoy that would be leaving tomorrow. He had to be on it: it was the safest and quickest way to leave the city– any other route meant running into guards or the marred. This convoy was probably going to be the last before Pasko attacked, or before Neil placed the city on complete lockdown.

Of course, the only way Jamie would be able to leave on the convoy would be to get rid of his stalker. Ivette would overpower him without a problem; he remembered all the times she had easily defeated him in one-on-one duels during his training.

Jamie was going to have to do what he did best. Deception.

He had prepped his route well– all he had to do now was execute it. She wasn't always following him, but Jamie knew that she would be vigilant in the hours leading up to the convoy's departure. Jamie finished stuffing the last of his equipment into a bag before slinging it over his shoulder, glancing towards the front door of his apartment.

Just as it had so many times before, Neil's obsession with public perception was working against him. By only sending Ivette to follow Jamie, she was beginning to tire.

There were going to be gaps in what she could monitor. Ways he could skirt around her watchful gaze. Jamie's eyes shifted towards the window on the other side of the apartment. He couldn't be sure which she had eyes on– or if she had set up a trap that let her know if either had been opened.

Jamie walked towards the window, pressing his head against the glass. He slowly lowered the blinds, glancing towards the roof. There was a slightly discolored patch of plaster in the space above his head: the remains of a fix from a leak.

A nearby chair served as a stepladder as Jamie felt for a soft spot in the ceiling. It buckled slightly under the pressure of his prodding. Jamie grabbed his knife from its hilt, stabbing it into the weakened area. Sprinkles of loose dust fell onto his face, which he wiped away as he continued cutting.

He continued to hack at the ceiling until there was a hole big enough to fit through and the material reached the undamaged region. It would need to hold his weight– at least for a few seconds. Jamie placed the knife away and sucked in a deep breath, jumping and throwing himself into the crawl space.

The impact caused a whirlwind of dust and powder. Jamie was sure he wanted to avoid inhaling them. He glanced a final time towards the hole: towards the life he was leaving behind.

Then he continued into the darkness.

It wasn't long before Jamie reached the end of the crawlspace. His lungs burned from the prolonged absence of air, and he was beginning to feel lightheaded as he reached for the grate at the end of the building. It was the final barrier to freedom.

A few good tugs, and the grate was released from its place. Jamie thrust his head outside and gasped for air. The crispness of the morning brushed against his face, thwarting the heat that was beginning to simmer beneath his skin. He wiped away the dust that had gathered on his hair before pulling himself closer to the edge. He looked over the side and towards the drop that awaited him.

It was a drastic fall– a lethal one, for sure. But this wasn't the first time he had needed to navigate the side of a building. Jamie pulled himself completely out of the crawlspace and held onto the ledge with his fingers. Just slightly beneath him was a widow. The trim couldn't have been more than two inches.

Two inches to hold on to. Two inches that were going to decide whether or not he fell to his death.

Jamie sucked in another breath and let go of the ledge.

50

When Jamie opened his eyes, he was still clinging to the side of the building, like a confused bat. He had caught the ledge. There was only about fifteen feet until landfall and another window he needed to catch. Jamie glanced up. His hands were beginning to tire, and he could feel that his forearms were pumped.

He let go of the ledge and landed just enough of his feet onto the window below to stick. The ledge was larger: five inches. Jamie turned his back to the wall and dropped his bag to the ground, sitting on the edge of the window. As much as he would have preferred to break into the room, he couldn't risk being spotted as he left that side of the building if Ivette was monitoring the front side.

Another drop and he landed cleanly on the ground. Jamie lay on the floor, looking at the open crawlspace he had descended from. He took a few minutes before pushing himself off the ground and taking his bag, navigating the sideroads as he advanced towards the convoy.

Now he just had to wait for the drivers to finish preparing for the trip, and he would be out of Neil's domain. Jamie rushed into the nearest car but was stopped before he could close the door behind him.

"Jamie!" A voice called to him. *Should he just pretend not to have heard the voice?* Jamie's mind started racing, and he could feel his heart begin to pick up speed. He had never felt so scared before– like he could simply keel over and die from stress.

Jamie begrudgingly looked up, over at the voice that called to him. It was Pat. He was wearing his usual aloof smile. "Yeah…?" He reluctantly answered, prying his fingers off the door handle.

"Well, aren't you going to ride with me?"

"Oh, right, of course," Jamie spoke quickly. He scrambled over to Pat's car, threw himself inside and pressed against the car seat, wanting to sink into it and disappear. His grip on his bag was enough to cut the circulation to the tips of his fingers, and they began to turn red. There was an irrational fear in Jamie's head that someone would steal it and further delay his escape.

Jamie's eyes were glued to the dash in front of him. His breathing had gradually slowed, slowed almost too much; that worried him too. Sometimes the shadow of a passerby would wisp through his window, and Jamie would almost jump out of his seat each time they did; nothing ever came of it: nobody stopped him, nobody even acknowledged him.

A few agonizing minutes later, Pat casually entered the car, oblivious to the suffering of the person to his right. He was humming a nameless tune, waiting for the final checks to be completed so they could continue on their journey. Jamie was glancing between the mirrors, watching out for Neil or anyone who was approaching the car. The drivers would walk past, laughing as they conversed.

Regardless of how happy or seemingly unthreatening the person was, it worried Jamie all the same. His skin felt cold and his head started to prickle. He wanted to throw the car door open and run away. He wanted to sink into the floor. He wanted to do anything: anything but wait, even though he knew waiting was the best option.

And wait he did. He waited until the car finally started to roll forward. After they had left the city and what remained of the buildings outside, Jamie finally calmed down. Resting his head against the seat, Jamie let out a silent sigh. He would be able to rest, at least for a while.

"You've been very quiet, Jamie. Has everything been alright?" Pat glanced at him through the corner of his eye. A mild concern was sneaking its way into Pat's normally jolly features.

"Yeah– yeah, no, I'm… I'm fine." Offering a half-hearted smile, Jamie was unable to force a genuine display to disprove his confliction. Hoping to avoid the uneasiness of the situation, Jamie looked out of the window again. There were many clouds in the sky, the kind that looked like cotton. Bright, white clouds, which bleached the sky and completely obscured the sun. It was drearier than Jamie had hoped.

"Well, it's just– you know. You were gone for a while. And now that you're back... you're *different.* It makes me worry about you. I know I'm– just some dude who drives you to where you gotta go, but... still. You really scared the hell outta me! I thought you had died. And then *suddenly* you're back– good as new. But you're not! It's," Pat sighed, gently tapping the steering wheel. "I guess I've just grown attached to you. You know? And every time I go to pick you up– I... I get scared. That you won't be there."

This startled Jamie. Of course, Pat was a nice guy. But he was nice to everyone. "Oh... that's..." Jamie had, for the first time, found himself at a genuine loss for words. He couldn't rationalize why Pat was so upset. Jamie had little impact on Pat's life. They hardly even saw each other. Had Pat had a friend in Jamie all this time?

"You understand, don't you? I mean– when you get all quiet. And just *stare.*"

"Well... the world is a beautiful place. What's life if you don't stop to smell the roses or watch the sunrise?"

"Yeah, but you... sit back and watch the journey. And you let the people pass you by. There's more to life than seeing it. You have to enjoy it. *With others.*"

"I find peace in solitude." The wind had started to pick up, causing the leaves on the trees to dance sporadically in the breeze. The clouds had started to part, revealing a bright, sunny sky. Yet Jamie didn't focus on any of that, and for the first time, he wasn't looking at the scenery; he was looking at Patrick. Jamie didn't spend much time looking at people's faces; it was harder to get attached that way, so he never noticed the small lines at the corner of Patrick's eyes or the wrinkles from his constant gentle smiles over the years.

"I just think you should give it a chance. I'll introduce you to some of the guys– they're curious about you."

The car fell silent for a while after that. Only the humming of the car and a quiet chime as rocks flung against its underside kept them company. Jamie had yet again been pulled from the present.

The trees seemed to dance during this time of year, their leaves giggling like happy children as they brushed against one another.

Who knew when the next time they were going to meet would be. That thought circled in Jamie's mind, and he said something without thinking. "You're a good guy, Pat. I'm sorry I couldn't… appreciate that sooner."

Pat's grip on the steering wheel tightened as he gulped down a wave of melancholy. He could feel the finality in the air, too. It was quiet for some time after that.

"Pat?" Jamie spoke up once more.

Pat glanced over at Jamie, elated that he had initiated a conversation. "What's up?"

"If… if you were a bee, and your queen was bad, what would you do?"

A bit confused by the question, Pat raised a brow, looking over at Jamie. "What do you mean?"

"Well, let's say that… the queen wanted more and more honey, no matter the cost. Even if it meant that some bees would die in the process. Would you leave the hive… even though you could never survive on your own?"

Under the guise of a seemingly innocent question, Pat happily answered. "Oh, is this a riddle? I love riddles. Or twenty questions? Whatever! I love these types of games." The radiant smile had returned to Pat's face as he continued. "The queen sure sounds incompetent to me. I mean, if your workers die, how are you going to get more honey? What I would do is join another hive. If I could, anyway. I guess we could always stage a bee-coup, though…"

"Is that what you would do? Then… what if you weren't sure if it really was the queen? What if a bear snuck into the hive every night? And… without a trace, stole most of the honey reserves. So, she works the bees so hard in order to keep everyone from starving. Then what would you do?"

This question seemed to stump Pat for a while, but was delighted to share his answer, nevertheless. "Then I suppose I would protect the queen and the hive with my life. If the queen's done so much for me, I'd repay it by protecting the hive."

Jamie listened intently to Pat as he answered, as if trying to memorize his reply. "*So the choices are between two extremes...?*" Jamie spoke to himself in a barely audible whisper, thinking about the scenarios.

"What was that? Another question? I love this game. Let's keep playing," Pat said with child-like glee.

This game of theirs lasted for some time. Once Pat figured out that Jamie had abandoned Crawford, he would look back at the questions with embarrassment; his friend had been telling him this plan and why he would be leaving for nearly thirty minutes, and Pat didn't have the slightest clue. It would be even worse when Pat would inevitably have to explain what happened to Neil.

Jamie waved goodbye to Pat as the car sped off into the distance, becoming obscured by the trees. He despised the finality that settled in the pit of his stomach. Instead of his usual routine of pulling out his map and compass to orient himself, he stood by the side of the road for a while.

He took in the nature surrounding him, breathing in the air one last time before his loyalty to Crawford truly frayed. While he had no trouble betraying the group he was with prior to Crawford, that didn't mean he took pleasure in double-crossing people. It was simply that he never had any loyalty to that group in the first place. He truly wanted to stay with Crawford: not just because of their network allowing him to traverse freely, but because of the people whom he would be leaving behind.

Jamie waited for a long while. Waited for someone, as he secretly hoped that Neil would drive up to where he stood and take him in his arms, assuring Jamie that this was just a mistake and that everything could be fixed. That it could all return to how it was meant to be. Explain away as Neil always had, but this time never could.

Finally Jamie would resign this foolhardy effort and accept that his only remaining option was to go and leave as he had originally planned. He set his bag down, readying his compass and a map. This time the destination was not his usually assigned city in the alloy zone, just a few hundred feet from the drop-off point.

Rather, he searched for a place that wasn't on any map. Not even his. It was a guessing game to pinpoint where it was, having to use his faulty memory and guesstimates to travel in its general direction. A long-expired military airplane hangar which should have been a museum if only there were time to finish it. Pasko.

The journey took several days, and Jamie had nothing much to think about. The choice had already been made. It was clear that Pasko was going to take control of Crawford or die trying– and take everyone one of Neil's associates down with them. Of course Jamie was friends with Prost, and he hoped that would grant him some grace, but he needed something more concrete than that.

On the dawn of his fourth day, Jamie stepped in front of Pasko's gates.

The sight of Pasko and the new sun behind it was the most beautiful thing Jamie had ever seen. Gentler than the silky sky and grander than the great wall of vines. Yet he couldn't shake a dark feeling inside himself. A bitterness in his mouth that soured the sight. Was he *really* paving a new path for himself?

Had he just traded one cage for another?

51

Two weeks later

Huddled around a table much too large, Leslie and the others loudly argued over their plans for the future. Jamie stood nearby, but far enough away to avoid joining the conversation itself. He had been withdrawn since his arrival. Prost– the only real connector Jamie had with these people– was stuck in bed from his injury. He wouldn't join them in the assault.

"We can't just do *nothing*!" Leslie insisted.

"We also can't go against *him.* We'd just be marching to our deaths," one argued.

"We could just make better defenses here," another suggested.

"We've come too far to sit back now. Besides, nothing we haphazardly throw up will make a difference against Napoleon's army." The conversation bounced from person to person. At first, the exchange was rather civil but started to degrade as the anxiety began to build. After all, nobody wanted to go against a Goliath.

"Then what *should* we do? We can't attack, and we can't defend. Should we just… run?" Colt asked, receiving a few disapproving but acknowledging murmurs.

"No. After everything we've lost– everything he's *taken* from us? We can't run. We've come too far. Paid too great a cost." Leslie shook her head. "The best thing we can do is take him by surprise. The only problem is that none of us knows the inner workings of Crawford. My information is too old and incomplete to be reliable, and there's only one person amongst us who can call that place home." Leslie looked over at Jamie expectantly.

Taking a small step back in a momentary retreat, Jamie watched as the others looked to him for guidance. "Are you serious right now…?"

"Look, I know it's not ideal. And I'm sure the last thing you want to do is twist the knife in your boss's back, but we need your intel. We can save Crawford from that tyrant's clutches. You must have friends within those walls who you'd want to protect," Leslie reasoned.

Jamie frowned, crossing his arms at the statement. He wasn't open to her suggestions; it seemed. "Let's say I gave you everything you needed, *which I won't*. There's something you're forgetting. The people love Neil. They'd never turn against him like I did. To them, you're just another bunch of raiders. Me being there wouldn't change their minds either; I was a stranger to most of them."

Smirking as though she had just outplayed Jamie, Leslie shook her head as if what she was about to say would be obvious. "We have irrefutable evidence. Ledgers. Attacks Crawford funded against other communes. All we need to do is get it in front of the people– the very same who came from the communities he helped destroy. Most of the people in Crawford are his victims."

Jamie's gaze fell to the table as his hand reached to cover his mouth, partially masking his expression. Leslie had brought out a few pieces of evidence that they had acquired and placed them on the table for all to see. Most of them he had already seen, but others were new.

The dealings between Myra's mercenaries and Crawford were not one-off, as it seemed. A few other jobs had been completed, mostly surveilling and a few instances of violence. Jamie's eyes squinted as he inspected the list of cities and communities that Myra's people had surveilled– he recognized the names. They were the very same that he had been sent to destroy.

Leslie took notice of Jamie's staring, starting to add her own commentary. "We noticed a pattern with several of these communities– they were all involved with the copper trade to some degree, more than most. They had also all been destroyed not long after the surveillance took place, but we couldn't find any evidence of payment for the destruction– just surveillance. You wouldn't happen to know anything, right?"

"No, no," Jamie shook his head, uncovering his mouth and recrossing his arms. "This must be something… one of those higher-ups did. Not something a lowly worker like me would do." Jamie met Leslie's gaze, trying to figure out if she believed his lie or not.

It was still for a few seconds too long, and Jamie worried that Leslie might have seen through him, though she nodded without voicing any additional concerns on the matter. But why would she be suspicious? Jamie had stolen evidence tying himself to anything of importance on the night they attacked Myra's compound. At least, all that he knew of. He became uneasy, but tried his best to keep his cool. "What if they don't believe you? Neil could easily spin your evidence against you."

"You need faith, Jamie. We already have a plan to deal with Neil."

"And..?" Jamie questioned, starting to be put on edge by how slowly Leslie was explaining her plan.

"That's where you come in."

"Again? You put too much *faith* in me."

"We just need you for the intel and to distract Neil."

"And how would I keep such a man away from people who were actively trying to bring him down?"

Leslie shrugged. "That's for you to decide, Jamie. But if… things were to get a bit *physical*, nobody would blame you."

"You want me to *kill* Neil?"

"I never said that. But you certainly can." Something in her voice told Jamie that this wasn't just a suggestion, though Leslie continued on before Jamie could dwell on the statement for long. "Just keep him away from us and his people for the rest of the night. Then we can handle him ourselves. But really, you can't tell us that you don't want revenge. After what he did?" The others glanced at Jamie.

Jamie didn't like the sudden shift in the conversation and the influx of eyes on him. The hairs on the back of his neck stood on ends and Jamie felt his blood run cold. There was nothing he could do with these expectations upon him, so with a frown he reluctantly resigned his protests. "I'll only help if you don't kill anyone. They don't deserve punishment for Neil's actions."

"I'll keep her in check," Ann assured. "Leslie may want revenge… but I think we must restore power to the well-intentioned. Sadly, I don't think that leaves any room for Neil and his corroborators. We won't be like him; the innocent don't deserve to be punished."

Jamie considered their words for a moment. He was nervous– nervous that his involvement would be uncovered once they infiltrated Crawford. His only hope of remaining below the radar was to destroy Neil's documents before the coup was completed.

"I don't know." Jamie sighed, looking away from the table. His words were filled with an air of uncertainty; everything had its risks, sure. But the timing of it all was too harsh for Jamie's liking.

They seemed shocked. After all, why wouldn't they be? Every person in that room had assumed that Jamie had switched sides, despite his long history with Napoleon. To Jamie, Neil was still the second king– he would never call him Napoleon.

But Jamie had fought alongside them not long ago– put his life on the line for them. Jamie's actions were illogical. "What are you– why? You wanted this too, Jamie," Colt stammered, confused by Jamie's sudden refusal.

"Damn it, man– what are you doing?" Valerie frowned, her voice dripping with anger from the sudden betrayal.

"You know this is the right thing to do. That it's moral," Ann added.

"Not to him, it isn't." The door swung open. A lady with a tired yet confident look on her face stood before them. Her eyes seemed as if they had seen centuries of turmoil. Her brain was crammed with decades of future plans. Leslie stood behind her, having led the stranger to the meeting.

52

Everyone looked at the strange lady with shock. The room had fallen silent upon her entrance. This meeting was supposed to be secretive; that way the chance of an ambush wouldn't be lost. "You can't–" Colt spoke up, though was silenced as Leslie raised her hand. She was the only one in the room who seemed to recognize the lady.

"It's alright, Colt." Leslie seemed unusually docile and accepting of the stranger's presence. As if she were privy to information no one else was. Jamie's face scrunched, almost instantly starting to scan the lady's features.

This was never the face of someone he had met, yet something about her seemed oddly familiar.

"If I may." The lady brushed past the others, barely giving a glance in their direction. Her target was Jamie, a warm smile present on her lips despite her swollen eyes and damp cheeks. "Our friend needs some convincing. I will speak with him while you all continue to finalize the placement of our forces." She offered a hand, which Jamie carefully observed.

His expression was one of deep fear, carefully yet unsuccessfully hidden behind a stoic mask. The way Jamie moved made it seem like he was worried the lady's hands might turn into razors at any moment.

Yet under the pressure of so many eyes, he would still take the stranger's offer. They looked at her with skepticism, though said nothing as the pair left.

Leading him away from the room with a content demeanor, she made sure to be far enough away so no prying ears could hear them. Then she turned to Jamie.

"Who are you?" Jamie asked, a skeptical and insecure tone in his voice.

"My name is Silvia. Silvia Oakes. Prost is my husband."

Jamie was silent for a moment. At first, he seemed clueless, yet Silvia could clearly see a hint of recognition as his brow furrowed. The muscles of his face contracted, scrunching as though he had licked a salt lamp. He looked away from Silvia. He looked back. "You?"

Remaining patient with Jamie, she would nod. "Yes. Me."

Jamie fell silent, thinking. *Silvia Oakes?* He had seen that initial somewhere. Feeling for his knife, he slowly pulled it out of its hilt.

"This is yours, is it not?" He held the knife in front of her. The initials *S.O.* were just as clear as the day she etched them on.

Though the blade was far more damaged since she had seen it last, this was certainly Silvia's knife. "How did you get this?" She questioned, carefully inspecting it. Jamie had taken good care of it.

"When I became a copper chaser. Guess they gave me all of your old stuff." Jamie watched Silvia skeptically, as if testing her reaction. She seemed overjoyed to have the knife again. Multiple inquiries with Neil about the meaning of the initials bore no results. Now he knew why.

"Yes, that sounds like Neil," Silvia scoffed, reminded of simpler times.

"But there's something I don't understand." Even Jamie, someone who had joined Crawford long after her death, knew of Silvia. Of the great feats she performed. Of her kindness and generosity. Her legacy outlived her in a way that seldom remained; in a world which quickly forgot the dead. Yet again, Jamie found himself staring at a ghost. "You've been dead for years."

"It is good that you don't understand," Silvia reassured him. "It means Neil is exactly as I remembered him. I know Neil, but you know his city. None of us have been there in ages, but you only left recently. We need you."

"I already said I wouldn't help with this. I can't..." Jamie wished to finish, yet felt his voice start to tremble. Neil had been his confidant for years, yet Jamie spoke of his murder without the weight deserving of taking a person's life.

"He's a monster. Whatever he is to you– whatever you *think* he's like, you're wrong. He'd stab you in the back if it meant he got even a penny from it. *I would know.* And I think you know it, too."

Jamie shook his head. "You're trying to poison me. Like he said you would."

"Because he knows I speak the truth. He's trying to turn you against me– leverage the years of trust he's built with you. I'm going to kill the bastard and free Crawford from his rule. One way or another." That last bit seemed to slip out, though Silvia seemed as composed as ever. "But his soldiers are loyal, like you. And a lot of people could die. But this can all be prevented if only we have someone who knows the rotation of the guards. Someone like you." Silvia placed a hand on Jamie's shoulder. It was tight– her fingernails dug into his skin even though the layers of clothes he wore.

It was at this moment, when their eyes held for a few seconds too long, that Jamie understood what she was getting at. This wasn't a pitch to join their merry band of misfits. It wasn't something he got to say no to. Jamie began to think– to weigh his nonexistent options.

"This lady is never going to stop hunting Neil because of what he did to her. If I don't join her, my name is going to be right under Neil's on her kill list. I did what she refused to do. My only hope is that she'll pardon me if I prove that I've changed."

Silvia said nothing, carefully watching Jamie's eyes as they gave way to his thoughts. The small flinch in the corner of his eye, the trembling of his irises as they were unable to anchor themselves on any one object.

Jamie had spent most of his life following a path that had already been laid out for him. Working at his father's tailor shop, serving the cultists. Even the very offer of becoming a copper chaser had been set in motion long before it was presented to him.

The small choices he did make were inconsequential by design. *Give Jamie enough power over his own life to make sure he never begins to question you–* that's how Neil handled Jamie; how he handled all of his workers. *When this can't work, ensure that he's been primed with enough suggestions so that when he's forced to make a decision, he doesn't even realize that it wasn't his thoughts that answered.*

Neil had been grooming Jamie for years, molding him into a perfect servant who never questioned orders, carefully ensuring that he wouldn't venture down the same path Silvia had.

"You know you must, Jamie," Silvia spoke gently, much as Neil did. "Deep down, you know what you must do to survive this war." She was silent for a moment longer, waiting until his eyes met hers. Yet she did not give Jamie a moment to question her words, continuing on. "Do you know why Neil tried to kill me?"

Jamie shook his head; a small "no" escaped his lips.

Silvia nodded. Of course. "I wouldn't follow his schemes. What he planned to do– to bury other communes for the sake of money and a workforce. It was vile, even for this world. And now? I finally have proof." Her voice squeaked in excitement. This was everything her life had amounted to since Myra attempted to kill her. "Not everything, but I know Neil has what remains. All that's left is to rally Crawford behind us. We can turn the page on this dark chapter; bury Neil's propaganda. *A monopoly isn't the answer.*"

Another moment of silence followed. It was unbearable and stuffy, as if they were being smothered by a wool blanket on a summer night. "I… I see your point." Jamie lightly strummed his fingers, hiding them behind his back before Silvia could see more of his tells. "But… how will I know that you won't betray me?"

"I can't claim to want to be rid of that man and then plant a knife in an accomplice's back." Silvia grinned, placing a hand over her heart. "You've done nothing wrong. Nothing other than to be deceived by Neil. For that, I promise I will shield you from the scrutiny of my companions."

Jamie nodded but couldn't keep down an uneasy feeling that swelled within him. His head spun with fear. Even if she wasn't lying, what was to say she wouldn't change her mind later? If Silvia had known how deeply implicated he was, she would not be so friendly– not so willing to protect him.

It was likely Neil kept some things about Jamie from Prost. Jamie did not know for sure. Through the years Jamie often brushed past the strange, the indecent, and the cruel without a second thought. It's what he had to do to survive and eventually what he had to do to keep his job as the copper chaser.

In truth, what scared him the most was that he recognized the names of the cities that had fallen. Some, he had told Neil of. Others, he had gone to the aftermath to collect the copper from the not long gone Mechatollies.

"Yes, I… I appreciate that." He was a pawn in a game he never knew existed– this, he realized. And although replaceable, he was nearing the end of the road. He held the key to destroy the king: the city layout, the soldier's rotations, weak points in the walls. All it would take were a few more turns, and Neil would find himself in checkmate.

Yet his moves were not his own, much like the other pawns in the game. Just like Colt, even Leslie and Prost: their moves had always been orchestrated by a higher power.

Yes, he saw it now; this game between Neil and Silvia.

Every move was a careful calculation. Every expedition for copper. The slow corruption of his morals, which pushed him to this point.

Maybe even this very conversation was part of her plan. Jamie was in too deep. Even if he tried to change directions, there was no leaving the path he had been pushed down.

The rope around his neck was beginning to tighten, and he only saw two hands extending him knives with which to free himself. *If* he played his cards right.

This dilemma could easily be pondered by Jamie for days, though they no longer had that kind of time. The longer Jamie stalled, the worse his odds became. "We should go inside then. You'll… like to hear what I have to say."

Silvia nodded, gently guiding him back to the room. The group was vigorously discussing tactics and did not at first notice the pair. Colt inched aside, allowing Jamie to enter. They fell silent, looking at him. They expected answers.

"There's a PA system," Jamie started, "it was fixed a few years back. It's rarely used for announcements, but almost every room has speakers. There's a broadcasting system outside, too. You'll be able to get your evidence in front of everyone that way, without having to worry about being gunned down in the central square."

"I'm assuming there's a catch to this?" Leslie questioned.

"You'll have to break into the sound booth and turn on all the systems in Crawford. Even if guards don't come after you right away, they might try to cut power to the building or even the whole grid. Even without Neil's instructions, they'd try to keep you from making a ruckus so no marred gets attracted to the walls."

"So how should we deploy our people?" Silvia questioned as Jamie turned towards the blackboard to illustrate where to go.

"The building where the equipment is was for a radio show in a mall; the signs are still up. *The Atom* Radio. You really *cannot* miss it." Jamie started scribbling where the mall was, making a large circle around it to represent the walls. He tried drawing the sign from memory. "There'll probably be a circuit breaker for that building nearby, so station a few people to guard that. Then there's the main power grid." Jamie drew another blob-ish building, which straddled the opposite wall. "They'll target this as a last resort, so by this time they'll be desperate."

"You think they'd shoot it out just to get us to stop?" Colt turned, approaching the chalkboard.

"If Neil gave them the go-ahead, maybe. But they'd likely be too scared to attempt something so consequential. They'd be plunging themselves into darkness too, after all."

"So how do you think we should get all of our people inside?" Silvia seemed preoccupied with the logistics of the plan. Getting so many people into Crawford and across town to defend the power grid undetected seemed nearly impossible.

"There's a highway which runs close to the walls and runs alongside it at some points. Most of it's been blown away, but it'll get you closer than entering through the front door. If you could hook onto the walls, then you'd be able to enter without a problem. There are some guards stationed around at watchtowers, but if you use the highway as cover while approaching, they won't be able to see you."

"So we'll need rope or a ladder to get in, then back down on the other side?"

Jamie nodded. "Rather do this quietly. Crawford's a bit lax on guards, but that's not to say there aren't people who are assigned to fight, should the need arise."

"Good," Silvia walked towards Jamie. "We'll leave by the end of the week." She extended a hand, confidently shaking his. "I knew we could count on you."

53

Crawford has always had a copper chaser, but their name was not always Jamie. Long ago, there was another; her name was Silvia. She was everything a person could strive to be. Beloved by all and damn good at her job. With her help, Crawford was able to usher in a new age of prosperity.

But that wasn't good enough. It was never good enough. At least, not for Neil. "We need more copper," he told her bluntly.

Silvia paused, looking at him with confusion. She had just gotten back from a week's deployment out in the alloy zone. "I came back with as much as I usually do?" She questioned, crossing her arms.

"Yes, you did. You've done a great job. But there's… competition. What I mean is– we'll lose our standing as one of the best cities. Not just that, but– I mean… we're really in a lot of trouble, Silvia. If– *when* copper becomes cheap, we'll lose everything."

"We still have plenty of copper remaining, and you're already making other industries. Like the car market *and* the biofuels."

Neil sighed, unsure of how to word his argument. "Silvia, remember what we used to do for work?"

Silvia looked on, waiting for him to continue.

"We may be on top now, but in the near future, that may change. If we can't capitalize on the copper trade as we do now, I'll never be able to finish making the auto industry, then our biofuel will be worthless. Crawford could fall to ruin. The first king– Amara and her city, already has us beat with fuels for the cars." Neil paused, recalling how the events had played out. "We started distributing our fuel only a few months after Minerva did, yet they're already miles ahead of us. If we can just get to the cars first. Then… then we can catch up. No, *surpass* them."

"Don't you remember how we lost our jobs?" Silvia retorted. "We reached for the moon before we were ready, and we crashed. We should be taking this slowly, Neil. Besides, if other people become wealthier, that'll be more people who can buy your cars and the biofuel to power them."

"We've already invested too much in the auto industry to let up steam now. If I just had another year, we could survive on the auto industry alone."

Silvia paused, her eyes narrowing with skepticism. "So then, what now? I can't possibly gather more copper."

Neil leaned back in his chair, as if having to consider the question, though they both knew that Neil had already planned what he was going to say long before this conversation started. "I don't know. I wish we had another copper chaser, but we don't. Nobody could be your equal– not even close." Neil leaned in, flattering Silvia before driving home the point of his spiel. "If only there were less copper on the market, then we could sell ours for more– at least, more people would buy it."

"I don't think I follow." Silvia crossed her arms, knowing that Neil being vague was never a good sign. "How *exactly* do you plan on manipulating the copper market?" There was an edge of suspicion, even accusation, in her voice.

"Nothing… permanent." Neil assured, trying to backtrack as if it were a stupid idea he had thrown out in the heat of the moment. "Just something that would *incentivize* more people to buy our products over our competitors. Long enough for us to break ground in the auto industry."

"I know where this road goes, Neil," Silvia spoke with a stern tone. "Upping the price of copper will help no one but ourselves. I won't have it. I don't know how you want to reduce the other's copper outputs, but I'll have no part in it."

"You're right– you're right. It was stupid. I don't know why I even said it," Neil shook his head and was quick to bring the conversation to a close. Not long after, Silvia departed from Neil's office, though the conversation hadn't left her mind. Everything Neil said was suspicious. Was the thought of power going to his head? Or was it that competitive spirit beginning to rot his morals?

That simple thought was how Silvia found herself breaking into Neil's office. It had been a week since then and presently the middle of the night.

She had gone through all of his ledgers and paperwork and eventually found a letter from a person she knew all too well; someone who had been cast out from Crawford because of her vicious habits: Myra.

Within the letter detailed several camps that participated in the copper trade, communes that had Mechatollies in their walls for harvesting, and any large-scale community that had even touched the industry in the past year.

There was also a long section noting compromises in the security systems of several of these cities. Ones which Myra would exploit– for a fee.

By the time Neil had gotten into his office the following morning, he found himself in a full-blown argument before he could even sit down at his desk. They had gone back and forth, Silvia waving the papers around in the air as if they were on fire and Neil wanting her to keep her voice down– fearful that others would overhear.

Neil kept trying to downplay what had happened, but Silvia wouldn't have it. Eventually, he gave in and admitted to what Silvia already knew to be true.

"They… they'll *manage*." Neil reasoned that if he agreed with Silvia, he could convince her that he had finally seen the error of his ways, and she would drop the whole thing. "This would help them! If we can make cars, people will be safer. Trade could expand. It's a necessary evil for progress. And we didn't leave those communities out in the cold; we gave them refuge here in Crawford."

Silvia was silent for a long while. Her face had returned to neutrality, with a small frown still present on her lips. Even if they had granted asylum to those people, that didn't deny the people who died on the journey to Crawford. The people who were murdered by over-eager mercenaries.

"Don't you ever do something like this again," she said in a stern voice. This incident wouldn't be forgotten. "If I ever hear about you scheming to destroy other camps, I'll tell everyone. And I'm sure the people whose camps you ordered destroyed won't take too kindly to the news."

Although Neil tried to stop her, Silvia stormed out of his office, slamming the door behind her. His head spun. The plan to suppress other camps had failed spectacularly. Neil clasped his hands around his head as if that could keep the paranoia from leaking out of his ears.

"*She can't.*" He pleaded as if someone were there to hear his distress. "No one can know."

54

There was only an hour before Leslie would begin marching her troops through the streets beyond Crawford's walls. Only an hour before they'd begin to scale the wall. Only an hour until the life Jamie once had would be gone forever.

But Jamie didn't have an hour. His assault– the *assassination–* started now. That's how he found himself in front of a decaying subway station only moments after the day's last light. He had stopped just a few steps shy of the descending stairs, staring into the deep black abyss beneath his feet.

Although Crawford had mostly severed its connection to the subway, there was one route they had neglected to close: the air vents. Jamie really wished that they had. Fear of a sneak attack from a few desperate scavengers wasn't why Crawford had sealed the subway.

It was the marred.

Jamie had only ever heard stories, each more horrific than the last. Several scavenger teams had been sent down for parts. None of them ever made it back. Even those who did survive were different. *Scarred.* Jamie took a harsh puff of the crisp night air and almost coughed it back up before managing to swallow the breath like a shot of vodka.

Even from his perch above the subway, Jamie could hear the skittering of small bugs and the Florid's distant hissing as they spoke to one another. He took his first step down the lifeless escalator, feeling the ridged handrails meet his palms. Though he had only begun his descent, this was but a small step on a long path of stairs that had led him down to this hell.

In a way, Jamie found the thought to be comforting– something he was in need of as the darkness of the subway began to envelop him. He could hardly see a foot in front of him. He took another step.

Challenges in life always got easier the more one faced them. Just like walking down the stairs, even if they were ones that led into the jaws of a beast beyond Jamie's ability to comprehend. Jamie wondered if that was what was happening to him now. He had already killed the cultists that retained him when he met Neil and Prost. It was the only way to survive at the time, just as killing Neil was the only way to survive now.

Why did the world always demand violence from him?

The entrance seemed light years away by the third step, despite it only being an arm's length away. Jamie considered the thought of turning back: of running into the forest and disappearing into the night. The stairs down seemed to stretch into eternity. Jamie worried that he might be descending for hours and miss his chance to speak with Neil for a final time.

Though Jamie wasn't a cowardly man, the idea of fleeing was tempting. His fears had gradually begun to lessen with each step he took down the escalator. Jamie realized that he had emerged through the thicket of his mind palace and arrived at the bottom of the stairs, firmly planting his feet onto the cracked tile.

It was brighter than he had thought, and Jamie realized that there was nothing to fear: he had gone through these motions before.

Jamie had snuck past a few Florids, most of whom were catatonic. It had been nearly twenty minutes since he reached the depths of the subway, most of which he had spent following the red line. This would take him directly beneath the heart of Crawford, directly to Neil.

He was walking beside the train tracks, just beneath the decaying concrete overhang. It had helped him pass a few crowded stops undetected until he arrived at his station. There weren't many Florids here– the few that remained were mere shells of their former selves. They would be about as impactful as a glove with a gaping hole in it.

With a cursory glance at the station, Jamie could see the entrance had been caved in and left no hope of escape for the trapped Florids. There was even one that had been pinned to the ground by ribbons of stray rebar, though the creature had perished a long time ago.

Jamie jumped onto the edge of the platform, swinging his legs over and pushing himself upright, swiping dust from the commute off of clothes. He made his way over to a bench that was propped against the wall. A lonely Florid was leaning against it and gave him a dejected chitter as he grew closer, though it was too weak to make any advances towards him.

The thought of putting the creature out of its misery crossed Jamie's mind, though he was quick to tuck it away. There was going to be a lot of killing today. Even if it would relieve the Florid's suffering, Jamie couldn't bring himself to do it. He crouched down beside it, staring into the creature's eyes.

Why did the road he walked have to be so cruel? Why did he have to take life from those who fought for it and leave it for those who rejected it? The Florid kept chittering away, but Jamie couldn't understand it. They seemed to understand each other, but there was nothing else within the station for the Florid to interact with.

It couldn't even make parasites because of the malnourishment. Soon, Jamie would be gone, too. Then the Florid would be alone once again. Jamie sighed, dragging a hand against the sturdy metal of his mask. The very one that Neil had gifted him. It was best not to think about things like this for too long– at least, not for someone like him. He pulled the knife from its hilt and began to unscrew one of the vent covers.

Once all the screws had been removed, Jamie gently lifted the cover from the wall and placed it to the side. He placed his feet forward but stopped before he could get halfway into the crawlspace. The Florid's eyes met with his. Jamie sighed, a mix of annoyance and sorrow. What was mercy? Maybe for the creature abandoned by the light, it was death. But was killing Neil really mercy? There had to be a better way.

By the time he closed the vent behind him, Jamie was the only living creature left in the station, and his knife was covered in blood.

55

Even for a man of smaller stature like himself, Jamie had trouble fitting through the crawlspace. If it had been easy, all of Pasko's forces would have taken the subway. The gap between the entrance and exit couldn't have been more than twenty feet, but progress was so slow that the distance felt much longer.

It was dark, even more so than the dim tracks he had just navigated, and the slick aluminum walls were cool to the touch. In this darkness, Jamie felt his mind begin to wander as his hands pushed him closer to the opposite end of the vent.

Of course, Jamie was well past the question of whether this was right or wrong: he had forgone ethics when he started releasing Mechatollies and their floral counterparts on innocent parties. And if he were to follow through with this course of action, he would have no choice but to complete it to a fault. If Neil wasn't dead by Jamie's hand, Jamie wouldn't have bettered his favor with Silvia in the slightest, and all of his mental suffering would have been for naught. This was especially important since he needed some sort of cushion for when she found out about the terms of his employment.

All this deliberation was beginning to hurt Jamie's head. But the alternative of escaping with Neil wasn't very appealing either. If he could escape with Neil, *and that was a big if*, what then? Look over his shoulder for the rest of his life? Looking out not only for Silvia, who surely wouldn't be content with just Neil's throne and would continue to hunt both Neil and Jamie for betraying her, but Jamie would also have to be wary of Neil.

Neil wasn't just paranoid; he was deeply attached to his position as the second king– it's why he found himself as Silvia's target. That's what all of Jamie's copper chasing, hunting, and sabotaging was ever for: *Neil's crown.* Neil would never forgive Jamie for being the one that ultimately brought down his house of cards, and it would only be a matter of time until Neil acted upon those feelings.

What ate Jamie up was that if he were in Neil's position, he wasn't sure if he would have played his hand any differently. Though it was difficult for Jamie to tell which thoughts were his own and which had been influenced by Neil. None of Neil's advances would have been possible if not for Jamie's assistance.

Even if Neil's motives were selfish, and Jamie didn't deny that they were, did that not ultimately improve the lives of the citizens of Crawford? Even all those years ago, the action which ultimately began Neil's undoing– the order to kill Silvia. If Silvia had gone public with those records, Crawford would surely have been in poverty *forever*. Its people would have starved, as escaping Crawford was harder than reaching it on account of the alloy zones which surrounded it.

Jamie could justify Neil's actions, just as he had justified his own for all these years. And he *hated* himself for it. If Jamie were to punish Neil, it would also punish him. Because then he lost someone too, just as so many others had.

Atonement? Retribution? It didn't matter what you called it. Jamie wasn't searching for forgiveness; only his own survival. If he spilt Neil's blood, he hoped to prevent the same from happening to his own. Neil's actions had returned to haunt them, and Jamie could now extend his life. It was a chance Jamie was ultimately going to take.

Kicking the exit out, Jamie dropped into the next room and resealed the crawlspace. He found himself in an electrical room. These vents were bigger than the previous but much more mazelike. He nearly got lost the first time he explored them– an exploration he had only committed to because of Prost's stories about the subway. Jamie scoffed, recalling all the times Prost had told Jamie about where to find the entrance to the subway. Maybe Prost knew that this was where their roads would lead, even all those years ago.

Not even Neil knew of the attachment between the building and the subway, which is why it was never blocked off. After a few twists and turns, Jamie reached the surface within Crawford's walls. A few harsh kicks later, Jamie was able to force the vent cover off and emerged in an unused building.

Slipping out of the building, Jamie dashed through the alleys of the streets he knew by heart, closing in on Neil's office.

It was difficult enough for him to slip by undetected, as Neil had numerous guards posted all around the city. Neil was as paranoid as ever, especially after the recent losses he had been suffering. Jamie could only imagine that Silvia's group wouldn't be nearly as fortunate as he had been, and that it was only a matter of time until fights began to break out around the city.

In a time like this, where was the one place in the entire city that Neil would feel safe? Nowhere else other than his office. Whether he was just sleeping, or working on a plan to climb out of a grave he had buried himself in, it didn't matter– he would be there.

56

Jamie wanted Neil to be mad. To curse his name and to give him a fight, so that he may give himself a sliver of relief and a modicum of justification for murder, beyond his selfish desire to survive. But Neil gave Jamie none of that.

Neil overlooked his kingdom and leaned against the white picket fence, with a bottle of whiskey sitting atop an equally pristine white flower bed.

He hadn't reacted when Jamie broke his office door down, nor when he had opened the doors to Neil's garden sanctuary. He hadn't given Jamie any reaction, knowing that in doing so, he could force Jamie's hand and hasten the conclusion of his life.

There were two bottles of whiskey on the fence: one was full and the other half-empty. Fingerprints of a sweaty hand littered the second.

"I knew you would return. Won't you share a drink with me, Jamie?" Neil asked without ever checking who it was that had approached him. He knew anyone else would have shot him instantly.

Silence was the immediate response, though Neil could hear the quiet sound of a gun being placed back into its holster, and relaxed footsteps soon followed.

Jamie took the untouched glass of whiskey, taking a single sip of the drink before returning the cup to its place on the fence. The liquid burned Jamie's throat as he swallowed it, though he knew the physical pain would be drowned out by the mental kind.

"Why did it have to come to this?" Jamie asked, pushing the bitterness of the drink out of his mind and focusing on Neil.

Neil raised the glass to his lips, seemingly unbothered by the turn of events. But Jamie could tell he was nervous: the tremors in his hands and the sloshing of the liquid in the glass told him all he needed to know.

"We're all going to die, Jamie," Neil said as he placed the glass down. He then moved both of his hands to wrap around the fence, as if needed to hold on, or risk being blown away.

"Why do you have to die by *my* hands?"

"I thought you would have figured that out by now." Neil looked at Jamie with a sad smile. The same one you'd give to your dog before putting it down: sadness with a hint of peace.

Just enough to soothe yourself and your dearest companion in their last moments.

There was a pause in the conversation as Jamie built up the courage to continue speaking. "Do you blame me?"

"No. I've never blamed you. This is the path I chose when I took you in," Neil stopped speaking, slipping his hands partly off the fence. "You acted just as I thought because you acted just like I would. And I made no move to stop you."

"Why?"

"I know this'll haunt you for the rest of your life. Just as how sending Myra after Silvia has haunted me. You'll punish yourself more than I could ever punish you, even though I wish for neither."

Neil tapped the pads of his fingers against the fence, feeling the imperfections of the wood as it brushed against his skin. "I know I won't be around to forgive you, and I'm not sure you'd care for an apology. So the best I can leave you with is acceptance."

"No matter how this plays out, this will be the last time we see each other. That's the price we pay, isn't it?"

Neil forced another sip of whiskey into his mouth to withhold what he truly wanted to say to Jamie. An apology was in order, one that Neil would never vocalize.

He wanted to say sorry for getting Jamie wrapped up in this mess– for forcing Jamie to act on violence despite his gentle heart. A kindness Neil knew was still there, even if buried deep inside Jamie. A kindness Neil knew was hurting.

More than anything, Neil wanted to reciprocate Jamie's feelings: to tell Jamie that he truly thought higher of him than he ever let on. But he wouldn't, if only to grant Jamie one last act of kindness.

"Your comrades expect results, Jamie. How much longer do you hope to stall the inevitable?"

"It won't be long now," Jamie said, carefully gripping the stock of his revolver. With a slow lift of his arm, Jamie pointed the gun in Neil's direction. "We're not good people, you know. And maybe we deserve what we have coming to us."

The gun in Jamie's hand began to shake, as if the iron was beginning to burn his palm. Like a holy cross burning the hand of a demon. No amount of fidgeting was going to stop that. If the gun were to go off now, it would miss Neil entirely. Something Jamie wasn't entirely opposed to.

Jamie silenced the shaking with a quick jerk of his arm. He pressed the cylinder against his cheek, rubbing the barrel against the side of his head.

It was cold now.

Shame washed over Jamie as he pulled away, turning back towards a city about to be reborn. To say it was his fault wouldn't be wholly accurate, though he was nonetheless a conspirator.

Jamie knew how many people had died to allow Silvia's efforts to reach this stage. Knew how many people died because of what he did, both before and after he gave Silvia an entryway to the city. One he doubted she needed; one she probably only wanted as a display of loyalty.

But Silvia didn't control Jamie. Neither did Prost– neither did Neil. Not even the cultists who held him captive, or the ghosts whose faces he could scarcely remember.

So no more.

No more would Jamie be a pawn in another's game. No more would he be some docile spectator, a role which he had played unconvincingly all these years.

"I feel something. I've felt it since Silvia first spoke to me. But I think it was always there. I just wasn't ready to feel it." Jamie glanced back at Neil as his gun fell to his side. Neil was ever suspicious of Jamie's movements but made no move to interrupt him. "Like I'm drowning– my head's being pushed under the water."

With a few swift steps, Jamie closed the gap between himself and Neil. They returned to their positions, just short of two feet apart.

Enough room for an arm and a revolver.

Enough room for a handshake.

"But I think I've taken a full breath of air for the first time tonight. It's like my eyes are finally *open*."

"Jamie–"

"I have a plan, Neil," he blurted. "A way for all of us to live. I know I can't change the past. But that doesn't mean I can't diverge from the path fate wants me to take. Will you follow me?"

www.ingramcontent.com/pod-product-compliance
Lightning Source LLC
LaVergne TN
LVHW041249110826
845146LV00005BA/1324